COINS AND CADAVERS

Murder Blog Mysteries #3

PAMELA FROST DENNIS

Coins and Cadavers
The Murder Blog Mysteries #3
Copyright© 2017 by Pamela Frost Dennis
All rights reserved
ISBN: 9780999349403

Printed in the United States of America
First Printing, 2017
For permission requests: pamelafrostdennis@hotmail.com
Cover: Bookfly Design

~ Thank You to ~

Mike Dennis
Thank you for always asking me how my
book is going—no matter how long it takes.

My supportive, loving family

My Friends
*A special shout-out to Nina and Jeri.
Chuck Ashton—thanks for nudging me
to keep going.*

My Readers
*Your kind comments on Amazon and
Goodreads make it all worthwhile.*

Dr. Dorothy Dink
Your wisdom and humor sustain me.

THIS BOOK IS DEDICATED TO:
My number one fan

WELCOME TO MY BLOG

Nine months ago, I reluctantly made my first blog post at the insistence of my best friend, Samantha. At the time I was suffering from a severe case of PDRD (post-divorce rage disorder). Sam said blogging would help me work through my bitter resentment. I thought strangling Chad was a better idea, but I agreed to try her idea first. And here I am, still at it.

Maybe someday, when I'm in my twilight years, I'll look back on my musings and chuckle at some of the things that I thought were so earth-shattering at the time.

Only a select few have access to my blog. My folks, Grandma Ruby, Samantha, and you—my closest friends.

CHAPTER ONE

Posted by Katy McKenna

For over a week now, my upstairs, furry "tenants" have been throwing all night ragers—jumping, thumping, and no doubt humping. I'm running on empty and have the dark circles to prove it.

————

My folks have complained for years about pesky squirrels getting into their attic, and I've always wondered what the big deal was. It's not like they're rats. But after several sleepless nights, I googled "squirrels in the attic" and learned that they're rodents, and like rats, could do severe damage to your home.

For example:

- A dear old granny in England died after squirrels gnawed through gas piping, causing her ancient stone cottage to explode.

- In Ireland, a family of four was crushed when their home collapsed after squirrels chewed through the attic timbers.

There's even a website dedicated to documenting the number of attacks on our power grid each year. In the site's first year of collecting data, there were nearly two thousand "cyber squirrel" attacks impacting millions of people across the nation.

"The number one threat experienced to date by the US electrical grid is squirrels." — *John C. Inglis, Former Deputy Director, National Security Agency*

I'm not making this stuff up.

Yesterday
Rodent Elimination: Phase One

I hadn't visited the gloomy, spooky space since the first time I looked at the house. But I couldn't risk having my home cave in just because I was too chicken to go in the attic.

After a trip to the hardware store to purchase ultrasonic pest repeller beepers guaranteed to drive away mice, cockroaches, rodents, spiders, ants, rats, and squirrels, I was ready to face the enemy.

In the hallway, I stood on a stepstool and unlatched the door in the ceiling to release the antique retractable stairs. After they had clunked into place on the wood floor, I gazed up at the exposed rafters.

"Really do not want to go up there." I pulled in a deep breath. "I mean, what's the rush? I can wait until my sister gets home, and we can do it together."

Mission aborted, I stooped to close the stairway when my cat zoomed in and tore up the stairs like her tail was on fire.

"Tabitha! Stop! Get back down here!" Her catnip mouse lay nearby on the floor. I clambered halfway up the wobbly steps and swung the fuzzy toy over my head. "Look what Mommy's got. Mmmm. Catnip. You know you want it, so come and get it."

Nothing.

"Dammit."

I stepped back down, grabbed the bag of sonic beepers, and climbed into the attic. Weak sunlight filtered through the grimy octagonal windows revealing a large and even creepier space than I remembered.

"Here kitty-kitty-kitty."

Something thumped in a dark corner, and Tabitha moaned mean and low.

Oh God, she's got a squirrel. Thoroughly pissed off now, I shouted, "Dammit, Tabitha. Leave the poor little animal alone."

Suddenly, she bolted past me and careened down the stairs, scaring the bejeebers out of me. I wasn't feeling brave enough to hunt around the spooky attic for the squirrel, so I switched on the beepers and placed them around the floor, then scrambled down the steps and slammed the stairway into the ceiling.

After getting my heebie-jeebies under control, I laughed at my silly behavior. I mean, come on, I'm a five-foot-nine, thirty-two-year-old woman, weighing in at one-hundred-thirty-six-ish pounds, and how big is a squirrel? A pound, maybe?

———

Around midnight, my half-sister, Emily, opened my bedroom door. "You awake?"

"No."

"There's a weird sound coming from the attic."

I switched on the bedside lamp. "It's the ultrasonic pest controllers I put up there to shoo the squirrels out. It's supposed to be too high-pitched for human ears."

"And you're saying you can't hear it?"

"Yeah, I can hear it. But if it works, it's worth it."

Emily sat on the end of my bed. "Well, from the sounds of it, whatever is up there—and I seriously doubt that it's squirrels—is enjoying it."

She was right. It sounded like they were having a gay old time, groovin' to the beat of the beep.

"Tomorrow I'm pulling out the big guns. Humane catch and release traps."

"So you're going to catch rats and—"

"Squirrels."

"Whatever." She shook her head. "And release them where?"

"In the woods, where they can frolic and live happy squirrel lives."

Today

Rodent Elimination: Phase Two

This morning, I went online and learned that most animals don't fare well when released in a new area. The humane society says that 97% won't survive. The frightened critters suddenly find themselves dumped in unfamiliar terrain, and it's too traumatic. Makes sense.

So I researched other ideas to humanely evacuate my pests and came up with peppermint oil. Supposedly, rodents hate it, but it won't hurt them, and my house will smell minty fresh.

Feeling bolder than yesterday, I climbed into the attic with a bag of peppermint soaked cotton balls and glanced around, thinking, *If this was finished it would make a nice office or guest room.*

A past owner must have had the same thought. The wall facing the back yard had three plywood planks, roughly four by six, nailed to the studs, the last one ending halfway between studs. I wondered why they hadn't finished the entire wall.

I tucked a few cotton balls behind the wall and something sharp gashed the palm of my hand. Curious about what cut me, I peeked in. Lodged behind the plywood was a rectangular wood chest about the size of a knee-high boot box. Its rusty handle faced me, and I tried to pull it towards me, but the box was wedged in tight. I gave it a hard jerk, and the handle snapped off, propelling me backward onto my rump. The heavy padlocked chest tumbled after, landing on my bony shins.

You know the agony of ramming your bare toes into a table leg? Well, this hurt like that times ten. The room turned bright white, and I knew I'd better lie down before I passed out.

Finally, I was able to sit up and tip the box to the floor. That move took me back to Ground Zero pain, and back down I went to wait out the accompanying nausea. When my head cleared, I rolled to a fetal position and considered lying there until my sister, Emily, got home from her shift at the Burger Hut.

Why didn't I bring my damned cellphone with me?

My yellow lab yelped frantically at the foot of the steps. Then the stairs thudded against the downstairs floor.

"No, no. Stay off the stairs, Daisy. Mommy's all right." *No, I'm not. My legs might be broken.*

I struggled to a sitting position again, biting my lip to squelch the shrieks of agony that would have distressed Daisy. The wooden chest was within reach, so I jiggled the corroded padlock, hoping it would pop open, but it didn't.

Standing was not an option, so I slithered my butt a couple feet across the rough wood floor, then reached back to drag the heavy box with me. One mighty tug and I wrenched my lower back.

I left the mystery box behind and worked my way to the steps wondering how I was going to get down without breaking my neck. I wound up jostling down on my rear end, one creaky rung at a time. By the time I hit bottom, I was in tears, and Daisy liberally applied first-aid kisses to my face.

Too bad she couldn't carry me to the couch, get some frozen peas for my shins, a heating pad for my back, several ibuprofens, and a glass of wine.

CHAPTER TWO

THURSDAY • JANUARY 15
Posted by Katy McKenna

Before my baby sister moved back to Santa Lucia, she'd been living in San Diego and working two jobs to pay the rent. Emily told our folks she wanted to come home and work a part-time job while she wrote a paranormal mystery series (she really is). She failed to mention that the main reason she wanted to come home was because she'd just broken up with her girlfriend. She also neglected to tell her family she's gay.

Mom was going through a trying time, so I offered up my guest room. Reluctantly. Very reluctantly. After the initial period of adjustment, it's been fun getting to know my sister. The nine-year age difference had always been a barrier between us, but now that we're all grown-up, more or less, the years no longer matter so much.

Last night, when Emily got home from her part-time job at the Burger Hut, she found me sprawled on the couch, shins smothered under thawed-out bags of veggies. Doctor Daisy sat on the floor by me, keeping a watchful eye on my vital signs.

"Good grief, Katy. What happened?"

"A heavy wooden treasure chest fell on me and almost broke my legs."

She shook her head with a hint of a smirk. "Sounds reasonable. For you, that is."

"I'm not kidding. Anyway, I took some leftover Vicodin from when I got shot in the leg, but it barely touched the pain."

She removed the dripping bags of peas and corn from my shins and took a good look. "Wow. That's gotta hurt."

"You could say that."

"I'll stash these bags back in the freezer for your next crazy escapade."

"You sound like Mom."

"That's because living with you is rapidly aging me." Emily laughed. "Oh, my God. I *do* sound like Mom." She scooped up Tabitha, who'd been weaving between her legs. "These guys must be starving. I'll feed them, then you can tell me all about your treasure chest."

"With the agony I'm in, it damned well better be a treasure chest."

After Emily fed the pets, she set a fresh batch of frozen veggies on my shins and then flopped in the armchair across from the couch. "So...a treasure chest. Really?" She pulled the elastic band out of her long goth-black hair and scratched her scalp.

"Yup." I sat up, pointing at the ceiling. "In the attic."

———

When I concluded my story, she still looked skeptical. "Get the flashlight and go see for yourself if you don't believe me."

"I believe you, but I will anyway." She went to the hallway and hollered, "How do you get up there? Do you have a ladder?"

"Use the stepstool to unlatch the door in the ceiling. Be careful not to let the stairs bang your head because I can't save you."

The stairway creaked down and struck the floor.

"Wow. This is so cool," Emily shouted as she climbed.

I wanted to watch, but when I tried to swing my legs to the floor, I thought better of it. "Emily! I need more Vicodin."

"In a sec. Okay, I'm at the top, and I see the box. Let me see if I can lift it."

"No! It's too heavy. We'll figure something out tomorrow." Emily is a petite little thing, and I was worried she'd hurt her back.

"Whoa. You're right. Darn it. I wanna find out what's inside." Then she shrieked. "There's a rat!" Another spine-chilling scream. "Three rats! I'm outta here!"

Emily squealed her way down the steps, then slammed the stairway into the ceiling so hard the house rattled a 4.0 on the Richter scale. Wish I'd gotten a video of her hopping around and shaking her head like she had rats in her hair. It would have gone viral on YouTube, for sure.

———

Emily woke me at eight this morning. "Wake up, sleepyhead." She handed me a steamy cup of French roast, perfectly doctored with sugar and a healthy dollop of half and half.

I sipped the tasty brew, giving thanks to the gods for inventing coffee. "What're you doing up so early?"

Usually Em sleeps past nine, then grabs a coffee and holes up in her bedroom to work on her book until it's time to go to her job. Her mystery takes place in a medieval fairy forest full of evil trolls and goblins. I'm proud of her for sticking to it. It can't be easy writing a book.

"Aren't you dying to see what's in the box?" she said. "I know I am."

"Oh my God! The treasure chest!" I flipped back the blankets, disturbing Miss Daisy. She rolled onto her back stretching her long legs with a big yawn, then smacked her lips and collapsed back to sleep.

"Eeew." Emily eyeballed my legs with a grimace.

Eeew was right. The blossoming bruises and lumps could win a spot in the Guinness book of world records.

"Maybe you need to see a doctor," she said. "Those bruises are the worst I've ever seen. You might have cracked something, you know."

"I was able to walk to the bathroom last night—"

"Yeah. Barely. Remember I had to help you."

"Anyway, I'm probably fine." I chugged my coffee, then stood, testing my limbs. Yes, it hurt big time, but I was pretty sure nothing was broken.

"I definitely could use three or four ibuprofens, though. I can't take any more Vicodin. It was making me nauseated. Then we need to figure out how to get that box down."

———

After debating several treasure chest extraction schemes, we settled on one of my ideas: a rope tied several times around the box with another long rope attached. Then slide the box down the stairs with Emily controlling its descent from the attic. Trouble is, I didn't have any rope, so we used extension cords.

"Okay, ease it down nice and slow," I said.

"I'm trying." She grunted with the exertion. "This thing weighs a friggin' ton. Probably full of gold bars, don't ya think?"

"Probably more like lead bricks." I reached for the box. "I got it, but don't let go yet." I guided the box to a comforter protecting the floor. "Okay, you can let go now."

Emily clambered down the rickety stairs, and then we stood contemplating the mysterious wooden chest.

"This is so Nancy Drew," she said.

"You're right. Did you read Mom's books?"

"The whole collection. Some more than once."

"I had a huge crush on Ned Nickerson," I said. "Did you know that most of the books were Grandma Ruby's from her childhood?"

"I did. It made them even more special. Did you have a favorite?"

"I liked them all," I said. "But a few of my absolute favorites were *The Secret at Shadow Ranch*—probably because I wanted a horse. *The Bungalow Mystery*, and *The Secret in the Old Attic*. Wow, I'm amazed I can remember the titles after all these years. What was yours?"

Emily glanced up the attic steps. "My favorite was *The Hidden Staircase*. Kind of ironic, considering I had no idea about your hidden staircase." She patted the mystery box. "You know, this could be a new Nancy Drew mystery."

"You're right. The Secret of the Old Box."

She crouched and rattled the rusty padlock. "We need to pick it."

And I needed to get off my feet. Emily dragged the blanket and box into the kitchen, and together we hoisted it onto the table. Then I collapsed on a chair, feeling lightheaded.

"It shouldn't be too hard to spring the lock, since it's so corroded," said Emily. "Got any ideas, Nancy?"

"Give me a minute. I feel like I'm going to be sick." I rested my forehead on my folded arms on the table.

"You want a glass of water?" she asked.

"Yes, and bring me a wet, cold face towel."

She did, and after I wiped my face and sipped the cool water, I felt revived. "Can you get my laptop? I think it's in the living room. I'm sure we can find a video on how to pick a lock."

First, we watched the one for how to pick a padlock with a paperclip. We followed the geeky prepubescent boy's methodical directions, but no luck. Then we tried how to pick a padlock with a screwdriver, and finally, "how to pick a padlock with a steak knife."

I tapped the lock. "Clearly, we'll never make it as burglars. So now what?"

"You got a hacksaw?" she asked.

"No. But I'm sure Pop does. He's probably at his shop now, but I have a key to the house. He won't mind if we borrow it."

A few years ago, Pop took early retirement from the police force after getting shot in the knee. Now he owns a quaint old-school fix-it shop near the downtown area of Santa Lucia. It's next door to Mom's hair salon, Cut 'n Caboodles.

"Or I can go to the hardware store and buy one," said Emily. "Then you'd have one of your very own. And the hardware store's closer."

After she left, I watched one more video, "How to pick a padlock with a paper clip for beginners" and voila! It popped open.

Now for the big reveal. I unhitched the lock and set it on the table.

Would it be riches? Or was I opening Pandora's box?

CHAPTER THREE

FRIDAY · JANUARY 16
Posted by Katy McKenna

I tried to ignore my phone vibrating on the nightstand at 6:49 this morning, but curiosity got the best of me, and I peeked to see who had the nerve to call so early. Ruby Armstrong.

Oh, crap. Who died? Grandma Ruby checks the obits every morning, and if anyone she was even slightly acquainted with has kicked the bucket, she calls to share with lucky me.

"Hi, Ruby. What's up?"

"I'll tell you what's up, little missy."

She only calls me that when I'm in big trouble. I scanned my groggy brain and came up blank. "What'd I do?"

"I always read your blog during *The Tonight Show*, and last night you ended your post on a cliffhanger. What the hell is in the damned box? I was up all damned night, wondering and worrying."

"Why don't you come over and see for yourself?"

"You know I have to go to work, Katy. Just tell me so I can get on with my life."

"Nope. You gotta see it. You're not going to believe it."

She heaved a testy sigh. "Fine. I'll be over in half an hour."

"Can you stop at Starbucks and get me a grande double shot latte, three sugars? And a cheese danish. Pleeease? You know you're my favorite grandma." For good measure, I added, "My legs really hurt, Grammy."

Ruby could be Attila the Hun and she'd still be my favorite grandma. Pop married Mom when I was a toddler. His parents had lived in Palm Desert but recently had moved to Prescott, Arizona because of lower taxes. Pop's folks are nice, but I rarely see them.

My bio-father, Bert McKenna, aka "plastic surgeon to the stars," never paid much attention to me while I was growing up. He was too busy running through trophy wives while making wads of money yanking up the faces of movie stars. His father had died when he was a kid, and his mother is hands-down the nastiest woman in the universe. Think Cruella de Vil times ten.

———

"Holy moly. Should you be walking?" Ruby eyed my legs clad in cut-off sweats when I opened the front door. She handed me a steamy latte and a little brown bag. "I brought a latte for Emily, too. Where is she?"

"Sleeping it off. We wound up drinking a little too much wine last night. It was a pretty crazy night. Let's sit in the living room so I can put my feet up and I'll fill you in."

Yesterday

After I'd taken the lock off the box, I looked at Daisy looking at me. I knew she thought I should wait for Emily, so to make my girl happy, I waited about ten minutes.

Finally, I couldn't stand the suspense any longer. "Daisy, let me take one teeny-tiny little peek to make sure there isn't something horrible inside. Like a nest of icky spiders."

Daisy wagged in agreement, then waited for my next move, eyes locked on the box, panting with anticipation.

I'd already sustained multiple injuries from the damned wooden box, so I wasn't taking any chances during the unveiling. I hobbled to the stove and grabbed an oven mitt, and then ever-so-slowly lifted the lid a few inches with a long metal spatula. A musty odor wafted out reminding me of old books and stale cigarettes.

"I'm *ba-ack*," sang Emily, slamming through the front door. "Let's do this!" She stopped at the kitchen entrance. "Hey. What're ya doin'?"

I let the lid drop. "I decided to keep working on the lock, and suddenly it snapped open." I shrugged my wide-eyed innocence. "I was just making sure there isn't anything dangerous that might hurt you."

"Yeah, right. Couldn't wait for your little sister." She set a shiny new hacksaw on the kitchen table. "So, what's in it?"

"I don't know. But whatever it is, it smells moldy and ancient."

She leaned over the box. "What are you waiting for? Open it."

"I think you should step back in case there's something unsafe in there," I said.

"Like what—a hand grenade from World War II? Ricin?"

Those things had not occurred to me. "Will you put Daisy out? I don't want her exposed to something hazardous."

"Oh sure, you care more about your dog than your baby sister."

"You can go outside with her, if you want, you know."

"As if." Emily opened the kitchen door. "Come on, Daisy. Your mean mother is banishing you to the yard."

Daisy shot me one of her well-practiced hurt looks, then slinked through the door.

"All right," I said. "Let's think about how we're going to do this."

"Katy. It's just an old wood box. Geez." Before I could stop her, she flipped the lid. "See? No bomb. No Ricin. No scary monsters." She waved at the contents. "Oooo. So scary."

A faded, pink satin-covered baby book lay on top. I lifted it out and opened it, taking care not to crack the old spine. "Ahhh. Baby Mabel. Born June fourteenth, 1903. Mabel Anne Sinclair. She weighed seven pounds, six ounces." I turned the yellow-tinged pages, savoring the precious keepsake.

Emily removed a bundle of papers tied with pink ribbon. "Oh, look." She held a paper under my nose. "It's Mable's marriage certificate. She married Harold Allan Petersen in 1921."

I set the baby book on the table and rummaged through the documents. "Oh no. Poor Mabel and Harold lost a baby in 1923 and 1925." I held up the death certificates. "Both died at birth. That's so sad."

Emily handed me a worn maroon velvet necklace box. "Maybe it's full of diamonds."

"Yeah, right."

Inside were three rings: a modest single-diamond wedding ring set, a light purple stone ring (probably a birthstone), and a man's gold signet ring with the initials H.A.P. inscribed on it. Also, there was a pearl necklace and a ladies watch: pink gold, two tiny rubies on both sides of the watch face, with an inscription on the underside.

"This is so romantic," I said sighing. "I will love you 'til the end of time –H." *Will anyone ever love me until the end of time?*

"Look at these." Emily held up a small bundle of yellowing newspapers.

"I love old newspapers. Especially the ads."

"No. Not the papers. Look in the box." Lined up side-by-side were neat rows of small, colorful art deco tin containers. "Those are definitely very collectible. They're in perfect condition."

"They're so cute," I said. "They're probably worth a lot. I bet I could sell them on eBay." I thought a moment. "No. I'd rather keep them and display them on the shelves in the living room."

Emily lifted one out. "It's awfully heavy. I wonder what's inside?"

"Probably those diamonds you were talking about."

"You wish," she said with a smirk. "I sure hope it's not something disgusting, like nasty old teeth with gold fillings. I've heard that people used to keep things like that." She placed the box on the kitchen table and then went to the utensil drawer for a butter knife to pry off the lid.

"Careful. Don't scratch it," I said.

"Oh. My. God."

"What? What?" I craned my neck, trying to see.

Emily tipped the open box toward me, revealing a neat stack of shiny gold coins.

"Holy crickets." I took one out. "This is a twenty-dollar coin. 1876. In perfect condition. I bet it's worth at least a hundred bucks." I glanced at Emily. "Why the funny look?"

"Holy crickets?"

"I've been trying to clean up my language."

"Whatever." She opened another box. "This one's filled with ten-dollar coins. This is insane."

She passed the tin to me, and I plucked out a coin. "Whoa. 1847. Before the Civil War. And yet it looks so new." Butterflies were skydiving in my stomach.

Emily now had several tins open on the table. "This is officially crazy. You have a friggin' fortune here."

"They can't be real." I shook my head. "No way. They're all too perfect. Too new looking. Like in mint condition. It's got to be counterfeit."

She removed another coin from a box. "Why would counterfeit coins be packed up with all this other old stuff?" She set the coin back in its container, shaking her head. "I think these are the real deal, and you, dear sister, are a very wealthy woman."

I placed my feet on the floor, achy legs forgotten. "No. No. It's not my money."

"You own the house, right?"

"Free and clear. Chad got the bookstore, and I got that mid-century modern monstrosity he had to have."

"Yeah, but when you sold it you were able to pay cash for your house," she said. "So, I think that anything in the house is yours."

"No, this money belongs to whoever hid it in the attic."

"Haven't you ever heard of the finders-keepers law?" Emily stood. "Do you think there might be more coins in the attic? You know, behind the plywood where you found this box?"

"Who knows? But now that you mention it, we should tear down that wood and take a look. But there's no way I'm getting up those stairs today."

"I can do it. Gotta hammer?"

"Yeah. Out in the garage there's a tool kit on the floor by the door out to the yard."

A few minutes later, Emily was upstairs prying the planks off the studs.

I waited at the foot of the stairs. "How're you doing up there?"

"Just about got the first one off. Just have to pull out one more nail. And… Nothing. Darn it."

I heard her grunting with exertion. "Do you want some help? I can call Pop."

"No. A lot of the nails were pounded in crooked, that's all. I've almost got it." The board thudded on the floor, followed by a shriek. "Oh shit!"

"What's wrong? Do you need me?"

"No. I'm okay." She came to the top of the steps. "There's a mummified cat behind the plywood, and it totally freaked me out. Unfortunately, there's no more hidden treasure."

On her way down, she said, "Why would somebody do that? That poor cat's been dead for years. Probably put there at the same time as the box. In the next day or so, I'll give him a proper burial."

"Wait a few days and I'll be able to help. But right now I need to sit down."

Emily helped me back to the kitchen table. "How about a glass of wine? I could use one."

"It's a little early, but sure. I don't have anywhere to be today. There's an open bottle of chardonnay in the fridge."

"Yeah, I know. I'm the one who opened it." She removed it from the refrigerator door and read the label. "Seriously, Katy. Now you can afford the good stuff instead of this cheap swill."

"Hey! I'll have you know I paid nine bucks for that at Costco."

She handed me a glass and sat down. "*Salud,* dear sister." We sipped in silence for a moment. "So. What's the first thing you're going to buy? A new car?"

"Are you kidding? Get rid of dear old Veronica?" Veronica is my 1976 orange Volvo DL wagon. Mom bought her before I was born and on my seventeenth birthday, she gifted the trusty car to me. "She's a classic." I nibbled a nail, gazing ruefully at the coins, then sighed. "Besides there's no way I can keep this money. Who knows? Maybe it was stolen."

The doorbell rang, and we froze, staring wide-eyed at each other like we were a couple of crooks caught red-handed.

"Who do you think it is?" whispered Emily.

"How would I know?" I whispered back, heart racing. "Just keep quiet, and they'll go away."

The bell ding-donged again. "KATY? Are you in there?" yelled my next-door neighbor, Josh Draper, also known (only to me) as Josh-the-Viking because he looks like a Nordic god.

"You going to answer it, Katy?"

"No way. I look like hell. I don't even have any makeup on."

"KATY?" Josh hollered from the porch. "I've got Daisy! Your gate was open."

"Oops. My bad," said Emily. "I may have forgotten to close it when I took the garbage out."

"Then you get to answer the door. If he sees these banged-up legs of mine, he'll ask questions, and the next thing you know, we're busted. Remember, he's a P.I. and a former cop."

She muffled a giggle. "It's not like we robbed a bank, ya know."

Emily shut the swinging kitchen door on her way to the front door. A moment later, I heard her say, "Hi, Josh. Sorry it took so long. I was in the bathroom, doing, uh, you know, bathroom stuff."

Wish I could have seen Josh's face when she said that.

"So where'd you find Daisy?" She sounded hyper-guilty.

"I saw her sitting on your porch, and I know she's not supposed to be loose."

"Thanks, Josh. I must've left the gate open. Katy would kill me if I lost her baby."

Daisy's nails clattered on the wood floor as she beelined to the kitchen. She barreled through the swinging door, wagging her tail and flashing me a guilty grin.

"You know you're a naughty girl, don't you?" I whispered, nuzzling her face.

Then Josh asked, "Is Katy home?"

"She's... taking a nap. "

"Well, tell her I said hi."

"Will do. And thanks again."

The door shut, then Emily returned to the kitchen and collapsed on a chair. "Well, that was certainly awkward."

I pointed at the money. "We gotta get this cash stashed before I have a heart attack."

"No way can I get that box back up in the attic. So where's a good place to hide the loot?"

"I have a fire safe in my closet, although I don't think it's big enough for all these tins."

"We could put the coins in plastic bags," she said.

"Still don't think it'll all fit. It's just for important documents."

"Then I guess we're going shopping." Emily pushed back her chair and stood.

I winced. "These legs aren't going anywhere. Besides, I think I've just about maxed out my credit cards with Christmas presents and all."

"Do you realize how funny that is? Considering what's sitting on the table?"

"I don't think we can walk into Office Mart and buy a safe with a gold coin that's a hundred and fifty years old. Could raise some eyebrows."

She laughed. "It's ironic. You're broke and probably crazy rich. Tell you what. You stay here and guard the booty while I go shopping. You can pay me back later."

"You better get two safes because I still need one for my birth certificate and other important papers."

Back to Ruby's visit today

"Well, my dear, that's a hell of a story." Ruby stood, smoothing her black pencil skirt.

I drained my latte and Ruby took our empties to the kitchen trash.

"I take it this is the treasure box sitting on your table in here?" she called from the kitchen.

I limped to the kitchen. "Good deduction, Sherlock."

She ran her fingers over the corroded metal edges of the chest. "I can see how this would have cut your hand. Are you up to date on your tetanus shot?"

"Yes." *I think. Not really sure. Maybe. Crap.*

"That's good. Now show me the money."

CHAPTER FOUR

SATURDAY · JANUARY 17
Posted by Katy McKenna

Last night, Mom and Pop brought over a pizza for dinner. Before we ate, I gave them the money tour, and then we settled in the living room.

"According to all the online legal experts," I mumbled through a full mouth of veggie pizza, "the money is mine, minus the mega chunk the IRS will claim is theirs."

"I think you should talk to Angela Yaeger." Pop headed to the kitchen for another beer.

Angela is the Santa Lucia police chief. We've been friends ever since I did a petition to stop the parole of a murderer last year.

The refrigerator door slammed, and Pop yelled, "You're driving home, right, Marybeth?"

"I am now." She shook her head at me with a smirk.

Pop returned. "Katy, I think you should also talk to Ben."

Ben is a retired attorney and Grandma's boyfriend. A while back I met him at the dog park. After several lengthy conversations,

I decided he would be perfect for my grammy, so I did a little matchmaking.

"He can advise you, or refer you to someone who can," said Mom. "If the money's yours, you're going to need expert financial guidance."

"And I don't think the coins should be sitting loose in the safes. They might get scratched," said Pop.

"They were in little tin boxes, but they won't all fit in the safes." I got one of the deco tins and showed them.

"Oh, that is so cute." Mom held it to the lamp light. "Such vibrant colors."

"I think you should wrap each coin in plastic to protect them," said Pop.

"You could get little snack bags. They have five-hundred-count boxes at Costco," said Mom. "In fact, I just bought a box the other day. I'll bring it over tomorrow."

The more we talked, the more apprehensive I became. *Maybe I should take the money to the bank and put it in a safe deposit box.* But the mere thought of transporting it freaked me out. *What if my car breaks down? What if someone crashes into me? What if I get carjacked? What if...stop it!*

———

There's an elderly lady down the street who has lived in the hood for eons. We're only on a "wave and a how-are-ya" basis, but last night, I got to thinking that she might have known my house's former owners. This morning I strolled down the block and invited her over for coffee this afternoon.

She accepted, and I dashed home to bake some chocolate chip cookies à la frozen Nestle.

———

After Nina Lowen was comfortably ensconced on the front porch swing, I told her about the mystery box, then handed her the baby book. I didn't tell her about the gold coins.

She slipped on the reading glasses dangling on a beaded chain around her neck and read the first page. "Oh, my. This is so precious. Mabel Anne Sinclair." She stopped, scrunching her eyes, gazing off into the past. "You know, there was a woman who lived in your house years ago, and her name was Mabel. Mabel, hmmm..." She snapped her fingers. "Mabel Petersen. Goodness, I haven't thought about her in years."

Score! The butterflies that have taken up permanent residence in my belly since finding the box fluttered awake, and I leaned forward in anticipation.

Nina turned a page. "This must be her baby book."

"Were you close?" I asked, thinking, *Say yes, say yes.*

"Oh, not really."

Rats.

"My husband and I moved into the neighborhood in 1981. Mabel was in her late seventies, so there was quite a big age difference between us. I had jet-black hair back then." She laughed, smoothing back her silver bob. "She was a heavy smoker, so I was always reluctant to invite her into my home because I didn't want my house to reek of cigarettes. In those days, you never could have said, 'Please don't smoke in my house.' It would have been considered rude." She paused to sip her coffee. "Mmm. This is good. What type of beans do you use?"

"I'm into Sumatra at the moment. One of these days I'd love to get a fancy espresso maker, but I'm holding out until I can afford a really nice one."

"Make sure to invite me over when that happens. Anyway, back to Mabel. She was a bit eccentric and didn't hold much trust in people, but who could blame her after what her husband had done?"

"What'd he do?"

Nina leaned toward me and whispered, "He ran off with another woman." She arched a brow, nodding a knowing look at me. "It happened ages before I moved in, but the neighbors told me all about it." Her eyes darted around as if she expected to see someone eavesdropping. "They say he got his secretary pregnant. Mabel and her husband had no children. I heard they'd lost two at birth. Heartbreaking." She shrugged, shaking her head. "Needless to say, it left her a very bitter woman, but who can blame her?"

Our conversation was interrupted by a cussing explosion across the street. Lately, my neighbors have been repairing motorcycles in their garage, so there's always a gang of bikers hanging out, and their language gets crude.

"I'd like to go over there and tell those potty-mouthed boys to cut it out," said Nina. "But it's a rough crowd, and I'm afraid of retaliation. In all the years I've lived here, I've never felt intimidated by anyone. Until now. I'm considering selling my house and moving into a senior community. I need to feel safe."

"I honestly don't think we're in any real danger, but we shouldn't have to be hearing that. At least they've stopped playing Lynyrd Skynyrd twenty-four-seven."

"Yes, I suppose I should be thankful for that."

"Can you tell me anything more about Mabel?"

Nina sat back and thought a moment. "Oh! This might interest you. I remember her talking about a wealthy paternal grandfather who didn't trust the booming economy of the 1920's and pulled all his money out of the stock market a couple of years before the big crash of '29. They lived in New York, and Mabel said everyone thought her grandfather was nuts, including her father, who wound up losing everything. She said the day after the market crashed he jumped off the building where he worked on Wall Street."

"I've read about the Depression. There were a lot of suicides at the time." I nibbled a chocolate chip cookie. "Was Mabel well off?"

"Heavens no. She was the most frugal person I've ever met.

And her coffee was atrocious. She'd reuse the grinds over and over until it looked like weak—"

Another long string of vulgarities having to do with women and their lady parts drowned out her last words.

I went to the edge of the porch and hollered, "Hey! Cut it out! There are ladies present."

One of the guys made a grinding motion with his hips while pumping his hands.

"Yeah, you wish," I yelled, knowing I should just shut up.

Of course, that got all of the scum-buckets hooting and grinding, and I turned to Nina. "Obviously, I should've kept my mouth shut."

Nina stood, brushing cookie crumbs off her slacks, came to my side, and shouted, "You boys should know better. Didn't your mother teach you any manners? Shame on you!"

The lowlifes immediately stopped, and a few called out, "Sorry, ma'am."

"You should be. Now behave," said Nina. "My goodness, Katy. That felt good. Why didn't I do that sooner?"

"I could learn a thing or two from you, Nina." I patted her shoulder. "Would you like another cup of coffee?"

"No. This has been lovely, but I must get home and feed my cantankerous old cat, or there'll be hell to pay. Guess I don't have to tell you who's the boss in my house." She turned to leave, then stopped. "I just thought of something that might interest you. When Mabel died, the house went on the auction block. I remember thinking how sad it was that there was no one to claim her estate."

CHAPTER FIVE

SUNDAY · JANUARY 18
Posted by Katy McKenna

My sister called her ex-girlfriend last night. I eavesdropped at her bedroom door long enough to see if the call was going well. When I heard her giggling, I tiptoed away. The reason they broke up was because Emily wouldn't tell her family about their relationship, and that hurt Dana. Who knows? Maybe they'll get back together.

Private
I have to make this private because Ruby reads my blog
and the last thing I want to do is hurt her feelings.

———

I was on my second cup of coffee while checking email on my laptop, half-watching *Good Morning America* and trying not to think about Mabel's money. Who was I kidding? That was all I could think about.

I checked in on my Facebook friends—something I rarely do.

Bio-dad Bert, now the proud father of a bouncing baby boy, had posted some cute photos that made me feel melancholy. I'll never really know this little half-brother of mine. When Aiden is my age, I'll be sixty-four. Wow.

A commercial came on about finding long-lost relatives on PedigreeTree.com, and it got me thinking. Maybe I could find someone deserving in Mabel's family and give them the money. I'd be like a fairy godmother.

I typed in the website, and darn! You had to pay a $19.95 monthly subscription fee to join. So now I was not only going to give away a zillion dollars, but I had to pay to do it. So not fair.

I filled out the registration form, crossed my fingers my credit card wouldn't be declined, and soon I began my search. A few minutes into my noble quest, Ruby called, and I told her what I was doing.

"Sweetie. The woman died *how* many years ago?"

"I looked up her obituary, and she died in April 1988."

"Probably any names you dig up now will either be already long dead or have never heard of her. So, why upset the apple cart? You bought the house, and anything left in it is yours. Enough, already."

"Yeah, but—"

"No buts about it, sweetie. If anyone were interested in what might have been hidden in your house, they would've come and gone long ago. End of story." She paused, and then, "Say, did I ever tell you the story about my bigamist grandfather?"

"No."

"My grandmother came to the U.S. from a little fishing village in Norway in the early 1900's. Marta Sandanger was her name. Isn't Marta a pretty name? You know, I thought about naming your mother Marta. But your grandfather was set on naming her Mary-beth after his favorite aunt, and since she was still alive, it made more sense to honor the living."

Why am I hearing about this now?

"Anyhoo, she wound up working as a housekeeper in Boston where she met a man, got married, or so she thought, and gave birth to my father. Then her ne'er-do-well husband told her that he already had another family and left her high and dry.

Back in those days, that meant my father was illegitimate. A bastard. Quite a stigma for both of them. Never mind the poor thing had been hoodwinked by the scummy scoundrel. Anyway, she moved to Minneapolis and became a housekeeper for a Norwegian widower with several children. Eventually, they got married and had a few more kids, and he adopted my dad."

"Uh-huh. Uh-huh." My dear granny was driving me nuts. I wanted to get back to searching for Mabel's relatives.

Ruby continued, "But what I started out to say is, we have relatives that we'll never know about because of that rotten bigamist. And they don't know about us, either. So, when I die, are you going to track them all down and share your inheritance with them?"

Is that it? All that back history, just to ask that? "No. Why would I? Besides, you always tell me you're going to outlive your money. And besides that, you're never going to die."

"Exactly."

We finally said goodbye. Ruby was probably right about the money, but I felt like I should make sure there was no one out there that might be able to claim the money before I started spending it. Besides, I'd already paid for the service.

I entered Mabel Petersen's info and within minutes found her parents, one sibling—no kids, all long deceased. Then I followed the family tree roots to her grandparents on both sides. From there the branches spread wider and deeper, but further and further from Mabel's side of the family. She'd had no children, nor had her sister, so no direct cousins.

My cell rang, and I was surprised to see that three hours had passed. It was Ruby again.

"Hi, sweetie. Say, I got thinkin'."

Oh, great.

"Since you signed up for that ancestor search site, why don't you see if you can find your great-great-grandfather, the S.O.B. Who knows? Maybe he was an oil baron, or the founder of some big company like Walmart or Coca-Cola. Ya never know."

"And then we lay claim to his estate?" I asked.

"No, I'm just curious. After all, that louse's blood runs in our veins. Tell you what. I'll scan some documents I have and email them to you. My grandmother's death certificate, my father's, too. Their birthdates will be on them and should be enough for a start. What do you say?"

"Why not? Could be interesting."

———

Good news! Emily is going down to Santa Monica to visit Dana next Saturday. Fingers crossed that all goes well. If it's meant to be, it will be.

CHAPTER SIX

TUESDAY · JANUARY 20
Posted by Katy McKenna

Late Sunday Night

PedigreeTree.com is extremely addictive. My family tree is leafing out nicely. One name leads to another and another. And you get little hints that point you to documents on other family trees that have opted to share.

I found out I had a great-great-great-grandfather on my father's side who was a coal miner in Kentucky. That makes me a coal miner's daughter, several times removed. Pretty cool.

I finally turned off the bedside lamp after midnight. As soon as I settled into my favorite go-to-sleep position, I became aware of the attic creatures skittering across the floor. Probably getting high on the minty cotton balls. Really have to do something about them before they bring down the house.

Monday, January 19

Yesterday morning, Ruby called at 8:15. "You dressed yet?"

"Yes," I lied. I'd been sound asleep when the phone rang. "Why?"

"Because I have a job for you."

Ruby works at Nothing Lasts Forever Temp Agency, a job that originally was mine until I bestowed it upon her after one day of employment.

"It's just a one or two-day gig, but I think you'll find it *very* interesting. And, sweetie? Wear something sexy and be at the office at ten for your assignment."

———

"Geez, Louise. Is that your idea of sexy?" Ruby gave me a snarky once-over.

"No. It's my idea of business casual." I wore dark-wash jeggings, a flowy white embroidered Bo-Ho top, ballerina flats, and a knee-length cardigan.

"Maybe you could ditch the ponytail and fluff it up a bit," she said. "I sure wish you'd kept the bangs."

"You know I hate bangs. I've spent months growing out the layers so I can wear a ponytail again and I finally made it. Besides, if I remove the elastic band, my hair will have a dent." I sat down on a gray, tweed loveseat. "So what's the mystery job?"

Ruby leaned her elbows on her desk looking like a teenager about to share some juicy gossip. "You, my dear, are going on a stakeout."

"A stakeout? Shouldn't a private investigator be doing this?"

"He is." Ruby arched an eyebrow like Dr. Evil. "But he needs some feminine backup, and you, my dear, fit the bill." There was a tap-tap on the office door. "That must be him now." She fluffed the crown of her short blond weave, then stood, smoothing her lavender cashmere sweater. "Door's open. Come on in."

Josh-the-Viking entered the office. Even though I recently had sworn off all men for the unforeseeable future, my heart still did a happy dance. He leaned over Ruby's desk and pecked her cheek.

He smiled at me but no peck. "Hey, Cookie."

FYI: The first time we met, I had been in my front yard dressed in Oreo print flannel pajamas. Cookie has been his nickname for me ever since, although sometimes he calls me Cupcake. I'm good with both.

"Hi," I said. *Oh my God. He has the most adorable dimples when he smiles.*

"Katy?" said Ruby. "You okay?"

I caught her salacious little smirk. She knows this guy pushes all my buttons and a few more I didn't even know I had.

"Sorry. I must've zoned out for a sec," I said. "Haven't been sleeping well."

"You sure you're up for this?" Josh sat next to me looking concerned. "I can do it without you."

"Or I could take Katy's place." Ruby pointed at her employer's frosted glass office door. "He can do without me for a few hours. Probably won't even notice I'm gone."

"No, no. I'm fine," I said. "Really. Yup. Let's do it."

Ruby stifled a snicker. She has such a smutty mind.

"Soooo. A stakeout. Sounds interesting," I said.

Josh angled toward me. His denim-clad knee bonked into mine, and he jerked it away. "I have a client who wants to get some dirt on her husband."

"Uh-huh." *He's so cute when he's serious.* I cupped my chin, resting my elbow on my other arm, trying to look all-business.

Josh continued. "She knows he's had affairs in the past, and he swore it would never happen again, but all the telltale signs are there."

"Like what?" I gazed at his tantalizing lips.

"He's working out at the gym, stylish new clothes, new hairstyle. She's pretty sure history is repeating itself, but she wants proof before she goes to a divorce attorney."

"So you need me to do what?" I leaned back on the loveseat and crossed my legs. "Schmooze him at the gym? Get a job where he works?" I stopped, scanning my TV cop show memories. "Try to pick him up at a bar?"

Josh chuckled, no doubt thinking how adorable I am. "We're just going to tail him and see where he goes. I may need you to follow him on foot, as a back-up to me. This guy's a divorce attorney and his wife is going to get hosed if she doesn't have some hard evidence of his infidelity."

———

Josh pulled his silver BMW sports coupe to the curb, killed the engine, and pointed at the single-story, dirty-white stucco building across the street. "That's his office."

The faded wood sign on the front said: "Above the Law Firm." Underneath were two names: Randall Goddard—Personal Injury and Timothy Nelson—Divorce.

"So what's our guy look like?" I said.

Josh leaned toward me to pull a file folder out from behind my seat, and I caught a whiff of his cologne. Spicy, musky, mind-bending.

He straightened, unaware of my mental drooling, and showed me a photo of Timothy Nelson. Pasty white, late forties–early fifties. Receding dark hair, lumpy nose, droopy mustache, aviator-style glasses—ordinary.

"Give me your phone, Katy. I'm going to put my number in it."

I scavenged through my purse and gave it to him, hoping he didn't catch the tremble in my hand. I couldn't help it. He was putting his number in my phone, and we all know what that means.

Josh nodded toward the building. "That didn't take long."

"Huh?" I'd been fixated on his nimble fingers typing his number into my phone.

"Our guy's leaving the office." He handed back my phone and started the engine.

Nelson yanked off his yellow tie and loosened his collar as he rushed toward a blue PT Cruiser. After buckling up, he finger-combed his stringy hair in the rearview mirror, then peeled out of the parking lot.

As a kid, I'd watched *Magnum P.I.* reruns with Grandma Ruby and dreamed of being a private investigator in Hawaii, and now here I was, almost living the dream in Santa Lucia. I wondered if we'd have a car chase. I snugged my seatbelt and set my feet square on the floor, ready for action.

Josh let Nelson pass by, and when he was about a block ahead, we pulled out, following at old-lady-speed, letting a few cars slip in between. Nelson turned right onto Muskeg Street, one of the main streets through downtown. Three blocks down he drove into the parking garage.

At the tollbooth gate, Josh said, "I'm dropping you off here. Then I'll park while you cover the exit door. If he leaves before I catch up, follow him and call me."

Oh. That's why he put his number in my phone.

I jumped out of the car and dashed for the door facing Muskeg Street. It's not the only door out of the building, but most people use that one. A few minutes passed while I lurked in the shadows of a nearby shoe store alcove.

"Come on. Come on," I murmured, tapping a toe.

The heavy metal door swung open, slamming into the concrete wall with a hollow clang, and the perp stepped through. There was no sign of Josh, so while I tailed Nelson, I rang my partner's cell.

"You following him?" he asked.

"Yeah. I'm eyeballin' the sleazeball right now."

I heard a chuckle. "Good girl. Where are you?"

"I'm at a stoplight at the corner of Muskeg and—"

An arm slipped around my shoulders, and I nearly jumped out of my skin. Then Josh murmured in my ear, "Let's pretend we're a couple."

Walking became virtually impossible, as if my rubbery legs had done a complete disconnect from my brain. The only thing I was aware of was the weight of his warm arm draped over my shoulders.

The light turned green, and Nelson scurried across the street. I stumbled off the curb, and Josh gripped my arm, keeping me upright. Halfway down the block, Nelson entered Victoria's Secret.

"Guess we're doing a little shopping." Josh held the door open for me. "After you, m'lady."

Inside, we loitered at the panty display table, perusing the wares. Nelson was studying a mannequin adorned in a black lacey bustier and red garters.

"This is cute." With an impish grin, Josh brandished an itsy-bitsy pink, polka-dot bikini.

I ripped it out of his hand and laid it neatly back in its slot on the table, thinking maybe I should get a pair. You know. Just in case.

"Look," whispered Josh. "He's talking to a clerk about that frilly thing."

"It's called a bustier."

"Well, it sure can't be for his wife. She's a pretty hefty woman. No way would she fit into that thing." He pulled out his phone. "Let's do a selfie."

"Seriously? Now? Here?" I said.

He put his arm around me and turned me around. In the phone screen, I could see Nelson behind us, holding the bustier, still chatting with the clerk. "Now tilt your head toward me so that I can get a clear shot of him."

I tilted.

"Little more. Little more."

I tilted until my temple was touching the nape of his neck.

"Perfect." He clicked several photos. "Okay, he's moving to the register."

We pulled apart and watched Nelson purchase the garment while Josh snapped more photos.

"May I help you?" asked a tinsel-teethed young salesgirl.

"We're on our honeymoon," said Josh. "The little wifey wants a —hold on." His eyes flicked to Nelson heading out the exit. "Sorry. Gotta go." He grabbed my hand, dragging me through the store.

Outside, Nelson was walking briskly toward the parking structure.

"I parked on the same level as him, so let's get up there before he does." We scurried past Nelson and raced across the street as the light turned red. Inside the building, Josh bypassed waiting for the elevator and opened the door to the stairs.

On the third level, he stopped and held the door, waiting for me. Good thing because one more floor and I would have keeled over. I'd been out of breath since halfway up the second flight of stairs, and my sore shins were throbbing. As I slipped by him, I tried to squelch my desperate gasps for air so he wouldn't catch onto how out of shape I am.

"Are you all right?" he asked, furrowing his brows. "You look like you're limping."

"It's nothing." *Don't make me talk. I'm trying to breathe.* "My legs are a little sore, that's all."

While I got into his BMW, he kept his eyes on the elevator. "I see Nelson getting out of the elevator." He climbed into the driver's seat.

I fumbled to snap my seatbelt buckle and accidentally grabbed his hand. A jolt of electricity zinged through me, and I wondered if he'd felt it, too. "Sorry," I muttered.

"No worries." He gunned the engine as we waited in awkward silence for Nelson to get in his car.

We followed the cheater through town to a tired looking gray house in a neighborhood of small cookie-cutter ranchers. Josh drove past the house, then did a U-turn on the next block and parked a few houses away. He reached behind my seat and hauled out an expensive looking camera with a telephoto lens and began snapping photos.

Nelson hopped out of the Cruiser, clutching the pink striped Victoria Secret box behind his back. He hurried up the weedy walkway to the front door and rang the bell. The door opened, and a middle-aged busty brunette flung her arms around him and planted a big, smooshy kiss on his lips. Nelson presented the gift, and she squealed with delight as she hauled him into the house.

"I would say he just nailed his coffin." Josh started the car.

"So that's it? That's private investigator work?"

"For the most part. Not like TV, huh?"

"No. But it was kinda fun."

"We got lucky today. These things can drag on and on. And then wind up going nowhere."

"But you still get paid, right?" I said.

"By the hour with an upfront retainer and expenses."

"How much is the average retainer fee?"

"Anywhere from fifteen hundred to five thousand, depending on the case," said Josh.

That got me thinking. *I could do this. I could be a private investigator. And it pays way better than graphic artwork.*

"What're you thinking, Katy?"

"Nothin'. Just thinkin'."

He chuckled. "You'd need training, a license, bonding. Or you could work some more cases with me and see how it goes. What do you think?"

I'm thinkin'....

When I got home from the stakeout, I found a note on the kitchen counter from my sister. *Working late tonight.*

Eager to regale my friend, Samantha, with an account of my undercover stakeout adventure, I curled up in my favorite chair by the French doors and called her.

"Hi, Katy," she said. "What's going on in your world?"

I got halfway through my story when the doorbell rang. "Hold on. Someone's at the door."

I checked the doorbell app on my phone and saw Josh standing on the porch. Daisy was whining at the door, so I should have known.

"Gotta go, Sam," I whispered. "It's Josh."

"Call me later!" she shouted as I clicked off.

With my heart beating an allegro tempo, I opened the door, and Daisy shoved past me, wriggling her tush around her boyfriend with no shame at all.

Josh petted her, but his eyes were locked on mine. "Hi."

I felt shy and barely able to breathe. "Hi."

He held out a bottle of red wine. "We need to talk."

I gulped as a shudder of urgent, delicious need overtook all rational thought. "No, we don't."

His soft smile collapsed, and his arm fell to his side, dangling the bottle.

I reached out, grabbed his blue button-down and pulled him through the doorway, then turned to him and leaned against the closed door.

"I brought a bottle of wine," Josh said, his voice quiet, intense. "It's supposed to be good. I know you like reds and...." He set the bottle on the entry table. "It's a petite...." He moved close to me and brushed a tendril of hair from my face, his fingers lingering on my cheek. "Syrah." He traced my jawline and then gently cupped my face with warm hands.

I was unable to move, to breathe, to think as he whispered

against my lips. "Katy, Katy, Katy. You crazy woman. What're you doing to me?"

Today

I whiled away most of this morning in a horny haze, reliving every delicious moment with Josh last night when I should have been working on what to do about the pile of gold stashed in my closet. Either it's mine or it's not, but if it *is* mine, then darn it, I wanna go shopping! I have a sudden need for sexy undies.

I logged into PedigreeTree.com and found several messages and hints waiting for me. Nothing regarding my search for Mabel, but there was a hint that led me to a family tree with my great-great-grandfather's name on it. Looking at the dates and location, it had to be him. I decided to send a message to a person on the tree who was in my age range and would also be Eugene's great-great-granddaughter.

Dear Erin,

There is a Eugene Horatio Cranston in your family tree, and he may be the same man who was my great-great-grandfather.

My grandmother's grandmother, Marta Sandanger, came from Norway to Boston in the early 1900's and wound up marrying a man by this name. They had a child in 1913, and then Eugene told her that he was already married and had a family. She insisted that his name was on their child's birth certificate because being an "illegitimate" child was a social stigma in those days.

His story may or may not have been true, as I am told this was often called a "poor man's divorce" using the "already married" excuse to abandon a family.

I hope it is all right to tell you this, but given how long ago it was, I have to think it is. I look forward to hearing from you.

Katy McKenna

Sam called around 11:45. "I'm on my lunch. Can you talk?" Her voice dropped to a whisper. "Or are you *busy*?"

"I know what you're implying, and yes, I can talk. Josh left early this—"

"Oh, my God." She squealed like a seventh-grader sharing secrets in the girls bathroom. "I want to remind you that besties share *everything*. So spill it, girl."

"Mmmm. It was *sooo* incredible."

"How incredible?"

"Like something out of a romance novel."

"How would you know?" she said. "You don't read romances."

"No. But you do. And you always talk about them."

"That's because it bugs you when I do. Can you come over for dinner tonight and tell me everything? Spencer's out of town, as usual; Chelsea's going hormonal on me, and it doesn't help that I'm PMSing. And Casey's been acting like a little butthead the last couple days. I desperately need an adult to talk to. *Puh-leeeze*?"

"Oooo. As fun as that all sounds, no can do, kiddo. Got a date." *With my boyfriend.*

"God, I can barely remember what sex is," said Sam. "Is it wonderful?"

"It was with Josh. And that guy had a lot to live up to considering how long I've been dreaming about him. But my dreams didn't even come close to the reality. It was beyond perfect, except for my sore ear, that is."

"What's that supposed to mean? Is he...kinky? Oh God, please say no."

"He's not kinky unless you call wanting me to dress in a clown outfit, kinky."

"What?" she screamed.

"Kidding. Boy, are you easy." I heaved another sigh to bug my BFF. And don't feel sorry for Sam because she did this to me when she hooked up with Spencer. "But he is—how should I put this? Exuberant. But in such a good way. A *really* good way."

"That doesn't explain the sore ear."

"You know how you told me it was a stupid idea to put those potted plants on the shelf over my bed?"

"Yeah. They look good there, but what if there's an earthquake?"

"Exactly. Thank goodness the pot was plastic."

"You know, I pretty much hate you right now."

CHAPTER SEVEN

WEDNESDAY · JANUARY 21
Posted by Katy McKenna

Josh cooked dinner for me last night. Halibut piccata, potatoes au gratin, baby green beans paired with a crisp pinot grigio. We got about three bites into the scrumptious meal when he said, "How about we put this under the warming lights on the stove and—"

I practically knocked my chair over scrambling to my feet.

Josh grabbed the wine and our glasses, and we raced to his bedroom. He won since he knew where he was going.

I'm so happy.

————

Sam FaceTimed me late this morning. "Hey, Katy. Watcha doin'?"

I know that means I'm supposed to ask her what *she's* doing.

"Nothing much. How about you?" I asked. "Hey, how come you're in the kitchen? Aren't you supposed to be at work?"

"I'm stuck at home with a sick kid."

"Which one?"

"Casey. Guess that's why he was acting bratty the last few days."

"What's wrong with my little buddy?"

Sam was walking toward the sofa in her great room. "I think it's a flu bug. He's running a fever, has an upset tummy, and sniffles."

Sam sat down, and Casey came into view. He looked adorable all bundled up in a blanket "He's watching his favorite show. Casey? Want to say hi to Aunt Katy?"

He took the phone. "Hi, Aunt Katy. I'm weally sick."

"I know, sweetie. I'm sorry you don't feel good."

His little mug looked so gloomy I just wanted to reach through the phone and give him a big hug.

"What's your favorite show, Casey?"

"*Paw Patrol*." His eyes grew wide. "Oh, I don't feel good." And then he hurled onto the phone screen.

Yuck. Did not see that coming.

———

This afternoon, I took Daisy to the Lago Lake dog park, hoping to run into Ruby's boyfriend, Ben. He hangs out there a few afternoons a week doing needlepoint and watching the doggies cavort. He says he's window-shopping and plans to get a rescue dog one of these days. He's leaning toward getting a Labrador. Says he's never met one he didn't like. I can attest to that. But then, I've never met a dog of any breed that I didn't like. Wish I could say the same about people.

After Daisy dragged me through the park's double gates, I wrestled off her leash and watched her make new friends before settling on the bench next to Ben. He was working on a yellow lab needlepoint project.

"Ooo. I like that. Kinda of reminds me of somebody I know."

"You weren't supposed to see this until it was done. I had a photo of Daisy made into a pattern. I thought it would make a nice pillow."

"Ahhh." I squeezed his arm. "That's so sweet. No wonder my granny is crazy about you."

Ben Burnett is a famous (as in *People* Magazine famous) retired criminal attorney from Los Angeles. He makes needlepoint pillows for the kids at the women's shelter in Santa Lucia, along with giving free legal advice. He said he's trying to make amends for all the guilty scumbags he put back on the streets during his long career.

"Did Ruby tell you what I found in my attic?" I said.

"She did. Have you moved forward on that yet?"

"No."

Ben pulled off his wire rims, set his needlepoint on the bench, and turned to me. "Ruby said you're trying to find the rightful owner. That would be you, Katy. You own the house, and that money had been sitting in the attic for years, which means there is no one living who knows anything about it. So there will be no claims."

"But—"

He held up a hand to shush me. "Even if someone did try to place a claim now, their connection to the money would be so dubious that no judge would take it seriously. Believe me, it's been tried. There was a case few years ago in Oregon where a homeowner found a coin collection in a kitchen wall when he was having his old house rewired. The collection was valued in the high six figures. The man had lived in the house for over twenty years, and no relatives of any former owners had ever approached him about the possibility of the coin collection still being in the house. However, when the story hit the newspapers, dozens of long-lost so-called 'relatives,'" he finger-quoted, "tried to stake their claims. Even the electrician went after him saying he found the money, so it should be his."

"Geez. That's pretty low. So what happened?"

"He got to keep the money. But he also had to pay huge legal fees to fight off those damned vultures. So the lesson here is—do not tell anyone outside the family circle about the money."

"Too late. I already told Sam."

"She's family. And I like to think I am, too."

"You are." I threw my arms around the dear man and gave him a hug.

He patted my back. "Thank you, honey."

As if on cue, Daisy ran up and kissed Ben's hand, then dashed back to her buddies.

"That does it. I'm getting a Lab. You know, she's the reason I met you, and then your beautiful grandmother. I cannot begin to tell you what that has meant to me after being alone for so many years." He brushed away a tear. "Let's get back to what we were talking about before we were so sweetly interrupted." He ran a hand over his perfectly trimmed silver goatee, shaking his head with a big sigh. "When I say do not tell anyone outside the family about the coins, I mean immediate family. The more people who know, the more likely it is that you're going to have problems. Maybe big problems."

I slumped on the bench, wishing I'd never found that damned box. "Got it."

"I don't mean to imply that, for example, your great-aunt Edith would try to extort you for money, but she might inadvertently tell someone who might. And you need to warn Emily, too."

"I will." *I wonder if she already told her girlfriend? Of course she has. I would've.*

His stern lawyerly look softened into a grandfatherly smile. "Okay, I'm done lecturing. Ruby asked if I would help you, and I'd be more than happy to."

"I'd love your help because I don't even know where to begin."

"Well, I do."

CHAPTER EIGHT

THURSDAY • JANUARY 22
Posted by Katy McKenna

Following Ben's advice, Pop and I took a twenty-dollar gold piece to a reputable coin dealer today. Upon entry, a portly senior gentleman waved from a recliner in the corner. "Howdy. How may I help you fine folks today?"

Not ready to commit, I said, "Oh, we're just browsing. Never been in a coin shop before."

"Well, take your time, and if either of you has any questions, I'll be right here, taking a load off."

I nosed around the dark paneled, memorabilia-crammed shop. Glass-topped counter cases displayed money from all over the world. There were boxes on top of one table overflowing with foreign bank notes selling for a dollar each. I selected one from the Cook Islands and admired the colorful illustration of a mermaid riding a ferocious looking shark. Another note showed a ferocious looking Tiki man with a very long you-know-what standing next to an outrigger canoe. Sure made our U.S. currency seem dull and stodgy.

"How long are you going to stall, Katy-did?" murmured Pop from behind me.

"Just give me another minute. At this moment, I may be a wealthy woman, but in another minute, I may be back to normal. In other words, broke."

He chuckled. "That's how I feel when I'm about to check my lottery ticket numbers." We approached the counter, and my father said, "Hate to get you out of your comfortable chair. Got a bum knee so I can sympathize, but we have something to show you."

"That's what I'm here for," said the jovial man, grunting as he stood. "Got a bad knee myself. One of these days, I need to go in for a replacement, but I'm not looking forward to the downtime." He jiggled his knee into place and then joined us at the counter. "Let's have a looksee at what ya got."

I removed the coin from its plastic snack bag and placed it on a black velvet pad on the counter. The man furrowed his bushy white brows as his grin faded.

Oh, crap. It must be worthless.

"My-oh-my, what have we here?" He picked up the coin and inspected it under a lighted magnifier. "Where'd you get this?"

I glanced at my father for an answer.

"It's been sitting in a drawer for years," said Pop. "I've been watching *Antiques Roadshow* for awhile now, and got to thinking maybe we should check it out. See if it's worth anything."

"Hold on a sec. I don't want anyone interrupting us." The shopkeeper locked the door, turned the Open sign to Closed, and shut the blinds. "I think it's time I introduced myself." He held out his hand. "Don Jacobs."

Pop introduced us, and we all shook hands, and then he said, "I'm getting the impression that it's worth a little more than twenty bucks."

"Oh yeah." Don twiddled the curl of his silver handlebar mustache. "You could say that. I should call my wife out. She's in back, doing the bills, and she'd kill me for sure if I didn't show her this." He hollered through the swinging saloon door behind the counter. "Jeri? You have got to take a look at what these nice folks brought in."

A petite curly redhead joined us, beaming a sweet smile. "This better be good, Donny. Those bills aren't going to pay themselves, you know."

Don handed his wife the magnifier. "Take a gander at this, honeybunch."

She gasped. "Oh, my word. An 1876 Liberty Head in mint condition. It's magnificent. Not a scratch on it." She turned it over several times, even checking the edges.

"We'd love to buy it," said Don, looking like a kid in a candy store. "But first I suggest you do some research, so you feel comfortable with what we offer."

"I did a little online research," I said. "But I don't know how accurate that would be. It's not like I know anything about old coins and—" I stopped, realizing I sounded like a gullible idiot.

The look Pop was pointing my way told me he shared that opinion. "Your shop has a good reputation," he said. "Of course, we understand that whatever you offer takes into consideration the fact that you'll probably resell it for a profit. That's to be expected."

"Thank you for understanding that, Kurt. These days, people do a little research online. Watch some of those pawn shop shows on TV. And then come in here and expect to get top dollar not realizing that to stay in business, we have to make a profit. We're just a mom and pop shop."

"With extremely high insurance," said Jeri. "Every year the premiums go up even though we've never made a claim. And then there's the IRS. You do understand that you'll have to pay taxes, right?"

"Goes without saying," said Pop. "But how does it work in a case like this?"

"If you were to bring in coins that are worth more than $10,000, we'd give you a federal form to fill out right here in the shop," said Don. "In the past, more than a few dealers have wound up in prison for not conducting proper business. Like paying a customer half in cash and the other half by check, then only reporting the check amount."

"And I think the fine may be up to $25,000 now, so it's not worth fudging on the tax issue," said Jeri. "If it's under $10,000, it's up to you to report the sale. We will, of course, report it on our end."

Don put his arm around his wife's slim shoulders. "If you'll excuse us a moment, I'd like to confer with Jeri before we make an offer. In the meantime, why don't you put the coin back in your purse."

They went in the rear of the shop. I could hear their buzzing voices, but couldn't make out a single word. Several nerve-wracking minutes had passed before they returned.

"We'd like to offer $8,500 for your coin," said Don. "You may be able to get more from a larger dealer, and we would understand if you'd like to shop it around. I could suggest some very respectable ones down in Los Angeles and up in the San Francisco Bay Area."

I tried to keep a poker face. "Pop? May I confer with you a moment?"

"Take all the time you need." The couple went to the back again.

I pulled Pop to the far corner of the shop and whispered, "That's way more than I expected. What should I do? I mean, it could be worth thousands more. Maybe we should go see one of those dealers in San Francisco."

Pop grinned all through my speech.

"What are you smiling about?" I asked.

"Confer? You want to *confer* with me?"

"Yeah." I rolled my eyes. "I *do*."

He set his hands firmly on my shoulders and looked me square in the eyes. "Here's the thing, Katy-did. Right now, you can walk out of here with a big fat check in your wallet and not worry about looking for another graphics job for a while. And don't forget, you have two safes full of gold coins at home. This is just the tip of the iceberg."

"So you're saying take the money?"

"And run!"

The woman I contacted on PedigreeTree.com responded.

Hi Katy!

What a fun surprise to hear from you!

I already knew that Eugene Cranston was a bigamist. He married my great-great-grandmother in California and then left her when my great-grandfather was a toddler. Told her he was already married. I wonder how many times he did this. My grandfather told my dad that years later Eugene contacted his father to make amends. He died shortly after.

So I guess this makes us cousins. I'd love to meet you someday. Where do you live?

Hugs,
Your new cousin,
Erin Cranston
P.S. Let's be Facebook friends!

We are now FB friends, bringing my total to thirty-six friends. She's single, really cute, lives in Palo Alto, and works at Google—how cool is that?

I can't wait to meet her.

Update on the squirrels in my attic

Life's been crazy lately, and they have become low on the

priority list. And yes, I know it's actually rats, according to my sister. But I prefer to think I'm sharing my home with adorable squirrels. No matter what they are, the pesky critters are still up there, and I know there's going to have to be a day of reckoning.

I hate the idea of killing any animal, but there doesn't seem to be any way around it. The beepers were a bust, ditto the peppermint cotton balls, and relocation would probably kill them. So, with a heavy heart, I called an exterminator and set up an appointment for an inspection next Wednesday. They wanted to come tomorrow, but I've got a lot going on. Or maybe I'm still hoping I'll get a brilliant idea on how to get rid of the pests without murdering them.

CHAPTER NINE

Posted by Katy McKenna

Emily left at the crack of dawn to visit her ex in Santa Monica. Sure hope all goes well. Since I have the house all to myself, I invited Josh over for a slumber party. Woo-hoo!

That also means I have to clean the house because his home is immaculate. Super tidy, and not a speck of dust (I checked). Drawers organized (I peeked). No clothes on the floor, no dishes in the sink, and get this—he caps the toothpaste. Who does that?

So my house has to be spotless—something it is never.

———

In the late afternoon, I hit up the Whole Foods deli because I was too pooped from cleaning to cook. Besides, you don't have to be a good cook to put on a good spread. You just have to be a good shopper.

When I got home, I popped the food in the oven to warm it, set the timer, and tossed the cartons, although who did I think I was fooling? When Josh rang the bell, Daisy dashed for the front door and woofed to her sweetheart on the porch. Guess who kissed him first?

"Whoa, Daisy. I'm glad to see you." He leaned over the squirmy girl and pecked me on the lips. "Happy to see you too. I brought another bottle of that red you enjoyed the other night."

That little kiss was like a double espresso for me, and as soon as the door shut, round one of the smooch-fest began. I finally said, "Really happy to see you too."

Josh followed me to the kitchen and set the Petite Syrah on the tiled counter. "Where do you keep your corkscrew?"

"Top drawer, left of the sink." Then I remembered the jumbled chaos in the drawer. "I'll get it for you." Doing my best to shield the mess, I fumbled through the clutter and pulled one out.

Josh filled two glasses, and we clinked rims and sipped the luscious wine. And that led to more kisses. And that led us to…

————

An hour later, Josh sniffed the air. "Do you smell something burning?"

"That would be our dinner."

There was no point in jumping out of bed to save the meal. Besides, that would have meant exposing my bare derrière in walk-away mode, and I wasn't ready for that, so I waited for him to make the first move.

"How about I get it out of the oven?" he said. "Maybe it's not as bad as it smells."

The food was worse than it smelled, so we strolled over to Suzy Q's for dinner. It's a neighborhood organic vegetarian cafe with a boho vibe and outrageously good food. After we were seated on the heated patio under a trellis of magenta bougainvillea, we ordered a bottle of local pinot noir, then read our menus in comfortable silence.

The waiter arrived with our wine, unscrewed it with a flourish, and after he filled our glasses, I said, "Remember the last time we had dinner here, Josh?"

"You'd just been nearly choked to death by that lunatic, and I'd lent you an ugly Christmas turtleneck sweater to cover the bruises. You sure looked sexy in it."

"Well…you're gonna laugh about this, but I thought we were on a real date until a few days later when you referred to me as your buddy and, um…."

Josh set down his glass and leaned in close, taking my hand. "I was crazy about you, but I didn't feel ready for you." He shook his head, looking forlorn. "I had hurt my ex-wife so badly, and I didn't want to take a chance on hurting you, too."

"Can you tell me about it? I remember you said your job as an undercover narcotics cop destroyed your marriage."

"It did. When you take on a job like that, you live and breathe it. I was hanging with lowlife scum, and after a while the lines got blurred, and eventually Nicole had enough of it. Said she didn't know who I was anymore." Josh shook his head, and his eyes filled. "Hell, *I* didn't know who I was anymore. I was drinking too much, scared most of the time, wouldn't talk to her let alone listen to her."

Josh broke eye contact, absently straightening the flatware. "After she left me, I realized I had to get out of it, so I quit my job and hit the road, finally winding up at my mother's house in Stockbridge, Massachusetts. I was broken, and it took a long time to heal."

"Do you ever hear from her? Nicole, I mean."

He turned his baby blues back on me. "All the time. We're still close friends. She's doing well. Has a good job as a paralegal at a big firm in Los Angeles. I hope she finds a decent guy one of these days. She deserves it."

His story wrenched my heart. "Do you think you two might, you know—"

Josh cupped my chin and pulled me in for a soft kiss. "No." Kiss. "We're friends. Just friends. Nothing more. She's my past." Kiss. "You, on the other hand…." Kiss.

CHAPTER TEN

SATURDAY · JANUARY 24
Posted by Katy McKenna

Everyone keeps telling me that Mabel's money is mine, so today I returned to the coin shop with a partial inventory of the coins.

"So let me get this straight." Don looked at me like I had a screw loose. "You're telling us that you have *how* many coins?"

"Nine hundred and seventy three." I handed him my list. "I wrote down the denominations, but I know I should've recorded the dates and where they were minted, but I was running short on time. But the list will give you an idea of what I've got."

Don's eyes practically popped out of their sockets, as he scanned the list with his wife. "If what you're saying is true—"

"And we don't doubt you, dear." Jeri patted my hand. "It's just that this is so astonishing."

"I'll say," said Don, waving the list. "It's amazing when even one gold coin is found, let alone this many. Some of the dates you've got here go all the way back to the California Gold Rush. And you say they're all in the same condition as the one you brought in the other day?"

I nodded, trying not to hyperventilate.

"This will cause quite a stir in the numismatic world," said Jeri, supporting her slender frame against the glass counter. "And to think that we get to be a part of the excitement. Oh my."

Numismatic? I had no idea what that meant. "Should I bring the coins here?"

"Oh no." Don shook his head, waving his hands. "No-no-no. Too risky. We'll come to you."

The shop doorbell buzzed, and he glanced at the security monitor. "It's Corky. He's an old and trusted friend, Katy, but I don't want anyone hearing about this. Why don't you and Jeri go in back and set up an appointment for us to come to your house on Monday."

CHAPTER ELEVEN

Last night Josh and I enjoyed Suzy Q leftovers and watched one of my all-time favorite quirky movies, *O Brother, Where Art Thou?*

Josh tickled my arm. "Hey, Cupcake. Got any more of that mint-chip ice cream? You've got me hooked on it, you know."

"There's a little bit left, and it's all yours."

He started to get up and then I remembered the clutter of boxes and bags jammed in the freezer.

"I'll get it for you." A few moments later, I handed him the carton and a spoon. "Here ya go."

"You sure you don't want any? We can share."

"Nope. I'm good." I wanted some, but I've been trying to cut back since seeing his firm, bare tushie.

When the carton was empty, he stuffed it in the garbage can under the kitchen sink and yelled, "Can you put it on pause while I take out the garbage?"

Oh. He's taking out the garbage. Who knew that domesticity could be so sexy? While he was outside, his cell beeped a text message. It was sitting in plain sight on the coffee table, so I leaned forward for a quick peek at the screen. It was from Nicole. His ex. Part of the message was visible without signing in. *I have bad news and need to...*

The kitchen door opened, and I sat back, acting nonchalant as Josh returned to the couch and snuggled close.

"Do you think it's time to go to bed?" He leaned close and nibbled my ear. "I do."

Usually, it's impossible to think about anything when he's doing that, but I needed to know what that message said. The tip of his tongue traced my ear as I said, "Um, uh. You got a... Ooo... Ummm...."

"Yes?" he whispered, his lips kissing their way into the crook of my neck as his hand snaked down my pants.

I was nearly incapable of coherent thought, but I needed to know what his ex's bad news was. The warm, wonderful hand was now approaching ground zero. Time was running out. *Concentrate, Katy!* "You got a text message. Maybe you should check it in case it's something important."

"It can wait, but I can't."

———

Josh untangled himself from my arms, threw back the blankets, and crept to the living room. I glanced at the alarm clock. 1:43. *He must be reading the message.* A minute later, he crawled back into bed and curled up to me.

"Everything okay?" I asked.

"I don't know. The text was from Nicole. She said she has some bad news. I'll call her in the morning." He nestled close and within seconds was softly snoring. I, on the other hand, lay there staring at the dark ceiling, consumed with curiosity about Nicole's bad news.

———

Today

Good news! Emily and her girlfriend, Dana, are getting back together. In fact, she's in her room packing as I write this. There's a light in her eyes that I've never seen before. Must be the look of love.

Dana works at Roxy Studios for some big mucky-muck in the television division and says she can get Emily a job there, too. Probably more like a "go-fer" job, since she has no work experience or education that would qualify her for a position like Dana's, but still it's an exciting opportunity.

I'm going to miss my little sister. If you'd told me I'd be feeling this way after she moved in last summer, I would have said you were delusional.

———

Josh called to break our dinner date. He's heading down to Los Angeles to see Nicole. Turns out her bad news was awful. She has colon cancer. I don't know how I'm supposed to feel about this. Of course, I feel terrible for her. But why does Josh have to go?

I just read that last line back, and realize I'm being selfish.

CHAPTER TWELVE

MONDAY · JANUARY 26
Posted by Katy McKenna

Don and Jeri Jacobs came over late this morning to see the coin collection. Even though they seem like good, honest people, I still felt anxious about being alone with them and all that money, so I asked Pop to attend. After everyone was settled in the living room with coffee, and green tea for Jeri, Pop set one of the fire safes on the coffee table, then opened it and sat back to relish their amazed reaction.

Don was the first to find his voice. "Even though I was expecting this, it's still mind-boggling."

"That's putting it mildly." Jeri held a hand over her heart, sounding breathless. She reached into her purse, and I'm embarrassed to admit this, but my back instantly stiffened with apprehension, as I envisioned her whipping out a gun and blowing Pop and me to Kingdom Come.

Instead of a gun, she pulled out a sheet of paper. "According to your list, you have eight hundred twenty-dollar gold coins, a hundred twenty-five ten dollar ones, and forty-eight fives with a total face value of $17,490."

"Wow." I already knew that number, but it still impressed me.

Jeri continued, "We won't know exactly what you have until all the coins have been catalogued and graded, of course. But there's no doubt in my mind that it will be in the millions. Even after taxes."

Pop patted my knee. "You okay, Katy-did? You look a little unsteady."

"Yeah." I took a shaky sip of coffee. "It's just so crazy. This kind of thing happens to other people. Not me."

"Look, Jeri," said Don, holding out a coin to her. "1847. San Francisco mint. Pristine."

Jeri cradled it in her hand. "It looks like it was never circulated."

"I gather there's quite a bit of work to do before Katy can start selling the coins," said Pop.

"There is," said Don. "But luckily, the coins don't need cleaning. That can be a very painstaking, time-consuming task. But I'll want to confer with someone more qualified than me. There's a man down in Santa Monica who's well regarded in the numastics field. He's dealt with big finds like this before. Even a sunken treasure from the Spanish Armada."

"Oliver Kershaw's his name," said Jeri. "He'll know how to proceed."

"When you have time," said Don, "go on Amazon and take a look at some of the coins they have listed there to get a better idea of what you have. I think you'll be pleasantly shocked."

"Amazon?" said Pop. "Are you kidding?"

Don shook his head with a chuckle. "Not kidding. They have a collectible coin department. In fact, go on there and type in Saddle Ridge Hoard—you know, the hoard that was discovered in the Sierras by a couple walking their dog on their property a few years back. Last time I looked, there were still several available for sale, ranging from $3,500 to $16,000."

"And while they are all in excellent condition, not one of them matches Katy's coins," said Jeri. "I guess you're going to have to come up with a name for your hoard, Katy."

After everyone left, I grabbed my laptop and settled on the couch to take a look at the Saddle Ridge Coins on Amazon. There weren't any 1847 gold coins listed, but there was an 1880 S Liberty Head twenty-dollar gold piece going for sixteen thousand bucks.

As soon as I saw that, I realized I needed to get the coins out of my house. But where? A safe deposit box? It would have to be a really big one. And I seriously doubt I could drag the fire safes into the bank without raising a few eyebrows. They'll probably think I'm a drug dealer and call the cops. Or the Feds. Or, God forbid, the IRS.

I sure hope those fire safes are as heat resistant as their labels claim.

———

"I'm not waking you up, am I, Cookie? I know it's late to be calling, but I wanted to hear your voice."

It was 11:25 and yes, Josh had woke me, but as soon as he said, "Cookie," I switched on the bedside lamp and piled the pillows behind my back, ready to listen and offer comfort.

"How's Nicole?"

He exhaled a sad sigh. "Not good. She needs to have a colectomy. Her mother and grandmother died from colon cancer at fairly young ages. I remember how sick her mother was. We were still in high school at the time."

"How bad is the cancer? I mean, what stage?"

"She didn't say. But she said her prognosis for a five-year survival is around eighty to ninety percent. She'll be doing chemo and radiation after the surgery."

The desolate tone in Josh's voice tugged my heart. "Ninety percent is really good, Josh. I don't think the doctors ever say one hundred percent, but ninety is pretty much that."

"You think so?" he asked in a small voice.

"I know so. My grandmother had breast cancer in her fifties, and her odds weren't nearly so good, and she's been cancer-free for over twenty years now."

"To look at her, you'd never know she's been sick a day in her life," he said.

"I know. But she was incredibly sick when she was going through the chemo. I remember how frail and old she looked. But as soon as she got through it and regained the weight, she was back to being my crazy, glamorous grandma."

"That's good to hear. I'll tell Nicole."

"Does Nicole have any family close by or friends who can help?"

"No relatives in the area. Nicole's dad joined the Peace Corps after he retired, and he's in Botswana. She has friends, but they all work full-time, and she's going to need round-the-clock care."

I know where this is going. He's not coming back.

"So I've volunteered to take care of her," he said. "It's the least I can do after everything I put her through."

"Oh...."

He continued. "I know. This is a hell of a thing to happen just when you and I are getting started."

"It's okay. I understand."

My head buzzed so loudly I barely heard him say, "I should be home in a couple of weeks, more or less."

"Huh? A couple of weeks? But you said she's doing chemo and radiation after the surgery."

"She is, but she's going to do it in Santa Lucia. In fact, she insisted, because she didn't want me to have to stay away from you for so long. I told her all about you, and she can't wait to meet you."

"Oh." *It's going to be okay!*

After Josh's phone call, I was wide awake. I opened my laptop and went on Amazon to look at coins again. Some of the "storefronts" had numerous pages of rare coins, while others had just one or two coins. And that gave me an idea.

Even though I still have a lot of money left over from selling that coin to the Jacobs, I have decided to put one coin for sale on Amazon. My hope is to get enough money to pay off my credit cards and still have enough cash stashed in the bank to cover my bills for the next few months.

However, I will wait and do it in the morning. I've learned through bitter experience that sometimes my late night bright ideas don't seem quite so bright in the cold light of day.

And that concludes today's post. However, I'm still wide awake, dammit.

CHAPTER THIRTEEN

TUESDAY · JANUARY 27
Posted by Katy McKenna

First thing this morning, I canceled the exterminator. I just can't be a party to slaughtering innocent little critters. There's got to be a better answer than that.

———

Last night's bright idea still seemed brilliant today, so I am now an "individual seller" on Amazon. I put an 1888 S Liberty Head ten-dollar coin up for sale in my shop. There's already one for sale in another shop for $5,250. Mine is in better condition—the other one has some tiny scratches, but I priced mine at five thousand to move it fast.

What really pushed me to do it was a call from Stinky's Muffler Shop this morning. They want me to design a NASCAR style logo that will be embroidered onto a jacket for their company mascot, an English bulldog named Stinky. They're not in a rush, so I said I'd check my calendar and get back to them.

Don Jacobs called and said the coin specialist in Santa Monica is eager to see my coins and wondered if tomorrow would be okay. So, things are moving along. Fingers crossed I don't have to do the Stinky job.

———

My newfound cousin, Erin Cranston, texted me. She's driving to Los Angeles on Thursday for a business meeting on Friday. She wants to stop on the way to meet me. She invited me to join her for dinner at Le Stella, a swanky restaurant in the fanciest hotel in Clam Beach where she's spending the night—just ten minutes from my house. Can't wait to meet her.

CHAPTER FOURTEEN

WEDNESDAY · JANUARY 28
Posted by Katy McKenna

The coin expert from Los Angeles arrived around one, along with Don Jacobs from the coin shop. In my mind, I'd pictured the numismatist as a scholarly gent in his sixties or seventies, and boy was I wrong. Oliver Kershaw, a tall, dark, and handsome Brit, looked like he'd stepped from the pages of GQ magazine. And his accent. OMG.

Oliver has a Ph.D. in numismatics from Oxford University. His original field of expertise was Roman and Greek coinage, but his real passion is for modern: 1700's to early 1900's. He consults on archeological digs around the world and is affiliated with several prestigious museums.

"Don told me that he believes your coins are second only to the recent Saddle Ridge Hoard found in the Sierras by that couple who were out walking their dog," said Oliver.

"From what I've read, their identities haven't been revealed. I would like the same for me."

"Of course, we'll be discreet. I was fortunate to be a member of the team inspecting the Saddle Ridge Hoard. Those coins were in excellent condition, and many appeared to be uncirculated."

"Where would you like to look at my coins? Right now, the fire safes are sitting on the living room floor by the coffee table."

"I think the kitchen table would be better for us," said Don. "Easier on our backs."

He bent with a groan to pick up a safe and Oliver said, "Here, let me do that. I don't have a bad knee. You grab my attaché case."

Don straightened, looking relieved. "You won't hear any arguments from me."

In the kitchen, Oliver removed a pair of latex gloves, a lighted magnifier, a laptop, and a microscope from his briefcase. "I'm very eager to see what you have, Ms. McKenna."

"Katy, please." I unlocked one of the safes.

He gazed at the contents for a long moment before removing a plastic-bagged coin. I glanced at Don, who was grinning ear-to-ear.

"Oliver? Was I right, or was I right?" said Don, chuckling.

"At first glance, yes." He removed the coin from its bag to inspect under the magnifying glass. "Extraordinary."

Don connected the microscope to the laptop, and Oliver placed the coin under the lens. The magnified image filled the computer screen.

The numismatist gazed into the eyepiece murmuring, "Astonishing. Brilliant, uncirculated. Lustrous."

"What does that mean?" I said.

"That means the coin still has its original mint bloom," whispered Don to me with a wink.

I exhaled the breath I hadn't realized I'd been holding, unclenched my hands, and sat in a chair to watch the men examine the coins.

Forty-five minutes into it, my stomach was growling. "Anyone want a snack?"

The men were so engrossed that neither heard me, so I

grabbed a bag of taco chips and settled in the living room to watch an episode of *House Hunters* on HGTV.

Finally, Oliver called me into the kitchen. "Katy. It is amazing and unprecedented to have two such significant finds within a few years of each other. Before the Saddle Ridge Hoard, the largest buried collection of gold discovered in the US was the Jackson Hoard, found in Jackson, Tennessee in 1985, and that one pales in comparison to yours."

"Wow. So now we have the Santa Lucia Hoard?" I asked.

"We do," said Oliver. "But it will remain a secret until every coin has been evaluated and you're ready to begin the arduous process of selling the collection."

Oh crap. "Uh, I kind of already put one coin up for sale on Amazon."

His pained expression made me feel guilty.

"I can pull it off the market if you think best."

"Let me see the coin," he muttered through tight lips.

Feeling like an idiot, I plucked a coin zipped in a labeled bag from the safe. "This one."

After a quick inspection, he said, "All right, we can let this one go. How much are you asking?"

"Five thousand."

"Ms. McKenna. You're giving it away at that price. It's easily worth seven thousand, so up it to $6,700 and do not take a penny less than $6,200." He gave the coin back to me, looking grumpy.

"I'm sorry. I'm between jobs and...." I slumped on my chair, mangling the plastic bag.

"I'm sure Oliver didn't mean to sound so gruff," said Don a little too jovially. "We just don't want you to lose money, that's all."

"I apologize for my tone, Katy," said Oliver. "But I do hope you won't sell any more until after we have analyzed the collection. Trust me, it will be well worth the wait."

That made me feel better, and I straightened up. "So, what happens next?"

"I'd like to have another colleague see the collection, and then if it is amenable to you, my firm would like to represent you. At some point soon, we'll need to move the coins. Of course, we will use an armored truck. Do you have an attorney?"

"Yes, I do. Ben Burnett. He's a retired criminal attorney from Los Angeles. But I'm sure he can do whatever I need."

The minute they left, I dashed for my laptop, fearing someone had already discovered the underpriced coin and bought it. Thankfully that hadn't happened, and I reset the price to $6,700.

CHAPTER FIFTEEN

THURSDAY • JANUARY 29
Posted by Katy McKenna

Josh called this morning while Nicole was still in recovery. The good news was the surgeon was able to reconnect her colon, which meant no colostomy bag. She'd been worried about that. Who wouldn't be? The bad news: the cancer had spread to her liver. However, they felt very confident that they got it all, and that she should have a good recovery.

"I can't stop thinking about you," said Josh.

"Neither can I. I mean about you, not me."

He laughed. "I love your quirky sense of humor—amongst other things."

Hadn't meant to be funny, but I let him think I did. "What other things?"

"You know.... Hold on a sec."

"Mr. Draper, your wife's in her room now. As soon as she's settled in, you can visit her for a few minutes."

Wife?!?

He came back on the line. "Did you hear that?"

"Yes." I kept my tone calm, controlled.

"It was the only way I would be allowed in. Maybe I should have said I'm her brother."

Ya think?

———

I wanted to look my best for meeting my cousin, Erin, but in all the excitement this past week, I forgot to do laundry, and that's where my favorite dressy outfit was. Crushed in the bottom of the jam-packed laundry basket. It wasn't actually dirty, so I sprayed the armpits with Febreze and tossed it in the dryer with a damp cloth and a softener sheet.

While my ensemble tumbled, I fluffed my hair with the blow-dryer, then freshened my makeup. My in-house cosmetics consultant, Madame Daisy, lay on the bath mat supervising my makeover with a discerning eye. When she sensed I was done, she woofed, "Maybe a tad more mascara and bronzer."

I finished with a spritz of Victoria's Secret "Pink" perfume and dabbed a little behind Daisy's ears. She accompanied me to the dryer, and I donned my toasty-warm and almost wrinkle-free clothes. "How do I look, Daisy?"

She waved her tail, but it lacked her usual gusto. Sometimes she can be so nitpicky.

———

When I entered Le Stella, the host gave me a snooty once-over, as his hairy unibrow twitched in disapproval. "Have you a reservation?"

"I'm meeting a friend." I looked across the nearly empty dining room and recognized Erin sitting at a window seat overlooking the ocean. "There she is."

"You're with her?" He looked dumbfounded that a country bumpkin like me could be meeting an elegant woman like Erin.

"Yup. That there gal's mah dinner date. We gotta *thang* goin' on."

He visibly shuddered. "Follow me."

Erin stood as we approached and after a quick hug, we sat. Let me clarify that: the snobby host helped Erin get seated and ignored me wrestling with my heavy chair. Then he snapped her napkin open with a flourish and placed it on her lap. "Your waiter will be with you momentarily."

Erin giggled. "That little twerp certainly seems to think he's something, doesn't he?"

"Oh good, it's not just me." It probably was just me, though. I doubted that Erin's exquisitely tailored pearl gray slacks had ever seen the inside of a hamper. Everything about her reeked old money: classic, understated elegance. Her tasteful silver jewelry had to be platinum. Her short curly brunette pixie set off her hazel eyes and made me want to whack off my shoulder-length auburn mess. Erin's makeup looked airbrushed (Daisy would approve), and her soft pink manicure made me curl my chomped fingernails into fists. I can't wait to reek of money.

A waiter approached our table and presented a bottle of wine for Erin to inspect the label. "I hope you don't mind that I already ordered." She nodded to the waiter, and he began the uncorking. "It's a Syrah."

I peeked at the label. Alban Vineyards, "Reva," Edna Valley, CA 2006.

"It's a local wine," she said. "I've never had it, but I'm told it's good." The waiter poured a taste into Erin's glass, and she sipped. "Mmm. Very nice."

After our glasses had been filled halfway, Erin toasted me. "Here's to my long-lost cousin and newfound friend." We sipped the rich red ambrosia.

"Delicious," I said. "Did you know that Edna Valley is just a few miles from here?"

"The waiter told me. He said they're known for their wines made from Rhône Valley varietals."

All through dinner, we shared our life histories, with the exclusion of The Santa Lucia Hoard, of course. Her parents have a mansion in Atherton, next door to Palo Alto. She's thirty-four, attended private schools, then college at Brynn Mawr. Liberal Arts major.

I doubt I impressed her with my stellar academic background. Roosevelt Elementary. Kennedy Middle School. Santa Lucia High School graduate without much honor. The University of Santa Lucia with a BA in graphic design—that seemed to impress her.

"I saw that on your Facebook profile. I always wanted to be a graphic artist. But my parents didn't agree, and they were paying the bills. Looking back, they were right. I have zero artistic talent. It seems like such a glamorous, exciting profession."

"Oh, it has its moments." I thought of my latest glam jobs. Acme Upholstery and Uncle Charlie's Clunker Carnival. "But tell me about your job."

Working for Google sounded like a dream occupation. Important, interesting, challenging. Everything I would want in a job.

"I travel quite a bit. Paris, London, Rome. Last week I was in Japan." Erin shrugged like it was no big deal. "But traveling gets old. It seems I'm always packing and unpacking but never settled. And don't get me going on perpetual jet-lag."

Oh, you poor thing. I've never even been to Canada. Or Mexico.

She refilled her glass. "I don't have to work, but I don't want to just be another rich brat with a fat bank account. I want to make something of myself." She dug a phone out of her black woven leather purse. "I want to show you a picture of my boyfriend, Tyler."

"I love your purse."

"Thank you. I got it on sale at Neiman Marcus. Twenty percent off. It's a Bottega Veneta."

I nodded, trying to convey a knowing look, but the truth is, I'd never heard of Bottega-whatever. Probably because they don't sell them at Marshall's, where I got my dark red handbag for fourteen bucks—which I get compliments on all the time.

Erin scrolled through a thousand photos. "Here's a good one."

"Wow. He looks a lot like Zack Efron," I said. "I mean, he could be his twin."

"I know." She sighed. "He's a few years younger than me. We've been dating for almost six months, and we're thinking about moving in together. Do you have a picture of Josh?"

"No. I need to do that." *Dammit. Wish I had that selfie he took at Victoria's Secret. Josh is way better looking than her boyfriend, and I want to show him off.*

We finished the wine with our shared dessert of salted caramel macaroons drizzled with dark chocolate. After a half-hearted argument over the bill that I let her win, we had a long chatty goodbye in the hotel lobby, and then I headed home driving extra carefully, fearing that two and a half glasses may have put me over the limit.

CHAPTER SIXTEEN

Posted by Katy McKenna

I've had several phone conversations with Josh over the last couple days. The topic is usually centered on Nicole. She's still recovering nicely. No complications have arisen, thank goodness. Just wish he would come home.

―――

I heard back from Oliver Kershaw yesterday afternoon. When he was here on Wednesday, he told me he wanted one of his colleagues to see the coin collection. That person, Rosalyn Perez, is out of town at the moment on a family matter. Oliver said he would call me to set up an appointment as soon has she returns.

I understand I must be patient. But I'm ready to be rich right now! Realistically, I already am...but not.

―――

Earlier this evening, I had a brilliant idea on how to eradicate the attic pests. Music. But not just any music. Head banging, in-your-face Heavy Metal. Since I've never been a fan, I did a little research, then put together a playlist in iTunes. Megadeath, Iron Maiden, Metallica, Slayer, Death. I downloaded the playlist onto an iPod, then got out my old boombox and attached the iPod to it.

I set the boombox on the floor in the center of the attic and turned the volume to max. The first song featured a singer who sounded like Lucifer on a bad acid trip.

"YEEEEEAAAAAHHH! DEATH! DEATH! DEATH!"

"I hope you enjoy the tunes!" I screamed, then dashed downstairs and closed the attic steps.

I went to my bedroom, and curled up on the bed thinking I'd watch a romantic movie on Netflix. But no matter how loud I cranked up the TV volume, all I heard was, "SCREAM FOR MERCY, SCREEEEEAAAAAM FOOOR MEEERRRCY—I WILL KILL YOOOOOUUU!"

What astounded me was Tabitha and Daisy slumbered right through the racket. I tried to hang in and give my plan a chance to work, but after twenty minutes of misery, I was ready to wave the white flag.

On my way to the attic, Randy, from across the street, rang my doorbell. "Dude!" he said with his eyes locked on my chest. "I didn't know—"

"WHAT? I can't hear you." I stepped out to the porch and closed the door. It was just as noisy outside. Probably should have given some thought to the neighbors before I set my plan in motion, because now they were gathering on the sidewalk looking mighty surly.

Randy straightened his t-shirt and puffed his chest so I could appreciate the clever slogan on it. *F_CKING isn't the same without U.*

"I didn't know you're a metal head," he said. "I had you pegged for more of a Barry Manilow—Kenny G fan."

"I like all kinds of music," I said. And then I shouted for all to hear before they lynched me. "Sorry about the ruckus. I'm trying to get rid of the squirrels in my attic."

'DEEEEEAAAAATHHHH!" screamed the music filtering through the attic windows. "Kill! Kill! Kill!"

A neighbor I've never met yelled, "Try an exterminator."

So much for my diabolical plan.

CHAPTER SEVENTEEN

MONDAY • FEBRUARY 2
Posted by Katy McKenna

Erin was leaving Los Angeles and heading back to Palo Alto yesterday, so I invited her to stop for Sunday brunch on the way and meet the family. I baked a broccoli and cheddar frittata recipe I found online that turned out to be a keeper. Samantha made her signature fruit salad—she adds a few shots of Triple Sec and a lot of sugar. Ruby and Ben brought the fixings for mimosas. And Mom and Pop stopped at the bakery and bought croissants and bear claws. After everyone introduced themselves, we gathered in the kitchen, and Ruby took mimosa orders.

"I still have a four hour drive, so none for me," said Erin.

"And none for me," said Samantha. "I'm working the second shift today."

"Sam's a maternity nurse," I told Erin, then turned to my bestie. "But you usually don't work on Sundays."

"I'm filling in for someone."

"I can make virgin mimosas," said Ruby.

"Then count me in," said Sam. "Make it a double."

During brunch, Erin reigned like a queen, telling funny anec-
dotes about her family. I could tell everyone was smitten with her
sweet personality. Sam admired her peach silk scarf, and later when
she was leaving for the hospital, Erin followed her to the door and
draped it around her neck.

"I want you to have this. The color looks much better on a
blonde." She turned Sam to look in the entry mirror. "See?"

"I couldn't, really." Sam threw me a pleading glance.

"I think it looks beautiful on you, Sam," I said. "Really sets off
your purple scrubs."

"Thank you, Erin. I love it."

Erin glanced at her watch and groaned. "I had no idea it was
already two-thirty. I need to get on the road. Wish I didn't have
to go."

"Do you really have to?" I asked. "I'd love it if you spent the
night."

"I'd love it too, but tomorrow's a work day." She paused a
moment, chewing her lower lip. "You know what? I worked at least
fourteen hours yesterday, and I usually don't work weekends, so I
earned this. I'm staying." We high-fived, and then she said, "But I
need to be out of here by six-thirty in the morning to make a lunch
meeting that I absolutely cannot miss. You know how traffic always
backs up through San Jose."

"I'd say this calls for another round of mimosas," said Ruby
from the kitchen entrance. "Corrupted this time."

———

Later, after everyone had gone I made coffee, and we sacked out on
the couch. Daisy had crammed herself against Erin, thrilled to
have a new friend who would scratch behind her floppy ears. And
Tabitha was curled up on my lap, delighted not to have to share it
with her sister.

"You're going to be covered in dog hair," I said.

"Oh, that's all right." She snuggled down into Daisy and cuddled her. "Right, Daisy? We don't care about a little dog hair, do we? I have a little Yorkie girl. Lulu. She only weights four-and-a-half pounds, but she's a little terror. It's kind of nice snuggling with a big dog that you can't break."

"That was so generous of you, giving your beautiful scarf to Sam. It looked expensive."

"It was, but that's what money's for. Through no fault of my own, I happen to have a lot of it. Besides, it was only a scarf."

"That has to be one of the joys of being wealthy. You know, doing nice things for other people. I can't wait until I can do that."

"Spending money on others is easy when you have it. I'm sure you do lots of nice things for people. I think that's more important than gifts."

"Yes, I suppose I do. But pretty soon, I'll be able to...." I realized I was running off at the mouth.

"You'll be able to what?"

Oh, what the hell. She's family. "Well, it just so happens that I have recently come into some money."

"Oh? Did you win the lottery?"

"Pretty much." I relocated Tabitha and grabbed Erin's hand. "Come on. I'll show you. You're not going to believe this." I led her to my bedroom closet where I pulled aside the clothes concealing the safes.

"So what'd you do—rob a bank or something?" she asked.

"Nope." I unlocked one of the fire safes.

Erin knelt, looking astounded. "Is this real?"

"Yup."

We sat cross-legged on the closet floor, and I told her how I found the treasure. When I concluded my tale, she said, "That has to be the craziest story I've ever heard." She put an arm around my shoulders and gave me a squeeze. "I'm so happy for you. But don't you think you should put it in the bank where it'll be safe? I mean, anyone could come in here and walk away with it. Doesn't that worry you a little bit?"

"Yes, it does. But pretty soon, it'll all be moved to the coin grading company in southern California that Oliver Kershaw, the coin expert that I told you about, owns. Besides, no one knows it's here. I mean, no one except family. So please, whatever you do, don't tell anyone. Not even your boyfriend."

"No worries," she said.

"Once I can start selling the coins, the money will go in the bank, of course." I locked up the safe, and we returned to the sofa.

"What's the first thing you're going to do with the money?" she asked.

"I don't know. Pay off all my bills for one thing. Invest in some safe stocks."

"Boring. Of course, you'll do all that. But what's the first fun thing you'll do?"

"Pay off my parents' mortgage and send them to Hawaii for a dream vacation."

———

Early this morning, over coffee and leftover bear claws, Erin said, "After I got in bed last night, I had the most fantastic idea." She picked up her phone from the coffee table. "After everything you've told me about your divorce from hell, and all that other crazy stuff that's happened to you over the past year, I think you need a vacation."

She flipped through photos on the phone. "My folks have a fabulous place in Belize, and I know they'd be happy to let you use it. It even has a staff and a car. Here…." She held out the phone. "Look at these pictures. Isn't it pretty? Your boyfriend could go, too. How romantic would that be?"

I scrolled through several photos of white sandy beaches. "Look at that water. It's like blue crystal. I've always dreamed of going somewhere tropical. But I don't know when Josh could go. You know, with his ex-wife having cancer."

"But even if he can't go, you still can. At least promise you'll think about it."

"I promise. Another thing I'd like to do is come up and visit you and go shopping. You always look so stylish, and I'm hoping some of it will rub off on me, now that I can afford to shop somewhere besides Ross and Marshalls." I stopped for a sip of coffee. "I'll stay at a hotel, of course, and—"

"No, you won't. You'll stay with me."

"But I thought you were moving in with your boyfriend."

Her sunny smile drooped. "No. That's not going to happen. At least not right now. We're having some problems."

"What kind of problems? I don't mean to pry, so don't feel you have to answer, but just the other day you seemed so happy."

"The thing is, I am, most of the time." She paused, searching for words. "All right, I'll just say it. Tyler has a temper. We had a huge fight on the phone on Saturday night. He was jealous because I'd been out with my coworkers down in L.A. It's not like I was cheating on him. We all went to the Whiskey a Go Go on the Sunset Strip and were just having fun."

I placed a hand on her shoulder and gently asked, "Does he ever hit you, Erin?"

"No." She hung her head, her voice hushed. "He hasn't hit me. But he shoved me into a wall a couple of weeks ago. Things have been hard for him lately. He lost his job, and he has massive school loans, and he won't allow me to help him." She choked a laugh. "At least I know he doesn't love me for my money."

I took her hand and squeezed it. "Erin. Shoving you into a wall is pretty much the same as hitting you."

She sighed. "I know. I was thinking about that on my drive up here. And then after listening to Ben talk about the battered women at the women's shelter, I realized I need to end this before something bad happens. I don't want to be one of those women."

———

At 6:45, I walked Erin out to her red Jaguar convertible parked at the curb.

Across the street, the front door burst open, and a busty bleached blonde with about three inches of greasy dark roots stomped down the porch steps shrieking, "We're done, you big pile of steaming dog shit. Done. D-U-N, done!"

Randy followed her to the edge of the porch. "Oh yeah? Well, you don't get to say when we're done, Darlene. We're done when *I* say we're done."

Darlene spun around, hands on ample hips. "Okay, pencil dick. Are we done?"

Randy nodded. "Yeah, you stank ho. We're done!" He went back into the house and slammed the door.

Darlene continued down the front walk, then spied us watching the show. "What're you two lesbos starin' at?" She yanked up her t-shirt and gave us a cheap thrill. "Like what you see?"

That sent Erin and me into hysterics, which did not sit well with Darlene.

"What're you flat-chested bitches laughing at?" Fists balled and spoiling for a fight, she got halfway across the street when Erin hollered, "One more step, and I'm calling the cops."

Darlene stopped, muttering, "Fuckin' dykes," then marched back to the foot of Randy's steps and screamed, "I need a ride home, dickhead."

Erin looked at me with a wry smile. "You know, now that you have money, you might want to rethink the neighborhood you live in."

CHAPTER EIGHTEEN

TUESDAY • FEBRUARY 3
Posted by Katy McKenna

My cousin called and asked if I'd thought any more about the Belize offer. I told her that I had a coin for sale on Amazon right now, and if it sells, then I could think about going.

"Here's a thought," she said. "I'll lend you the money. All you actually need is airfare and some spending money. And it's not like you won't be able to pay me back."

"With everything that's happening, I don't know if now is the right time."

"But when is it ever the right time?" she asked. "Just go for a few days and relax in the warm, tropical sun. I promise you'll be glad you did. You will come back totally recharged."

"Let me think about it."

"Please know it would make me happy, and I could use a little cheering up right now."

"Why? What's wrong?"

"Tyler didn't appreciate me telling him I wanted to take a time-out." She paused, and I heard her sigh. "Katy, he hit me."

"Oh my God, Erin. I was afraid this would happen."

"That's not all. Now he's stalking me. Last night I saw him standing down on the street below my bedroom window. I may have to get a restraining order."

I thought about when my ex had been constantly calling and texting me, begging to get back together. It was annoying, but I never felt the need for a restraining order.

"What're you going to do?" I said.

"I may go stay at my parents' house. They have round-the-clock security guards on their estate. I really don't think Tyler would hurt me—"

"He *hit* you. If he's done it once, he'll do it again."

"I know, but it wasn't that hard. I mean, nothing's broken." She laughed. "Oh, God. How pathetic is that? You always say you would never take this kind of treatment from someone and then when it happens and you love the guy, you become pathetic."

"I don't think you're pathetic. But you need to protect yourself."

"I will. And you need to go to Belize. Come on, Katy. Put a smile on my face and say you'll go."

———

Ruby invited me over for Taco Tuesday at her independent living senior village, Shady Acres. I love tacos, and I love free meals, so I said, "Count me in."

At dinner time, I parked in front of her cottage, and we strolled over to the dining room.

"So what's doin' with you, kiddo? You going to take Erin up on her offer to go to Belize?"

"I'm thinking about it, but this probably isn't the right time. You know, with Josh's ex-wife going through cancer."

"Sweetie, you can't do a thing about that, and we're only

talking about a few days. You could go and be back before Josh gets home, you know."

"Yeah. Maybe. But then there are the coins. That numismatics expert is sending one of his colleagues to see them, and I'm not sure when that's going to happen. And I can't afford the plane ticket, anyway. Erin offered to loan me the money, but I'm not comfortable with that. It's too much."

At the dining room entrance, I said, "Time to switch subjects. I don't want anyone hearing about the hoard."

"Oh, pish. No one has hearing good enough to hear anything you say unless you shout at them. But I hear ya. Mum's the word."

We entered the room, and several women waved. One of the ladies motioned us to sit at her table.

Ruby hollered, "Not tonight, Iris. I haven't seen my grand-daughter in days, and we need a catch-up."

"At least you have a granddaughter," said Iris. "My son never had kids. I'd be a great-great-grandmother by now. Come give me a hug, Katy darling."

I did, and she whispered in my ear, "I'm planning a little surprise birthday party for your grandma. You know it's coming up soon. The big seven-five."

"Yeah, but she doesn't want to be reminded."

"She's still a kid, for crying out loud. I'm ninety-two."

"Well, you sure don't look it."

She patted my cheek. "You're such a good girl. You know exactly what to say to an old lady, and I'll take it. Now scoot before your grandmother shoots me."

I returned to Ruby and sat.

"I ordered margaritas while you two were chatting. What was she saying to you?"

"She said she loved your outfit."

Ruby sat up straighter and flashed a sunny smile at Iris. "I like yours, too!"

Iris looked at Grandma like she was bonkers, and Ruby whispered, "She should never wear green, it clashes with her red hair. Makes her look like an ancient elf."

While we waited for our drinks, we talked more about Erin's Belize offer.

"You have to go, kiddo," she said. "And before you start in again about not being able to afford it, I'm lending you the money. End of subject."

CHAPTER NINETEEN

FRIDAY · FEBRUARY 6
Posted by Katy McKenna

Last night I phoned Erin and accepted her Belize offer. She was thrilled and said she'd email all the info about the house.

I also talked to Josh, and he said Nicole is healing well and has been approved for travel next week. I want to see him before I go, so I booked my plane ticket for next Friday. Five glorious, sun-filled days of snorkeling, exploring, eating, and relaxing on the beach. Actually, three days, since I'll be traveling on two of them. I can't believe I'm doing this. I finally get to use my passport!

Everyone knows I'm not a big Facebook person, but I had to share the Belize trip. It always amazes me how fast you start getting "likes," and emoji hearts and smiles. Even Erin left a comment before I clicked off: *Maybe I'll join you!*

Private

I'm constantly fretting about someone stealing the coins, so until Oliver Kershaw arranges for my hoard to be hauled away in an armored truck, I need to move the money to a safer place—preferably offsite. I probably shouldn't be worrying, considering the gold has been stashed in my house for decades, but until now, no one knew about it.

So, today I went to the bank to inquire about a safe deposit box. The bank officer handed me a form to fill out and here's what it said: *The box is leased solely for the purpose of keeping securities, jewelry, valuable personal papers and precious non-currency metals, and the Renter agrees not to use the box to store money, coin, or currency....* So much for that idea.

I left the bank and drove to the nearest Starbucks for a grande cappuccino, no whip. Really wanted a cheese danish, but next week I'll be strutting my stuff in a bikini, so I don't need any extra calories.

I sat at a table for two on the patio and pondered my next move. Since the bank idea was a no-go, I thought I should at least find a new hiding place, and then only tell Mom and Pop the secret location.

When I got home, I grabbed my shovel from the garage and went out back to survey the yard for a burial site. I decided that the easiest digging would be in the planting bed along the back fence, near my office shed.

Each safe measures 16x18x8 inches high, so, to accommodate both safes, the hole needed to be almost two feet deep by roughly forty inches long and eighteen inches wide. I scratched a line in the dirt and then commenced the digging.

The first few inches were easy since most of that was bark chips. Then it got a lot harder. I chipped away at the dry dirt, tossed little rocks aside, then dug some more. I could only sink the shovel about one inch into the ground. I'd jam it in as hard as I could, then balance my feet on the shovel-head and wiggle it back and forth, trying to break up the solid, parched earth. The layer under the top soil looked like sandstone. Pop has complained about it in his yard. Calls it hardpan. I call it concrete. At the rate I was going I might have the safes planted by summer.

After a water break, Daisy followed me out to the back yard to help inspect my eight-by-ten shed for a good hiding place. Halfway through the yard, she was diverted by a trespassing squirrel. She chased the little guy into the gnarly, old pepper tree. Once he was up high, he stopped and gave Daisy a good verbal thrashing, then scurried along a branch and slipped under the eaves of my house.

"Ha! I knew it was squirrels in the attic."

I unlatched the shed door and swatted several cobwebs away, before stepping inside. Over in a corner were a few cardboard cartons filled with art supplies and other odds and ends that I haven't needed since moving in. I opened a large one labeled "I have no idea what to do with this stuff" and remembered why I wrote that. I rummaged through it and decided there was nothing I couldn't live without, so I dumped the contents in the garbage can by the garage and flipped the lid down before I spotted something I couldn't live without. I returned the box to the shed, then retrieved the hand-truck leaning against the shed (really should return that to the folks), rolled it into the house, and loaded the fire safes onto it.

Back in the shed, I set them inside the carton, shoved it snug into the corner with the other boxes, and set a few boxes on top. Then I got crafty and smeared cobweb residue on the edges to make it look like they hadn't been opened in a long time.

Halfway through the yard, I stopped, gazing up at the attic window, feeling a burst of inspiration bubble up. I could turn the attic into an art studio. Since I wouldn't have to do graphics for a living, I could do art for the pure joy of it. And then I could make the office into a she-shed like the ones I've seen on HGTV. Paint it and decorate it girly bo-ho chic. Put a daybed out there with lots of pillows, and string lights across the ceiling. A perfect place to read and relax.

I crouched and gave Daisy a hug. "It's going to be so much fun being wealthy women, huh, girl?"

CHAPTER TWENTY

WEDNESDAY · FEBRUARY 11
Posted by Katy McKenna

I wish I could say that Josh's ex-wife is horrible, but I can't. When we met this afternoon, she greeted me like we were long-lost besties.

"Josh has told me so much about you. In fact, you're pretty much all he talks about."

Here's the low-down on Nicole Draper. Brunette shoulder-length shag-cut. Creamy skin, and startling blue eyes that I would've said were enhanced with lenses if she hadn't been wearing horn rims. Without even a stitch of makeup, she's drop-dead beautiful. To be honest, after seeing her, I couldn't help wondering what Josh sees in me.

We were in Josh's living room, and she patted the sofa for me to sit beside her. "I know how awkward this must be for you, but trust me, Josh and I...." She shrugged, smiling up at him. "We're like brother and sister. Family. And right now, I don't know what I would have done without his help."

"Does anyone want a coffee?" asked Josh.

"None for me." Nicole wrinkled her nose. "No caffeine and no alcohol until I'm done with radiation and chemo."

"I'll pass, too," I said. "Nicole, I know your father's in the Peace Corps. Will he be coming home?"

"She hasn't told him about the cancer," said Josh from the kitchen.

"Why not?" I said.

"I just can't. My mother died of colon cancer when I was a junior in high school."

"Josh told me. That must have been hard for you."

"It was," she said with a melancholy smile. "I used to get annoyed when my friends complained about their mothers, and I'd think how lucky they were to still have one."

That made me feel guilty. Of course, I complained about my mom when I was a teenager. She didn't let me pierce my ears until I was fourteen. Wasn't allowed to wear eye makeup until I was fifteen. Couldn't date until sixteen—not like anyone was asking, anyway. What a mean mother!

Nicole continued. "I don't think Dad could handle knowing his little girl has cancer, although the doctors say they got it all. My prognosis is good, so why put him through the worry?"

"My father would have a fit if I didn't tell him," I said.

"Mine will too, but it'll be after I'm a hundred percent well."

"When do you start chemo and radiation?" I asked.

"I check in tomorrow and will have my first round on Friday. Can't wait," she said with a snort.

We chatted a while longer, and then Nicole said, "I hate to be a party-pooper, but I'm exhausted. I think I'll go take a nap." She winked at me. "And you two probably could use a little alone-time."

She was right about that.

My cousin called late, just as I was nodding off. She was bawling and barely comprehensible.

"Erin. Calm down." I switched on the bedside lamp and sat up. "What're you trying to tell me?"

"Tyler. Oh God, Katy. It was so awful."

"Tell me what happened."

"He called, begging me to talk to him. He sounded so sad, so broken. So, like an idiot, I said okay." She inhaled a shaky breath. "I told him he could come over."

"You're staying with your parents, right?"

"No," she murmured.

"You're kidding. I thought that's what you were going to do."

"You sound mad at me."

I softened my tone. "I'm not mad. Just concerned, that's all."

This was going to be a long conversation, so I stuffed a pillow behind my back, and got comfortable.

Erin continued. "Anyway. I ordered his favorite Thai takeout. Opened a bottle of wine I know he likes. I thought that would make things easier."

"And did it?"

"At first. But Tyler kept begging me to take him back. I said I didn't trust him. I told him you said that if he hit me once, he'd hit me again and I couldn't take that chance. Anyway, after I said that, Tyler was furious. He flung the food at the wall, poured the wine on the floor. I was afraid he was going to hit me with the bottle, but thank God he threw it into the fireplace, instead."

"I said, 'See? This is why I can't trust you.' And he shouted, 'But I didn't hit you, did I?'" She stopped, choking on anguished sobs.

When her crying subsided, I asked, "Then what happened?"

"I told him to get out or I'd call the police, and that's when he started hitting me. Over and over."

"You called the police, right?" I got out of bed and paced the room.

"Yes. As soon as he left. God, it was humiliating. They made me feel so foolish."

Yeah, you were foolish. "Do you need me to come up there?"

"God, no. You're going on vacation. I would never ruin that. But—"

"But what?"

"Could I come down there?" she asked, then rushed her words. "While you're in Belize, I could take care of Daisy and Tabitha, and water your plants. I know it's a lot to ask, but I'm so scared."

"The police haven't arrested him?"

"I didn't press charges."

I stopped pacing. "Why the hell not, Erin?"

"Because I was afraid that would make things worse. You know, he'd get out on bail, then come back and," her voice dropped to a murmur, "and maybe kill me."

"Of course, you can stay here. But Daisy will be spending those days with my folks. She's their canine grandchild, and they already have fun outings planned with her. They're picking her up tomorrow. Tabitha will be here, though. But she's easy. She has a feeder with a timer, so she's pretty self-sufficient." I was upset and rambling to cover it. "Does your boyfrie—I mean, does Tyler know where I live?"

"He knows you live in the Santa Lucia area, but he doesn't know your address or even your last name. So no way will he know where I am. He's a hothead, but I don't think he would come searching for me all the way down there. I mean, why would he? Besides, I told him you're going to Belize."

"I not worried about me. I'm worried about you. Can you drive?"

"So I can come?" She sounded like a frightened little girl.

"Yes, of course you can come. Try to leave in the morning so we can have some time together. I have to be at the airport on Friday at five a.m."

And yeah, truth be told, I'm worried about me. Tyler might blame me for Erin breaking it off with him.

CHAPTER TWENTY-ONE

THURSDAY · FEBRUARY 12

Posted by Katy McKenna

This has turned out to be really bad timing for a trip. I'd like to cancel it but I'd never get a refund on the plane ticket, and my dear granny talked me into flying first class.

"Sweetie," she said, "you're a millionaire now. No, make that a multimillionaire, so you might as well start living the life. Besides, I know how much you hate flying."

"But I don't have the money yet, so who knows when I'll be able to pay you back. This is going to be a long process, Ruby. Could take a couple of years. So as of now, I'm still broke, and my cards are pretty much maxed out."

"But you *will* have the money. And sweetie, when you fly first class they keep you so busy with champagne, warm nuts, delicious meals, and ice cream sundaes that you don't have time to worry about," she shot me a devilish grin, "being trapped in a 450-ton tin can 35,000 feet above the ground."

Samantha came over this afternoon to lend me her swimsuit cover-up. Erin arrived just as we were sitting down on the porch to enjoy a cup of coffee.

The previous times I've seen my cousin, she was elegantly put together, but today she looked like a forlorn little street urchin. Mussed hair, wrinkled clothes, no makeup. Eyes puffy and bloodshot. And her left cheek and lips were bruised and swollen. It's a miracle she made the four hour drive without crashing.

After a warm embrace, I got her seated on the porch swing. "Do you want coffee? Tea?"

"No, I'm way over my caffeine limit. Maybe a water?"

I stepped into the house, then leaned back out. "Ice?"

"No. More like lukewarm. My front tooth hurts. It was loosened when Tyler punched me, and it's pretty sensitive right now."

"Shouldn't you see a dentist?" Sam asked, as I went into the house.

"I'm sure it'll be fine in a few days."

I returned with her water. "I feel awful about leaving you alone."

"Don't you dare feel bad," she said. "I want you to go and have fun. If I'd taken your advice and stayed with my parents, this wouldn't have happened."

"You *sure* you'll be all right, all by yourself here?" I said. My inner Mother Hen was clucking, *How can you leave this sweet, thoughtful girl all alone?*

"Erin, give me your phone," said Samantha. "I'll put my number on it, in case you need anything."

Erin dug it out of her handbag and handed it over. "I really appreciate that, Sam. But please don't worry about me. I'll be fine."

"What about your job?" I asked.

"No worries," said Erin. "I have loads of sick leave accrued, and now I'm going to take advantage of it." She touched her bruised cheek. "If my boss saw this, she'd go through the roof. Probably make me go for victim counseling."

"Erin, you *are* a victim," said Sam, looking stern. "Maybe it would be a good idea."

"I'm fine. Really. It's my fault for allowing Tyler to come over. I should've known better."

Sam gave me a look, and I knew she was thinking about how often battered women blame themselves. I was about to say something to that effect when Erin said, "Would you mind if I go lie down? I'm worn out."

Sam stood. "I have to run anyway. Chelsea is at a swim meet and needs a ride home." She leaned into me for a squeeze. "Take lots of pictures and gain at least five pounds."

We always rate how good a vacation was by how many pounds we gained.

———

Josh and I had planned to spend the evening together, but with Erin's arrival, I had to cancel. I'll only be gone for five days, but I'm going to miss him so much.

I woke Erin at seven with a glass of wine and a plate of Triscuits and cheddar cheese. "Wake up, sleepyhead."

"What time is it?"

"Seven. I need to get to bed early. My flight's at six-thirty, so I need to be at the airport by five, which means I have to get up at three-thirty. Ugh. There're some things I need to go over with you, and I don't want to wake you at that ungodly hour."

"It's a good thing you woke me, or I might've slept till ten or eleven and then been up all night." She sipped her cabernet. "I didn't pack much, so you better show me how to run the washer."

"It's ancient, and on certain cycles sounds like it's possessed, but it gets the job done." I led her to the laundry room and opened the cabinet over the washer and dryer. "Here's the soap, softener, bleach. Just spin the dial to whatever cycle works for you."

Erin nodded. "Simple enough."

"Now I need to show you how to work the alarm," I said.

"I have one at home, so it shouldn't be a problem."

I took her to the front door, where the main panel is located. "The code is one-two-one-two"

"Seriously? One-two-one-two is a pretty common code. Right up there with one-two-three-four."

I hadn't thought of that, but she was right.

"Do you have a lucky number?" she asked.

"Hmmm." I've never thought about this. What would my lucky number be? "How about the day I found the coins?"

"What day was that?

"Let me think. It's been.... Wow. I can't believe it's almost been a month. Hold on. The date will be on my blog."

"You never told me you have a blog," she said. "May I read it?"

I've only known Erin a few weeks, even though it seems like forever. But am I ready for her to know everything about me? Like all the petty, snarky stuff? I was not.

"Actually, it's more like a personal diary and—"

"No worries." She patted my arm. "I understand. Must be very cathartic."

"It's funny you said that because that's exactly what Sam said to me back when I was still seething over my divorce. She said a blog would be cathartic. I thought it was a pretty stupid idea at the time, but now it's a part of my daily life."

"Does it help?"

"It does."

"Then maybe I'll give it a try. I brought my laptop, so it'll give me something to do. While you get the date, I'll refill our glasses."

A few minutes later, I reset the alarm to 0114.

"Much better," said Erin, with a nod. "No way would anyone

ever think of that code. What time did you say you're getting up in the morning?"

"Three-thirty. That'll give me plenty of time to put on makeup and have some coffee. I don't like rushing."

"You're going to have so much fun. I really appreciate you letting me stay here."

"And I really appreciate you inviting me to stay at your place in Belize."

We sat on the sofa, and Erin pulled the red throw over her lap.

"After I finish this glass of wine, I'm off to bed," I said.

"As much as I love you, I won't be up to wish you a bon voyage." Erin leaned in for an embrace. "You have all the information I gave you?"

"It's on a piece of paper in my purse, and on my phone and my laptop. When I land in Belize, I'll call the house like you said, and someone will come get me."

"It'll probably be Sophia. She's a sweetheart. But watch out for her husband, Raul. He's a huge flirt—but totally harmless. They fight a lot over that, so just ignore them. Sophia is very jealous. Trust me, you don't want to get on her bad side."

CHAPTER TWENTY-TWO

THURSDAY · FEBRUARY 19
Posted by Katy McKenna

So much has happened since I last posted. It's going to take a while to catch up, and I'm not sure I'm up to the task, or ready to even try. Please bear with me if I lose it.

Friday, February 13
Part One

I woke at 3:11 in the morning, nineteen minutes before my alarm was set to go off. I considered catching a few more winks but was too excited-nervous about my trip.

After a strong dose of caffeine, I showered, did my makeup, and dressed in comfortable travel wear. Black leggings, a long loose, sleeveless red top, black cardigan, and sandals. I left the house at 4:40. The local airport is small, so I'd be on a commuter flight to L.A.X., where I had an hour-and-a-half layover before flying first class to my final destination.

After parking, I spent twenty-plus nerve-wracking minutes in the pitch-dark figuring out how to pay for extended parking at the kiosk. Finally, at 5:18, I dragged my suitcase and carry-on up the hill into the airport. I checked in and breezed through the short airport security line with no hassles. After strapping my sandals back on, I situated myself where I could watch other folks coming through security. A few minutes into my blatant people-watching, a middle-aged, amply-endowed woman crowned with a flaming red bouffant, stepped through the scanner and set off the alarms.

"Oh my *gawd*," she hollered in a southern accent so exaggerated, she sounded like Forest Gump on estrogen.

"Please step over there, ma'am." A female TSA officer ushered her to the side for a pat-down.

"It's my *braaa-ssiere*," shrieked the woman. "This *always* happens."

"I still have to check you, ma'am." The officer ran the scanning wand around the woman's body. As she swept it down the lady's back, the thing went berserk.

"I'm tellin' you, it's my *braaa-ssiere*." The redhead gestured to a short, skinny man waiting on the sideline. "Tell her, Carl. It's my brassiere!"

The bashful looking little man nodded, looking resigned to his fate.

Two minutes before the scheduled boarding time, an announcement came over the intercom: "Attention. Flight 724 has been delayed due to dense fog."

What fog? I turned in my seat to glance out the window. *Where did that come from?*

By 6:35, panic set in. *It's an hour flight to LA. My flight to Belize is at 9:15, so if we leave within the next half hour, I'll still have plenty of time.*

The flight was officially canceled at 7:10.

I spoke to the airline counter clerk about my options, and he said, "I can get you out on a flight to Los Angeles this afternoon, and then...." His fingers tapped the computer at warp speed.

"Hmmm... Let's see. There's a flight to Belize at midnight. Do you want me to book it or do you want a voucher for travel at a later date?"

"Go ahead and book it." I didn't want a voucher; I wanted my money—I mean Ruby's money, back.

I decided to treat myself to a big breakfast at the airport restaurant before going home. I was on my second cup of caffeine when the waitress set my veggie omelet, crispy hash browns, and rye toast in front of me.

Halfway through the meal, I texted Sam and my folks. *Guess what? Flute cackled due to flog. Going home for a nip and leavening later this afternoon.* I hit Send and then read my message. Boy, I hate autocorrect.

———

I unlocked the front door and dumped my purse on the entry table. I was feeling a fat headache coming on, so I went to the kitchen and swallowed two acetaminophens. And then I heard Erin giggling.

I strolled through the house toward the guest bedroom. At her door, I was about to say, "knock-knock," when I heard her laugh again from my bedroom. I thought that was kind of weird. Then I heard a male voice and assumed she was watching TV.

"Erin?" I said, with my hand on the knob. "You'll never guess what happened."

The stunned expression on Erin's flushed face mutated into ugly hostility as she peered at me over a man's broad tattooed shoulder. "What the hell'er you doing here?"

The two were naked, wrapped in each other's arms. From the tangled mess of sheets and blankets, it must have been a fast and furious romp. Tyler, her Zack Efron doppelgänger boyfriend, turned to gaze at me.

I was so dumbfounded, all I could say was, "My flight was

canceled." Yeah, dimwitted I know, but I hadn't yet fully processed the scene before me.

"That kinda sucks for you," Tyler said in an amiable tone. He rolled off the bed, stood, and lazily stretched his lean, muscular body.

Mortified, I averted my eyes. "What's going on?"

"What do ya think?" He smiled, slowly advancing toward me.

I stepped back until I was flat against the wall and glanced at Erin. She looked different. How to describe it? It's like she was still Erin but with a rough, trashy edge. She shook a cigarette from a pack on the nightstand, lit it with a gold lighter, and sucked a long drag, exhaling through her nose.

I was fixated on the cigarette, thinking, *She smokes?*

"Oh well," said Erin. "It's not like you would've had a good time in Belize, anyway."

"What do you mean?"

"That house in Belize? Never existed." She puffed the cigarette, and the smoldering tip dropped onto the bed. "Whoopsy." She brushed the ash away, leaving a black hole in the sheet.

"But you showed me pictures."

"Everything I told you was a lie. There's no mansion in Atherton. No vacation home in Belize. No ski cabin in Tahoe. No villa on Lake Como."

Tyler leaned one hand against the wall beside my head. "You can still have a good time. Here. With us." He trickled a finger down my neck, into my décolletage. I jerked away, and he snickered. "Relax. It's all good."

"I want you both to get out of my house. Now." I edged my way to the open doorway.

"What? Like this?" Tyler held his arms outstretched, clearly proud of his generous endowment. I'm talking porn-star generous. Sorry, but it was impossible to ignore.

"Get dressed and get the hell out." I backed into the hallway, wondering if I should run for it. *No, goddammit This is my house!*

Erin stubbed out her cigarette. "Cut it out, Tyler." She stood and slipped on *my* pink robe. "Katy's not supposed to be here, but that doesn't change our plans. In fact, it's actually a good thing she's here."

I stopped my slow retreat. "What plans?"

Erin tied the robe belt with a yank. "Katy? Where's the money? It's not in the closet, so where is it?"

"The money's not here. I put it in a safe deposit box at the bank, and now you both need to get out of my house, or I'll call the police." I dashed for the front door, but just as I was opening it, Tyler slammed it shut and jerked me away, shoving me into the wall.

"We'll leave when we're good and ready to leave, bitch."

"Tyler, go put some clothes on while I talk to Katy," said Erin.

I turned to the door, placing my hand on the lever.

She said, "You might want to rethink that. I'm pointing a gun at your back and one way or another, I'm not letting you go out that door."

I took a deep breath and turned to face Erin and her big, black gun. "Are you going to kill me?"

She rolled her eyes. "Well, that would be pretty stupid. If you're dead, you can't tell us where you hid the money, can you? But it would be a helluva lot easier if you tell us before I'm forced to hurt you. And Katy, we both know it's not at the bank."

I must have looked terrified because she smiled, allowing me a brief glimpse of the Erin that I knew—make that, thought I knew. "Look at all the trouble you've gone through trying to find the rightful owner. And from the looks of it," she brandished the automatic pistol, "that would be...me." She sighed, shaking her head with a rueful grin. "Isn't it funny how things work out?"

Tyler returned to the room dressed in jeans and a tight white t-shirt. "What's funny?"

"That Katy went on PedigreeTree.com to search for someone to give the money to, and she found me. Her long-lost cuzy." She glanced at me. "And yes, I truly am your cousin. Probably won't be your favorite one after this, though. But you'll always be my favorite."

I flicked a glance at the alarm by the door. *Maybe I can set it off.*

Erin read my thoughts. "Forget it, Katy. Even if I let you get to it, all that'll happen is the alarm company will call and ask for the password." She stepped close and tapped my nose with the cold gun. "Which you gave me last night, remember? The password is Daisy." She moved back a step. "Go sit on the couch. Tyler will bring you a drink to calm your nerves, and then you'll show us where you hid the money."

"Erin," I said. "I thought you were afraid of Tyler. He hit you. You have bruises on your face."

She touched her cheek. "He didn't want to hit me. I forced him to do it. The poor baby cried afterward. Everything has worked out just as I planned. You felt sorry for me and let me stay in your house." She cocked her head. "Well, almost everything. The money was supposed to be in the closet, and you're supposed to be on your way to Belize." She shrugged. "Oh, well."

Tyler handed me a rocks glass half-full of vodka. "Drink up."

My hand trembled as I took it and set it on the coffee table. "Not in the mood." *Probably drugged or poisoned.*

He picked up the glass and chugged it, ending with a belch. "Your loss."

Erin flopped into the chair by the French doors. "Why'd you move the money, Katy?" She slung a sleek, tanned leg over the chair arm. "It's not like there were that many people who knew about it. Your folks. Samantha. Emily. Ruby. And those coin shop people. Oh! And me." She frowned, looking hurt. "Don't you trust me? Wow. That hurts."

"It had nothing to do with you. I just didn't want it in the house anymore."

"Aha. Clue number one. The money's not in the house."

"I already told you that. The coin dealers have it."

"I thought you said it was in a safe deposit box." She swung her feet to the floor. "You and I both know the money's still here." She came to me and squatted. "Where's the money, Katy?"

"I'm not telling you."

She ground the gun muzzle into my toe. "Don't make me do this."

It was nearly impossible to speak, let alone string together a coherent sentence. "If you–you shoot me, the neighbors will hear it and call the police."

She gazed at me with a cold smile that scared me more than the gun. "What do ya hear, Tyler?"

He cupped his ear. "Motorcycles gunning their engines and loud music. Allman Brothers, I think. Classic."

"So ya really think anyone's gonna hear one little gun pop?" asked Erin. "Seriously?"

"I can get a pillow to help muffle the shot," said Tyler.

"It's up to Katy," said Erin. "You got ten seconds to decide, Katy, and then it's goodbye big toe."

She racked the gun like a pro. The ratchet sound made my bladder instantly release the three cups of coffee I drank at breakfast.

"One. Two."

I've always said that if someone pointed a gun in my face and said, *Give me your purse,* I would. I'm not about to give up my life for money. Of course, there's never more than fifty bucks in my purse, and it's usually more like three or four. Now I had a gun pointing at my foot, demanding I hand over millions.

"Five. Six."

If she pulled the trigger, I would immediately tell her where the money was hidden. There was no point in losing a toe for nothing.

"Eight. Nine."

"All right," I shouted. "You win. If I tell you where I hid it, will you leave?"

Erin crossed her heart with the gun. "Scout's honor. All we

want is the money, and as soon as we have it, we're out of here, and you'll still be able to wear cute sandals. I'll even leave you some cash to get a pedicure, 'cause, girl, you need one. Bad."

I closed my eyes and murmured, "The money's in the garden shed. You'll find it inside a big cardboard box."

Tyler started for the French doors facing the backyard. "Come on, Erin. Let's go get it."

Yes! Go! As soon as you're outside, I'm out of here.

Erin glanced at me, reading my thoughts again. "You really think we're going to leave you alone so you can call the cops? Get up and show us." She waved the gun in the direction of the doors.

I stood, leaving a wet stain on the couch.

Tyler pointed at the spot, laughing. "Looks like we really pissed you off."

Back in the kitchen, Erin ordered me to sit at the table while Tyler unloaded the heavy safes from the hand-truck onto the floor. I remember how disconnected my thoughts were: *Still gotta return that hand-truck to Pop. I hope Tyler doesn't dent the floor.* Looking back on it, I think I must have been in shock.

"Where's the keys?" asked Tyler.

"Good question." Erin held out her hand, snapping her fingers. "Keys, please."

"They're in the gadget drawer, left side of the sink," I said.

She opened the drawer and snickered at the jumbled mess. "Seriously, Katy? I'm supposed to believe you put the keys to the Kingdom in a junk drawer?"

"Yes."

I guess my defeated tone convinced her because she began rummaging. In a few seconds, she pulled out a little metal ring with one key on it, waving it triumphantly. "Aha! Got it."

"That's not it. And it's two keys. I'll find it." I reached to the back of the drawer and felt my fingers connect with my red rhinestone heart keychain—a girlhood gift from Ruby. "Here."

Erin snatched the keys and sent me back to the table. Tabitha curled through my legs, then jumped into my lap, nuzzling me. The hair along her back was raised as if she understood we were in serious trouble. "It's okay, baby." I stroked her, trying to reassure both of us.

"Prepare to be amazed, Tyler." Erin simultaneously lifted the lids on each safe.

"Holy shit. Babe, you weren't kidding." He unzipped a plastic bag and dumped a twenty-dollar coin into his hand. "Check it out. 1874. Looks like those coins they sell on TV." He flipped it into the air and grabbed for it, missing the catch.

"Tyler! Cut it out." Erin snatched up the coin and set it back in the bag. "This coin is probably worth thousands, but not if it's all dinged up, you bonehead."

"Sorry, babe."

"Let's leave the money in the safes." She squatted to lock them. "Would you put these in Katy's closet, Tyler?"

"For *safe* keeping, right, babe?" He leaned over Erin from behind and slid his hand inside the front of her robe.

She swatted his hand away. "Not now. Go put the safes in her closet."

Tyler left the room carrying one of the safes. Erin sat down at the table, still aiming the damned gun in my direction. "Is there more gold in the house that you haven't told me about?"

"If there is, I didn't find it, and believe me, I searched."

"I'd hate to find out later you were holding out on me."

"I'm not, Erin. You have it all."

"Oh, I have it all, all right. A crappy education. A crappy job—"

"How is going to Bryn Mawr a crappy education? And you work at Google. Not exactly what I'd call a crappy job."

"Like I said before, everything I told you was a lie. I wanted to impress you. You want to know the real story? I got a bookkeeping certificate at a community college. I'm a loser receptionist in a real-tor's office, and I rent a room in a dingy, low-rent house with four other losers." She smacked the table making me jump. "You don't need this money. Your life is great. You have this nice house," she swept her hand through the air, "and a wonderful family. Great friends—I don't have *any* friends."

I wonder why.

"God, even your pets are nice." Her eyes shimmered with tears. "Me? I've got nothing."

Tyler returned to the kitchen and massaged Erin's shoulders. "Hey, babe, you got me. For richer or poorer."

She groaned and grabbed a paper napkin to wipe her eyes.

"What about your parents?" I asked.

"They're both dead." Erin tossed the crumpled napkin on the table. "Tyler? Find some rope and tie her up."

"You got any rope?" he asked me.

"No." *Oh God, if I'm tied up, I am so screwed.* "Listen. Just take the money and go. It sounds like you need it more than me."

"What's to stop you from calling the police?" Erin shook her head. "Sorry, Katy. I like you. I really do, and under different circumstances, we could've been friends. Too bad you told me about the money, huh?" She shrugged, and then snapped at Tyler, "Look for something to tie her up with."

He wound up strapping me to the chair with two long exten-sion cords. Talk about déjà vu. Not too long ago, a woman who was completely bonkers tied me to that same damned chair.

"Now don't run off," said Erin. "We're going to look around for a while, just to make sure we haven't missed anything, then we'll be on our way." She glanced at Tyler. "Katy found the gold in the attic, so let's start up there."

Erin left the gun on the counter by the sink. The moment I heard their footsteps on the attic floor, I began working to loosen the cords.

Precious minutes ticked by. My wrists were rubbed raw from the stiff cord digging into my skin, and sweat was trickling down my back. I heard footsteps on the stairs and froze.

Then Tyler said, "We need to get rid of her."

CHAPTER TWENTY-THREE

FRIDAY • FEBRUARY 20
Posted by Katy McKenna

Friday, February 13
Part Two

"Well, Katy. It looks like you were right," said Erin. "About the attic, anyway. I saw where you pulled the wood off the studs. So, that leaves the rest of the house to explore. Ever since you showed me the coins, I've been reading online about hidden fortunes found in the walls of old houses. I'm betting this house has a few more secrets to reveal. By the way, from the looks of things up there, I don't think your beepers or peppermint cotton balls have taken care of your rat problems. There's poop all over the floor."

The staircase screeched as it fastened into the ceiling.

"Tyler!" yelled Erin. "Why'd you close the attic? I told you we're taking Katy up there."

"Oops. My bad," he called from the hall.

She saw the panicked look on my face and patted my shoulder. "Relax. We're not going to hurt you."

"I heard what you said."

"That was Tyler. If you haven't noticed by now, he's kind of an idiot. I'm not going to kill my cousin. We're family."

The steps were creaking their way down again, so I had to talk fast. "Why'd you invite me to dinner that night at Le Stella? At that time you didn't know about the money."

She sat down facing me, knees close to mine. "You're not going to believe this, but I was looking for a fresh start. I've always liked the Central Coast, and let me tell you, the Bay Area is not a great place to live when you're broke." She shrugged. "With you being a graphic artist, I thought I needed to impress you, so you wouldn't think I'm a loser. That fancy car? It's a rental. All my credit cards are maxed out." She crossed her arms, with a chagrined expression. "When I met you I liked you right off and realized that just being me would have been good enough for you."

"That's true."

She sighed. "And here's the really pathetic part. You know the night you showed me the coins?"

"Yeah." *How could I ever forget the dumbest thing I've ever done?*

"I had decided I was going to tell you the truth about me." She laughed, shaking her head. "I even hoped you might ask me to live here. You know, be your roommate, since your sister had moved out. But then you showed me the coins, and that was a game changer, for sure."

"It doesn't have to be like this, Erin. I could share the money with you."

Tyler entered the kitchen, and Erin said, "It's way too late for that, Katy. You know that."

"Too late for what?" asked Tyler.

"Nothing," said Erin, gazing at me.

"The sad thing is, I would've," I said. We locked eyes, and I could tell she believed me. And for a split second, I thought maybe she would let me go. Then she retrieved the gun from the counter.

"Tyler, untie her." She aimed the weapon in my direction.

He unraveled the extension cord wrapped around my ankles. While he untied my hands, I glanced around for a weapon. I didn't believe Erin would shoot me, especially after everything she said, but what about Tyler? He wanted me dead.

The knife block by the stove! I'll grab one and jam it in his stomach. He'll never know what hit him. I steeled myself, ready to act.

"Stand up, Katy," said Erin.

I stood. It was now or never.

Erin jabbed my ribs with the gun. "Please don't do anything stupid. I know I said we wouldn't kill you, but I will if I have to. So don't make me have to."

The cold resolve in her voice deflated my daring plan, and I decided compliance was my only hope of survival.

"Tyler, bring the extension cords," said Erin. "Katy, do you have any duct tape? I need to make sure no one can hear you screaming for help after we leave."

"No."

"Oh, please. Who doesn't have duct tape?"

"It's either under the sink or in the bottom drawer on the right of the sink."

"Got it," said Tyler. "Let's go."

"Wait," I said. "Before you take me up there, I need to go to the bathroom. Please." This was not a ruse to escape. That big airport breakfast was grinding in my gut and needed to be eliminated before I got sick.

Erin ushered me to the hall bathroom. Before she left me to my business, she checked the high window over the tub. "No way you're getting out through there." She looked in the sink cabinet for anything that I might be able to use as a weapon and removed the toilet plunger. "Three minutes, Katy," she said as she closed the door. "Then I'm coming in."

In the attic, they told me to lie down on the rough wood floor, and Tyler trussed me up again.

"I can't get this damned extension cord tight enough." He gave the stiff, plastic cord a hard yank, and I yelped when it pinched my ankles. "Hand me the duct tape. That'll work better."

Tyler removed the cord, tore off a long length of the gray tape, and wrapped it several times around my ankles. Then he shifted me onto my side and jerked my bare arms behind me.

"You're hurting me," I cried.

"Tyler. You don't have to be so rough," said Erin.

"Sorry. It's not like I do this sort of thing every day, you know." He taped my wrists together.

"Too tight," I said.

"Too bad," he said.

Erin tore off a short length of the duct tape and squatted beside me. "Close your mouth." She set the tape in place, smoothing it against my skin. "Please know I don't like doing this to you." She stood and clasped Tyler's hand. "After we are far away from here, I'll call your parents and tell them you're up here. So relax. No worries."

Thank God.

She gazed at me lying bound like a rodeo calf. "You don't deserve this, Katy." She shook her head. "But I just can't walk away from millions of dollars."

They stepped down the stairs. A moment later, as the stairway shut, Tyler said, "Are you really going to call her parents?"

She snickered. "No. That'd be kinda dumb, don't ya think? When her parents don't hear from her, they'll come looking. I read somewhere that you can go for three days without water, so she'll be fine. And we'll be long-gone in Costa Rica, living the life I've always dreamed of."

"It's going to be at least five or six days before anyone starts looking for her, you know," said Tyler.

"Oh, well. That's a bummer."

———

I lay on the attic floor for God knows how long, using the damned sonic beepers as a rhythmic mantra to soothe myself.

Beep: Breathe in.

Beep: Breathe out.

Long, slow, cleansing breaths.

The aroma of the peppermint cotton balls triggered soothing memories of Mom smearing Vicks VapoRub onto my chest whenever I had a bad cold.

Breathe in. Breathe out.

I hadn't heard a peep from downstairs since Erin said they wouldn't be calling my folks, so I assumed they were gone. Judging from the sunlight filtering through the four-paned, hexagonal windows, I figured it was around three p.m.

My bladder was feeling the diuretic pressure of all the coffee I drank that day. I really hit a low point when I realized that I would have to urinate. I held it as long as I could, because I kept thinking about Josh rescuing me and my mortification when he saw my wet pants. Silly, I know, considering that I was probably going to die there.

The motorcycles still rumbled across the street, which meant there had to be at least a few guys in the front yard. If I could get to the window, perhaps I could catch their attention.

I was lying on my side, twelve to fourteen feet from the window. How could such a short distance look so far? So impossible?

Maybe I can roll to the window.

The first roll over onto my stomach was pretty easy but trying to get the momentum to turn to my back was a different story. I kept banging my chin and nose into the floor and wound up sniffing what I'm pretty sure was rat crap. Holding my chin high, I tipped over onto my back again and came to the conclusion that rolling was not the ticket. I was pretty sure my grazed chin was oozing blood, and I could feel poop pellets stuck to it. *Probably will get blood poisoning and have to amputate my chin.*

That goofy thought actually gave me a little chuckle. Then it dawned on me that I could bend my knees and shove my body across the floor! Mental fist pump!

Big mistake. My bare arms were tethered behind my back, and after one push, they felt like they were on fire.

The throbbing pain gradually backed off, and I planned my next move. *If I can pull myself to a sitting position, I can try to shimmy on my butt to the window.*

Sitting up with your hands tied behind your back isn't easy, especially when you haven't done a sit-up in a while. A very long while. Like since high school P.E. class. My nonexistent stomach muscles strained mightily, but it wasn't happening.

Finally, I got the idea to roll over to my side with knees bent in a fetal position and curl my way up to a sitting position. It wasn't easy, but I did it.

I began the long trek to the window. Lift one butt cheek and wriggle forward. Lift the other side and wriggle forward. Repeat until mission accomplished. My leggings kept snagging on the wood floor. Sweat trickled down my forehead, stinging my eyes. Finally, I was peering out the window. To an empty street, devoid of all human life.

I was disheartened to see Erin's rented sports car still sitting in my driveway. The longer they hung around, the more chance they might change their mind and kill me. I decided to keep watching out the window, and if I saw anyone, I'd bang my head on the glass, even though it meant risking my captors hearing me.

Four cars and a truck cruised down the street. Fred, the escape-artist old beagle that lives on the corner, strolled by, pausing to poop on my dead lawn.

I heard a booming thud downstairs. And then another. And another, followed by a cracking-ripping sound. Another bang and the window glass rattled.

Shit! They're tearing down the walls. Why couldn't they believe me? I went over the entire house with Pop's metal detector. There's no more damned gold.

Erin shrieked in the hallway, and Tyler hooted. "Don't be such a girlie-girl. It's just an old dead rat."

"I don't care. Get that thing out of my face," she screamed. "It's disgusting."

"Looks like it's been dead for years," said Tyler. "It's practically a mummy."

"Katy said she had rats," said Erin, now giggling.

I said I had squirrels.

"You know, we could knock out these walls a helluva lot faster if we had another sledgehammer. You're not making much progress with that little hatchet," said Tyler.

"I'm amazed she had a sledgehammer in the garage. I thought we'd have to go to the hardware store."

"Maybe your cousin is planning on doing some home remodeling."

No, I'm not. The former owner left those behind.

"I know she watches a lot of those HGTV shows," said Erin.

"So do I. I've always wanted to buy an old fixer-upper and do the work myself."

"Uh-uh. No way," said Erin. "I'm not living in a dump ever again. I'm going to buy the biggest, fanciest house on the Caribbean coast. I wish I could buy a ski chalet in Vail or Aspen, too, but it's not going to be safe coming back to the U.S."

"Babe, the only thing stoppin' you is Katy. She's the only one who'll know we stole the money. If she can't tell the cops it was us, how'll they ever know?"

"No, it's not right. Can't do it," said Erin. "Besides, I can buy a chalet in the Alps."

Oh, thank God.

"Babe. Get real. I'm tellin' you we need to get rid of her. Then we can do whatever we want."

"I really can't. Besides, her friend knows I was here."

"No problem. I can waste her, too."

Oh, God no! Sam has nothing to do with this.

"Tyler, stop it. I'm not murdering my cousin, and her friend has kids."

"You don't have to. I will. She's not my cousin, so what do I care?"

"You said she'd only last three days without water," said Erin. "Remember? So she's going to die anyway. By then, we'll be long gone."

She's right, Tyler. I'll die anyway. So leave me to it.

"Yeah, but it'll be a long, slow, agonizing death," said Tyler. "Is that what you want for your cousin? One bullet in her head. BAM! She won't suffer. And to make you happy, we'll leave her friend alone."

"How do you know she won't suffer?"

How can she ask that? Is she changing her mind about killing me?

"I go hunting with my buddies all the time. You shoot a deer in the head, and they drop like a bag of rocks. Hardly any blood. BAM!"

"Stop with the bams, Tyler. I can't think."

"What's to think about?" he said. "One pop, and it's done, and then me and you—"

"You and I."

"That's what I said."

"No. You said *me* and you."

"Same diff."

"No, it's *not*." Erin's tone was terse.

"Whatever." Tyler resumed tearing down the hallway walls.

After about an hour, Erin said, "I guess there's nothing here, so...."

So leave!

"Let's rip out the walls in the living room."

"Don't you think we should get out of here pretty soon?" said Tyler.

"What's your hurry? No one expects her back until next week."

"I know that, babe, but the longer we stay, the higher the risk of this whole thing blowing apart."

"Tell you what," said Erin. "Let's work on these walls today and then tomorrow morning we'll drive to L.A. and get on a flight to Costa Rica."

"I was thinkin' we could make a pit stop in Vegas. Live like high-rollers for a few days."

"I kind of like that idea," Erin said. "We could sell a few coins to private collectors in Las Vegas. Then we'll have plenty of money to travel in style."

"How about you bankroll me in a high stakes poker tournament, and I parlay it into big winnings?"

She snorted. "More like big losings. You've never played in a tournament, goofball."

"What do ya mean? I play in tournaments all the time."

"Online. I meant you've never played with live, in-your-face people, and real money. Big difference." She paused. "Oh, stop with the puppy eyes. Okay. You can play poker while I shop for new clothes. Then we can charter a private plane from there. I've always wanted to fly in a Lear jet."

"I've never been on an airplane," said Tyler.

"It's not like I've done it a lot. But when I was a kid, my parents took me to visit relatives in Michigan a couple of times, and we flew."

"I was a foster kid, remember? So no family to visit."

"Oh, God, I'm sorry. Poor baby. Come to Mama."

Judging from the next sounds, he was coming to Mama.

———

I must have nodded off because the next thing I knew, the demolition derby was back in full swing. Now that they weren't directly under me, I thought it might be safe to try to break the window.

Then I'll can yell at anyone passing by. Except my damned mouth is taped shut. Shit! Shit! Shit!

I forced myself to stay calm and think. I really wanted to blubber and feel sorry for myself, but I'm proud to say I managed to hold it together.

Okay, new plan. I'll break the window and see what happens after that. Not exactly a plan, but it beats doing nothing and meekly waiting to die.

I lay on my back and with bent knees, shimmied my butt close to the wall. Then lifted my legs and aimed my feet at the window. I listened to the rhythmic wall whacks downstairs and counted.

One.

Two.

THREE!

I thrust my feet against the window and shattered one of the panes. Shards of glass dropped to the porch roof. I froze, listening to hear if my captors had noticed.

The wall-busters continued, so I steeled myself to break the pane next to it and after that, kick out the wood framing. Then I'd be able to lean out of the opening. Surely a passer-byer would see me.

One, two, THREE!

The glass cracked but didn't fall out. I pushed my bound feet against the pane, and the glass snapped off, slicing the top of my right foot. Blood snaked its way down to my duct-taped ankles.

I remembered Pop telling me about one of his cop buddies bleeding out within minutes when he got shot in the leg during a domestic dispute call. *Oh, God. Did I sever an artery?*

I lowered my feet to the floor, waiting to see if I was going to bleed to death. I wriggled around to get a look at my foot. The wound was seeping, but not gushing, so I decided I wasn't going to die. Yet.

My head and shoulders wouldn't fit through the one open pane, but I could stick my head out and make as much noise as one can when their mouth is duct taped.

——

It was long past sunset, and not a soul had passed by my house. Holding myself upright for the last few hours had strained a muscle in the right side of my lower back, and my aching body screamed to lie down and sleep. A chilly breeze gusted through the window, making my teeth chatter.

Next week at this time, all of this will be behind me. Just a bad memory. I'll be sitting on my sofa, wrapped in a warm blanket, cuddled up with Daisy and Tabitha on one side. Josh on the other. As long as I'm alive, I still have hope.

——

I was slurping a melting double-decker chocolate cone, and the ice cream dribbled down my chin. Daisy licked the drips off my feet. Her tongue felt raspy like a cat's, and I tried to tell her to stop, but I had a mouthful of ice cream. I strained to twist away from her relentless licking, but my legs wouldn't budge.

My body jolted suddenly like I was tumbling off a cliff, and I woke up, but the scratchy sensations didn't stop. Something heavy shifted on my chest and scraped my sore chin. I tilted my head up and met the glinting eyes of an enormous rat. My body shuddered, and the rat crashed to the floor and scuttled away with his buddies.

My horrible day just got a whole lot worse. I had no idea how many rats were in the attic. Was it a few? Or hundreds? I recalled that scene in *Willard* when the rats swarmed over the man's body to devour him. Sam and I had thought it was pretty cheesy-funny at the time, but now I wondered if that could actually happen.

Try to think happy rat thoughts. I inhaled a long quivering breath, then slowly released it. *Okay, got one:*

When I was six, I had a pet rat. He was white and gray. I named him Ernie after the Muppet on *Sesame Street*. He had a cute pink nose, and he went nuts when I gave him Cheerios. Ernie had a tiny red teddy bear toy that he cuddled when he slept. He was an adorable, sociable, lovable rat.

I need another happy rat thought.

Five years ago, I was in Disneyland with Chad. We were near the castle, and a cute packrat was sitting in a bed of purple and yellow pansies nibbling on a piece of a churro. Children gathered around, shouting, "Look at the funny bunny!" The moms and dads smiled, all knowing this was not a bunny. But so what? He was a cute little creature.

I said to the little guy, "You're going to have such a tummy ache from eating that greasy food."

And then my was-band Chad had to say, "Get real, Katy. It's a goddamn RAT!"

The kids shrieked, and the packrat dropped his churro and dashed into the bushes.

That memory didn't end well but not because of the rat.

CHAPTER TWENTY-FOUR

SATURDAY · FEBRUARY 21
Posted by Katy McKenna

Saturday, February 14

As dawn illuminated the sky to a soft pearl gray, a cool breeze washed over my face and woke me. It took me a second to realize where I was and another few to remember the rats. The instant I did, I squirmed and struggled to sit up. Mercifully, the nocturnal rodents must've called it a night.

I broke a sweat as I shifted my stiff, aching body so I could peer out the window. I was shocked to see Erin's car still parked in the driveway.

A toilet flushed. Then a shower turned on. A few minutes later, the tantalizing aroma of coffee wafted through the attic air.

Maybe Erin will give me a drink of water before they leave.

Then it struck me that if she came up to the attic, she'd see the broken window. *Please don't let them come up here. Wait, I know! I'll say it's been broken for a long time and I'd forgotten to get it fixed. They'll realize there's no way I can get anyone's attention anyway since I'm all tied up...right next to the damned window. Shit!*

I began the slow, agonizing scoot to the spot where they left me yesterday. Once there, I sagged against the wall, trying to squelch my hyper-breathing.

"Hey, babe," hollered Tyler. "Pour me a coffee, will ya?"

"I already did," said Erin. "It's on the counter."

"We sure made a mess here." Tyler sounded like he was right below me. "Man, she'd be pissed if she saw this."

"While you were in the shower," said Erin. "I loaded all the coins into a carryon. It's in Katy's closet, but it's pretty heavy, so I need you to put it in the car."

"Whoa, babe. Do you know what today is?"

"No. Should I?"

"It's Valentine's Day. I feel bad I didn't get you anything."

At that point, Erin and Tyler took a break to acknowledge the day.

———

Erin's voice grew louder as she neared the hall. "I want to check on Katy, then we can go."

"Babe. We need to get rid of her. I know you don't want to, but it's too dangerous leaving her alive. I was thinking it would be better to get her out of here, then dump her somewhere where she won't ever be found. No loose ends, you know."

Oh, my God!

"And how do we do that?" asked Erin in a sarcastic tone.

"Easy. We'll put her in the car and—"

"You do remember my rental's a two-seater, right?"

"How about we take her car, too?" said Tyler. "We could push it over a cliff with her in it."

"Not a good idea. Katy's car is supposed to be sitting at the airport. What if her boyfriend next door, or one of the other neighbors, sees us driving it down the street? There's not a lot of old orange Volvos running around these days, so it might get their attention."

"Yeah. You're right. I didn't think of that," Tyler said. "I just wanna get her out of here, so nobody can find her before she's dead. What if her friend comes over to see how you're doing?"

"I'll take Katy's phone, and in a couple of days, I'll use it to text her family that she's decided to stay away a little longer. Later today, I'll text her friend, Samantha, on my phone, and tell her I'm doing better and decided to go back to the Bay Area."

"Works for me," said Tyler. "Let's get out of here."

"You go ahead and take the money out to the car, while I make sure we haven't left anything behind."

A minute later, Tyler said, "Whoa, you weren't kidding about this being heavy."

Are they really leaving now? I waited, holding my breath. I didn't think I'd be able to breathe again until I heard the Jaguar drive away.

The front door slammed, and Tyler yelled, "I put the suitcase behind the seats. You ready to go, babe?"

"Not quite yet," said Erin.

"What do ya mean? We need to get outta here."

"I've been thinking about what you said, and you're right. It's too dangerous to leave Katy alive. We have to kill her," said Erin. "Not just for us, but for her sake, too. No matter what, she's going to die, so let's do this and spare her the misery."

Oh, God. No, no, no. Crushing terror seized me, and my bowels discharged everything I'd been holding in since the night before.

"Give me the gun," said Tyler, "and I'll do it while you look for her phone."

"No, let's do it together. I owe her that much."

"Whoa. You really are a bad-ass girl."

"More than you know, Tyler."

The attic floor trembled as the ceiling staircase creaked down.

Tyler entered first, singing in a creepy-sweet tone, "Kaaa-teee? How're you doing?" He crouched beside me, and ripped the tape off my mouth. "Got any last words?" His nose wrinkled. "You shit your pants?"

My cousin stood a few feet behind him. "Please, Erin. You have the money." I paused, striving to make my raspy words sound composed, sensible. "You *don't* want to be a murderer. Right now, you can get away and live the life you were meant to live. I'll die in a couple of days anyway, and when someone finds my body, they're not going to connect my death with you. Besides, if he shoots me, somebody might hear the gun go off. Why risk it when you don't have to?"

Tyler laughed. "Your loser friends across the street are working on their cycles, so kinda doubt they're going to hear one bullet timed to the revving engines. Vroom, *BOOM*, vroom." He placed his index finger on my forehead. "Right there in the center. Won't even mess up your pretty face."

Over Tyler's shoulder, I caught and held Erin's eyes. "I'm begging you. Think about my family. This'll kill them, too. And they all adore you."

She gazed at me, her lips hard-pressed like she was holding back tears.

Tyler, still hunkered beside me, his back to her, held out his hand, snapping his fingers. "Come on, babe. Gimme the gun. Let me put this reeking bitch outta her misery."

Erin shook her head slowly—eyes locked on mine—and whispered, "I'm so sorry."

The gun lifted, aimed at my head, and I closed my eyes for the last time.

I waited for death, each passing second fractured into long milliseconds. The rumbling motorcycles faded into the background. The only thing I heard was my heartbeat whooshing in my ears, driving life-sustaining blood through my veins, not ready to concede.

My only thought was, *Shit. So this is how I die*. I didn't think about whether it would hurt. Or if there were an afterlife waiting for me. There was no montage of my thirty-two years on this earth. Nothing. With no way out, I resigned myself to my fate. The utter, mind-bending fear that I'd felt only moments before had evaporated. I felt almost peaceful.

The gun exploded, my body jerked, and everything went silent.

A few seconds passed, and I opened my eyes. I assumed I was dead until I focused on Tyler hovering over me, looking dumb-founded. An oozing hole split his forehead. Then he collapsed on top of me, grinding me into the floor. His rough cheek mashed into my face and warm spittle drizzled down my cheek.

Tyler's dead weight crushed my chest. "Help me. Can't. Breathe."

Erin held the gun pointed toward me, her eyes wide, vacant.

The weapon slipped from her hand. For a moment she didn't seem to notice. Then she retrieved it, her gaze never leaving mine.

"Please, Erin," I whispered. "Please don't."

Her lips moved, but all I heard was a high-pitched *eeeee*, like the last time I experienced a gun blast at pointblank range.

I shut my eyes and waited for my bullet.

Suddenly, Tyler shifted. In a jerky motion, he slithered down my body until his head burrowed into my crotch. I sucked in a lungful of air and saw Erin dragging him off of me. She hauled his limp body to the other side of the attic, then returned to me and squatted. Her lips were moving.

I shook my head. "I can't hear you."

She left the attic. She returned with a glass of water and lifted my head to drink. My lips were cracked and sore making it difficult to sip. It trickled to the back of my tongue, and I choked and sputtered the liquid down my chin.

Erin withdrew the glass.

"No, please. Water."

She tipped it into my mouth again, and I willed it to go down my throat. At the halfway mark, Erin set the tumbler on the floor and glanced around for the roll of duct tape.

"I have to go now, Katy," she yelled in my ear.

She smoothed a piece of tape over my lips, picked up the water, and left.

This narrative is about to go from bad to worse, so I'm taking a break to decide if I want to continue or not.

Two hours later

I've decided to cut to the bare bones. It'll be too hard to write and too awful for my family to read.

The scurry of rodent feet woke me, re-stoking my trepidation. In the moonlight spilling through the windows, I saw rats gamboling around Tyler's head. Thankfully, none of them were glancing my way. Being a glass-half-full kind of girl, I appreciated my tenuous good fortune.

CHAPTER TWENTY-FIVE

SATURDAY · FEBRUARY 21

Guest Posted by Samantha Drummond

*Katy asked me to fill in some of the gaps in the story,
so I'm guest posting.*

When Katy's flight to Los Angeles was canceled, she texted me from the Santa Lucia Airport: *Guess what? Flute cackled due to flog. Going home for a nip and leavening later this afternoon.*

Katy's texts are often indecipherable, thanks to autocorrect. Really wish she'd read them before she hits Send. I read it while on duty but was too busy to think up a sarcastic reply. Two nurses had called in sick, and of course, it was also an unusually busy day. I don't know what was going on in Santa Lucia nine months ago, but we are running about 27% above normal in the maternity department.

And now that the hospital has all but phased out the nursery, the new moms get no recuperation time. For some, this is fine, but my heart goes out to the ones begging for a nap. I know how they feel!

One of the moms on my shift went through thirty-six hours of labor before the obstetrician did a C-section. The exhausted mother desperately needed some rest, so I kept her baby at the nurse's station for a few hours because we had no one staffing the obsolete nursery. It has gotten ridiculous, and I'm seriously considering a career change.

Two hours of overtime and three babies later, all I wanted to do was to put up my feet and have a glass of wine, but my step-daughter, Chelsea, was having a sleepover, so neither was happening.

I finally crawled into bed around eleven-thirty, resigned to a long night of giggling and ear-splitting shrieks. When Katy and I were teenagers, we vowed never to tell our kids to quiet down when having a slumber party. I was determined to be the cool mom and keep that stupid vow, but at one in the morning, I lost my cool and broke it. A fat lot of good it did.

While up, I thought of Katy and checked my phone for a text. Of course, there wasn't one, but I didn't give it much thought. Instead, I went back to Chelsea's room and broke the vow again.

———

Saturday morning, I texted Katy. *Hey, girl! Having a good time.??*

Late that afternoon, Katy's mom called. "Have you heard anything from Katy? There haven't been any plane crashes, but I'm getting worried. I've heard of young women being abducted and sold into slavery, and—"

"Marybeth. I don't think that sort of thing happens in Belize. But maybe she doesn't have good cell reception. I'm sure she's fine."

"You're right. I'm probably overreacting. It's just that she's never traveled alone before, or out of the country, for that matter."

"I'm sure I'd be worrying too if it was my kid," I said.

"You'll let me know if you hear from her?"

"Will do, and you do the same, okay?"

A few minutes later, Katy's grandma called. "I haven't heard from Katy, and I'm getting pretty darned p.o.'d at that girl. Has she called you?"

"No. I just spoke to Marybeth and promised her that if I hear anything, I'll let her know."

"Well, you can add me to the list," she said.

"I don't think there's anything to worry about. She probably just doesn't have good cellphone reception."

"I bet she's swilling fancy umbrella drinks and too damned drunk to give a hoot whether we're worried or not. That's what I'd be doing. If I'd been invited to go, that is. Which I was not."

"Neither was I, Ruby, although I couldn't have gone anyway."

"So, what do you think about this new cousin?"

"Erin seems nice enough." I recall feeling guilty at that point, remembering the lovely scarf she gave me. But the truth is, I'm a little resentful about how fast Katy and Erin have bonded.

"You don't sound so sure about her."

"I like her. I really do."

Ruby snorted. "Oh, please. I can read you like a book. But don't you worry, honey. You'll always be Katy's best friend. What do you girls say nowadays? Your BFF? Sounds so silly. Why can't people just say the words, so the rest of us have a clue what you're saying?"

After talking to Katy's mom and grandma, I felt a little concerned, too. But a couple of hours later, Katy checked in with a short, annoying group text to all of us. *Having a goooood time, wish you were here! I may never come home!!*

CHAPTER TWENTY-SIX

SUNDAY • FEBRUARY 22
Posted by Katy McKenna

Hard to believe this was just a week ago.

Sunday, February 15

Watching the dawn slowly light the attic rafters, I recalled Tyler's dire prediction that tomorrow would be my last day on the planet. Then I thought, *Just because Tyler said that people couldn't live longer than three days without water doesn't necessarily make it so. Besides, Erin gave me some water, so that's got to count for something.*

I was determined to survive this ordeal and spend the rest of my days savoring every blessed moment. I even swore to any God willing to listen to me that if I survived, I would never again be petty, ungrateful, snarky, bitchy, thoughtless, unkind, or jealous. I'm sure there were a lot more character flaws that should have made the list, but I was too drained to think.

By this time, the stench in the attic was becoming unbearable. Tyler's body had released its waste when he died and the foul odor mingling with my own stink was disgusting. But now I was catching another revolting smell from his end of the room that was growing stronger by the hour. His body was decomposing. I was thankful that I couldn't see the progress and that a fresh breeze was blowing through the broken window.

Late in the day, the sky clouded over, and I caught the delicious scent of rain in the air. Pretty soon, it turned into a torrential downpour. It hadn't rained in nearly a year, and I was crushed that I couldn't run outside and get soaked to the skin and dance in the puddles.

A cold, drip splashed onto my head. Then another and another. Drip. Drip. Drip. My roof was leaking life-sustaining water to me, and I couldn't open my mouth to receive it.

I tried to shimmy away from it but didn't have the strength to power through it, so I gave up and accepted the bitter irony.

CHAPTER TWENTY-SEVEN

SUNDAY · FEBRUARY 22
Posted by Katy McKenna

Monday, February 16
Part One

Monday, Monday.... The few lyrics I knew from the old Mamas & the Papas' song kept looping in my head. My resolve to break the three-day rule was dissolving into a puddle of dry tears. *Monday, Monday... My final day....*

———

Something woke me. A muffled, scuffling sound. *Probably the damned rats again.* A flicker of anger ignited in my gut. *Leave me alone. Can't you at least wait until I'm dead?* Then I heard something that stabbed my heart. Daisy was whining. I opened my eyes thinking she was beside me. But she wasn't there. It was just me, dead rotting Tyler, and maddening little flies buzzing everywhere.

And yet, I could hear her as if she were right next to me. *She must know I'm dying, and she's connecting with me. Oh, my sweet baby. I'm so sorry. Mom and Pop will take good care of you and Tabitha. I promise. They love you almost as much as I do.*

"Daisy! Mind me! You're making Grandma very cranky," yelled my mother. "It's time to go."

Mom?

Daisy erupted into a manic barking frenzy.

"Fine then. I give up. You can stay, but I'm leaving."

The front door closed.

No, no, no! Don't leave. I'm up here. Mommy!

I lifted my feet and banged them on the floor, and Daisy howled. I stomped again, not feeling a twinge of pain. No way would my girl leave me up here.

"Daisy, you're scaring me," said Mom.

Oh, thank God. She came back. I thumped the floor and screamed, straining against the tape. "Mmmmm!" I slammed the floor again. *It's me, Mama. I'm here.*

Mom called in a scared voice, "Who's up there?"

I moaned as loud as I could. "Mmmmm."

The front door slammed. I'd scared my mother away. My last chance.

There was no reason to keep hanging on. It wasn't even worth trying anymore. I just wanted to sleep. I gave in and closed my eyes.

CHAPTER TWENTY-EIGHT

SUNDAY • FEBRUARY 22

Guest Posted by Marybeth Melby

My daughter asked me to post about when I found her in the attic. I'm not much of a writer, but I'll do my best.

Monday, February 16

That morning, Kurt made a lovely breakfast. Scrambled eggs, bacon, sourdough toast. He was trying to make me feel better, but I had no stomach for food and was in no mood to feel better.

"You'd think she could at least take the time to call," I said.

Kurt shook his head, as he buttered his toast. "You'd think."

"I mean, this is so unlike her."

"I know."

The phone rang, and my anger instantly evaporated, as I stood to answer it. "That's got to be her."

"Give the brat hell," said Kurt.

Then the caller I.D. announced it was Mom calling, and I sat back down, even madder. "Will you talk to Mom? I can't deal with her right now."

Mom had been checking in every few hours, and I couldn't handle another tirade about taking Katy out of her will if she didn't call soon. Kurt took the phone into the living room, and I could hear him trying to smooth her ruffled feathers.

Daisy must have felt the tension in the house, because she nuzzled her head into my lap, gazing up at me with her soulful, brown eyes. "Sorry, baby. Grandma's cranky. And I'm sure this darn peri-menopause isn't helping my mood one bit. I'm probably overreacting. Your mother's a big girl and can take care of herself."

Daisy sighed, and I said, "Once a mother, always a mother. Doesn't matter how old your kids get, you never can turn off the worry switch."

She groaned, and I took it as agreement. "How about some breakfast?"

Her ears perked at the word "breakfast," and she scampered around the kitchen as I opened the sack to fill her bowl. "Hey, Daisy, we're almost out of food. I know your mommy has another full bag in the laundry room. Later, when I get back from the salon, we'll get it, and you can say hi to Tabitha. Probably need to check on her food and water, too, since Erin went home yesterday."

The salon is closed on Mondays, but I always go in for a few hours to catch up on the previous week's paperwork and place orders. I finished up around two-thirty and drove straight home. Daisy greeted me at the door clutching her stuffed alligator in her mouth.

After a good hug and a lot of sloppy kisses, I got her a doggy treat, and then it dawned on me. "Oh, baby. I forgot you're out of food. You know what? Granny's exhausted. How about we spoil you tonight and give you people food?"

Her tail wagged and she spun in circles the second she heard me utter those wonderful words.

"And we won't tell your mother because we know how fussy she is about what you eat."

And then I remembered that darned cat.

———

Daisy pawed at Katy's front door as I inserted the key. "Honey, stop it. You'll scratch the paint, and your mother will kill me." I barely had the key pulled out when she shoved through and disappeared. I stepped inside and called, "Hey, kitty! Granny's here!"

Tabitha raced to the entry and tried to climb my legs. Thank goodness I had jeans on. I scooped her up and cuddled her. "What's wrong, honey? You lonely? Let's go check your food, sweetheart."

As I write this, I can't believe I didn't notice the disaster in the living room or hallway. I guess I was so intent on soothing Tabitha, that I simply beelined to the kitchen without looking at anything other than the cat. But when I stepped into the kitchen I got a nasty shock.

Dirty plates were stacked on the counter and in the sink. The refrigerator door was wide open. A milk carton on the counter had gone sour. The drawers were all pulled out, and a couple were dumped on the floor. The garbage can was knocked over. Flies everywhere. It took me a good minute to comprehend the chaos. I could not fathom how Erin, no matter how spoiled she may be, would do something this rotten to Katy. Little did I know....

"Oh, Tabitha, you poor baby. No wonder you're so upset."

I opened a window to air out the smelly kitchen, dumped the sour milk, set the trash bin out the back door, then tackled the dishes. I broke all my rules about wasting water and set the crusty dishes to soak in a sink full of hot, sudsy water. But as soon as I stepped away from the lemon-scented dish detergent, I still smelled a revolting stench.

"What is that? It smells like something died in here."

Daisy whined in the hall, and I left the kitchen to see what her problem was. That's when I caught sight of the living room. It looked like a wrecking ball had swung through, randomly smashing into the walls. Broken plaster was strewn everywhere. A thick film of chalky dust covered everything, making the room look eerie.

Daisy woofed and I found her perched on a pile of rubble in the hall, eyes fixed on the ceiling, whining and pawing the pile of plaster. The walls had been stripped down to the studs, exposing the underlying shiplap and electric wires. A putrid stench wafted from the attic.

"My, God! What died up there?" And then it dawned on me. "Rats. Daisy. It's time to go."

The stubborn dog would not tear her eyes off the ceiling.

"Daisy, it's just a dead rat. Or several. That's all it is. Nothing to worry about." I wanted to get out of the house—not just because of the smell, but because I was frightened. It had to be vandals who broke in after Erin went home, and I was nervous they might return while I was there.

"Let's go, girl." Daisy ignored me, completely fixated on the ceiling. "We'll call an exterminator in the morning. It's time to go now." I patted my thigh, and she continued to disregard me, which was so unlike her. I stepped into the debris and tugged her collar, and she lay down, refusing to budge.

"Daisy! Mind me! You're making Grandma very cranky," I yelled, then threw up my hands. "Fine then. I give up. You can stay, but I'm leaving."

I wasn't really leaving Daisy, but I needed to get out of the house before I vomited from the overwhelming odor. On the porch, I called Kurt's cell, figuring he'd still be at his shop. As it rang, Daisy's whining took on a tone that chilled me to the bone, so I hung up and went back inside.

"Daisy, you're scaring me."

Something in the attic thumped the floor and let out an

unearthly sound that sent shivers down my spine. Daisy responded with a low, throaty whimper that grew into anguished howls.

Petrified, I forced myself to yell, "Who's up there?" Something or someone needed help, but I didn't have the nerve to go into the attic alone. Then I remembered Josh, so I ran to his house and pounded on the door.

He looked annoyed when he opened the door, until he recognized me from our one brief meeting months ago. "Marybeth? What's wrong?"

"You need to get your gun and come with me."

The dear man didn't even question my unusual request. "Hold on." A few moments later, he ran with me to Katy's house. At the front door, we heard Daisy wailing, and he motioned me to stay behind as we entered.

He stopped when he saw the living room chaos. "What the hell happened here?"

"I have no idea. Vandals, I guess. But there's something in the attic that has Daisy frantic, and I'm terrified to go up there alone."

Josh followed me into the hall. "It smells like something died."

"At first, I thought it was rats," I said. "But then something pounded on the floor and moaned, so whatever is up there is a lot bigger than a rat. It could be an opossum, and I'm afraid it might be injured or rabid."

Josh took Daisy's collar and coaxed her off the mound. "Come on, girl. Let me go see what's upsetting you."

She seemed to understand and stepped away. I helped him clear the pile of plaster out of the way, and then he stepped on the stool Katy keeps in the hall and unlatched the ceiling door. As he pulled down the steps, I half-expected some horrible monster to leap upon us.

When the stairs locked into place, Josh took his gun from his back waistband and set his foot on the first rung. "I want you to stay down here and hold onto Daisy. I don't think she can manage these narrow steps, but the way she's acting, I'm afraid she might try."

"Please be careful, Josh."

Three-quarters of the way up the steps, he yelled, "Call 911!"

"What is it?"

"It's Katy! She's hurt!"

I ran to the kitchen phone, dialed 911, and screamed, "I need an ambulance."

The dispatcher calmly asked the nature of the emergency, and I came unglued. "It's my daughter. She's..." I didn't know what to say. "...my daughter's been injured."

After answering his unending questions as coherently as possible, I hung up and dashed for the stairs.

In the attic, Josh was crouched beside Katy, his back to me. Daisy stood beside him, nudging her girl's limp legs.

I hung back, terrified that my baby was dead.

CHAPTER TWENTY-NINE

MONDAY · FEBRUARY 23
Posted by Katy McKenna

Monday, February 16
Part Two

Something tugged at my mouth. It hurt, but I didn't bother opening my eyes. Didn't care.

"Katy. Open your eyes, Katy. You're safe now."

Josh? I opened my eyes. *Is this real?*

He worked the sticky duct tape from my mouth, then tenderly traced my raw lips.

I drank in my Viking's beautiful face, praying he was real and not a delirious, dying illusion. And then he faded away. *Oh, God. It wasn't real.* I shut my eyes.

A warm hand smoothed the hair away from my forehead like Mom did when I was a child. I opened my eyes again. She was crying.

"Mama?"

Daisy nosed Mom's arm aside and kissed my face.

"Daisy! Stop licking Katy's sore face," said Mom.

This is real.

"Who did this to you, baby?" Mom asked.

"Erin." But all that came out was a croak. I tried to swallow, but instead my throat constricted, like the sides were stuck together. "Water."

"Oh, honey, I can't understand you."

"Katy?" said Josh. "Who's the dead guy?"

"What dead guy?" Mom glanced around the gloomy attic. When she caught sight of my rotting roommate tucked in the dark shadows, she shrieked. "Oh, my God! Oh, my God!"

She turned back to me, trying to act composed like she saw corpses every day. But her freaked out eyes were telling a different story. "Oh, my poor baby. Did he do this to you?" Her warm hand caressed my brow.

Again, I tried to say, "Erin," but I sounded like a dehydrated frog.

"It's okay, sweetie. Don't try to talk," said Mom, then snapped, "What is taking that ambulance so damned long?"

"It's only been a few minutes." Josh leaned into my view. "I'm going to take the tape off your ankles, but I may hurt you if I do your arms. We'll have to wait for the paramedics."

I must have faded out because the next thing I knew Mom was cradling my head and holding a water bottle to my mouth. She drizzled in a few drops. "Just a little bit, Katy. I don't want to risk choking you."

My shriveled tongue felt like it was inflating. I opened and shut my mouth a few times, cautiously working my stiff, creaking jaw. "More, please."

Mom poured enough for one swallow. My parched throat was caught unaware, and the water slid down the wrong pipe, sending me into a wretched coughing spasm that hurt so, so bad. Like the worst case of strep throat, times ten.

"Oh, sweetie, I'm so sorry," said Mom. "I knew I shouldn't give you more. I knew it. I knew it."

Daisy plunked herself along the length of my body, pressing close, giving me warmth. The coughing eased, and I sputtered, "More."

My next memory is lying on a gurney in the front yard with an I.V. poked into my arm. Not long ago, I was in another front yard on a gurney. I really need to get a new hobby.

I tried to sit up, and Mom patted my shoulder, persuading me to relax. "You're safe now. I called your father, and he'll meet us at the hospital." She shook her head with a wry smile. "You'll be the death of us yet."

I glanced around as best I could from my prone position and saw several cops on the porch. Police cars blocked the street on either side of my house. Beyond the blockade were three TV news vans. I was grateful that a police officer was holding back the nosey reporters. My yard was decorated with yellow crime scene tape, and my redneck neighbors were lounging on the tattered sofa in their front yard, watching, "The Katy Show."

"Time to get you to the hospital, young lady," said a clean-cut, good-looking EMT, as he and his partner hoisted my gurney into the ambulance.

Mom climbed in and sat on a bench next to me. Before they closed the door, Josh said to her, "I'll take Daisy to my house, and Nicole can watch her. I'll catch up with you at the hospital, as soon as I can. I know I'm going to have to answer some questions before they'll let me out of here. It would help if I had something to tell them."

I said in a raspy whisper that hurt like hell, "It was Erin, and the dead guy's her boyfriend, Tyler." I shut my mouth, not wanting to utter another painful sound.

"Erin?" said Mom. "I can't believe it. She seemed like such a nice, sweet girl. And her boyfriend? I thought she was hiding from him."

"Got a last name?" Josh asked.

"Cranston," said Mom. "Katy, do you know her boyfriend's last name?"

I shook my head.

"He'll probably have ID on him," said Josh.

During the ride to the hospital, Mom called Pop. Five minutes after they had me situated in a curtained cubicle, he rushed in, looking like he'd aged a hundred years. "Katy-did, are you all right?"

"Hey, Pop." My gravelly voice didn't seem to convince him.

He kissed my forehead. "Who the hell did this to you?"

"It was Erin." Mom popped another ice chip in my mouth. "And her boyfriend. The one who was *supposedly* abusing her."

Before Pop could ask questions, a familiar-looking doctor with a fringe of silver hair joined us at the foot of my bed. "Hello. I'm Dr. Prendergast. I don't know if you remember me, Katy. I was on duty the day you came in with a gunshot wound. Your friend, Samantha Drummond was attending you and—"

"Oh, good grief," said Mom. "I better call her, or we'll never hear the end of it."

"What about your mother?" said Pop.

She thunked her head. "Talk about never hearing the end of it."

"Don't feel bad. It's not as if you've had much to think about." He squeezed her shoulder. "You call Sam, and I'll call Ruby."

They stepped out of the room, and the kindly-looking doctor moved to my side. "I don't suppose you remember much about our last encounter."

"Not really."

"No surprise. You were high as a kite from pain meds. But I'll never forget you. You propositioned this old grandfather. Made my day, let me tell you," he said, chuckling. "My wife got a real kick out of it, too." He glanced at the tablet he held. "All righty, then.

We're going to do some bloodwork, then take you upstairs for x-rays. How's your pain level, on a scale of one to ten?"

What would a ten be? Run over by a garbage truck? And a one would be cramps? Sometimes my cramps are more like a four–five, not counting the accompanying migraine. I felt way worse than that. "Seven–eight." I wanted to say eleven, but I was trying to be positive.

"We'll get you something for that before we send you upstairs."

———

By the time Josh arrived, I was back in the curtained cubicle. Two police officers stood guard nearby. Mom was sitting in the only chair available, tucked between my I.V. pole and the blood pressure monitor, and Pop was perched on the end of the bed.

My elevated feet were puffy from the constricting duct tape. My arms were scraped raw, and some of the oozing wounds looked infected. I hadn't seen my face yet, but Mom said I was not a pretty sight. I'd already absorbed two bags of saline, and every cell in my body tingled with hydrated joy.

"Katy." Josh grasped my hand and lifted it toward his heart but saw me wince and stopped.

"Why are those cops here?" I asked.

"To keep you safe," said Josh.

That frightened me. "Do you think she'll come back and try to—"

"No, no. It's just a precaution." He paused, shaking his head, his blue eyes bright with welling tears. "I'm so sorry this happened to you. I was right next door and had no idea. I could've lost you."

"I'm fine," I murmured.

"No, you are not fine," said Mom in a sharp tone.

Josh turned to Pop and extended his hand. "Hello. I'm Katy's friend, Josh. I live next door to her."

"Good to meet you. I'm Kurt."

Dr. Prendergast pushed the cubicle curtain aside. "I've got good news and...."

And bad news?

He continued, oblivious to my negative thoughts. "...more good news. Your x-rays looked good. Vital signs are good. After you've finished this," he tapped the saline bag hung by my bed, "and urinated, we can send you home. In the meantime, how about some gelatin?"

Not a gelatin fan, but at that moment it sounded like ambrosia.

"I'll take that look as a yes. We'll get you some apple juice, too."

A few minutes later, an aide set a tray on the table next to me, stabbed a straw into a juice box, and held it to my lips.

"Here you go, hon," said the rosy-cheeked woman with a warm gap-toothed smile.

My first sip of the cold, refreshing, sweet nectar made every high-end wine I've ever tasted seem like pigswill in comparison.

"Not too fast now," she said. "How about we try some of that gelatin?"

"I can do that." Mom picked up the plastic container and dipped a spoon in.

I tried to reach for it, but my arms weren't having it. "Ow!" I slowly inched my hands to my lap and rested my head against the pillow. "I hurt."

"Honey. Let me help you." Mom spooned the red gelatin into my mouth. "Mmm. Good, huh?" she said, like I was a toddler.

After a few bites of yummy, rubbery cherry gelatin, I drained the carton of apple juice, wishing someone would bring me a gallon of the stuff.

"Katy, you know you won't be able to go home," said Josh, looking grim.

"What do you mean? The doctor said I could." I searched his troubled eyes, and a chill quivered down my spine. *Oh, my God. There's something wrong with me, and now that they've got me high on gelatin and juice, they're going to break it to me.* "Is there something I should know?"

A smile tugged the corners of his mouth. "Honey, your house is a crime scene. A forensics team will be there, and it could be days before they're done. They haven't even...." He hesitated, then plowed ahead. "Removed the body yet."

I struggled to sit up straighter but my decrepit body protested, and I leaned back against the pillows. "Why not?"

"They can't remove it until all the evidence is photographed and bagged. They have to go over the entire scene inch by inch, and it's a slow, exacting process. It could be days before the body is removed."

"Days? Are you kidding? That's disgusting."

"Bodies are never removed until the investigation of the crime scene is complete," said Josh. "Inside or outside."

"But what if it's raining or sweltering hot?" said Mom.

"Then they try to hurry up the investigation," said Josh. "Because the weather conditions can alter the evidence."

"What if the body is lying in the street where everyone can see it?" she said.

Pop shook his head. "Doesn't matter. Still a crime scene. And unlike the TV shows, the body is never covered."

"Why?" I asked.

"It could contaminate the evidence," said Josh.

"That must be awful for the victim's relatives," said Mom.

"It is, and they can get very hostile about it," said Josh. "You've seen the riots on TV about this. People are shocked, hurt, grieving, angry, and they don't understand that the procedure is the same for everyone regardless of who the victim is."

"So, Katy-did, until they finish at your house, you'll be staying with us," said Pop.

Seems like every time I turn around, I'm back at the old folks' home.

"Kurt," said Mom. "You haven't seen the mess in her house. The walls have been torn down."

"Why in the hell would Erin do that?" he asked.

"Searching for more money," I said.

"But why would she do that? She's rich," said Pop. "Didn't she say her parents live in a mansion in the Bay Area? Atherton, right?"

My throat was too raw for a lengthy, detailed explanation, so I went with, "No, she's not." *And now she is because she has all my money.*

"So that's what this was all about?" said Pop. "That girl left you for dead for the damned coins."

"What coins?" said Josh.

I hadn't told Josh about the money, and now it felt really awkward. Like I hadn't trusted him.

Pop saved me the uncomfortable explanation. "Katy found a boxful of valuable old coins in her attic. She was cautioned to tell *absolutely*," his voice climbed a surly decibel, as he swung his eyes to me, "*no one* until they were removed from the house and put up for sale. That would've included Erin."

I shook my head, trying to keep my words to a minimum. "Mistake." I gazed at Josh, trying to convey my regret with my eyes. "I'm sorry."

He returned my look with a soft smile. "At least no one can accuse me of loving you for your money."

Love? He loves me? I gazed at him, feeling a dizzying fusion of joy, love, and desire bubble through me. Without thinking, I raised my arms to him and screamed, "Oh shit! Shit! Shit!" Josh took my hands and eased them back onto my lap as I whimpered, "Oh, oh, oh."

After I had myself under control, I noticed my parents staring at us, looking gobsmacked.

I knew Mom was close to giving Josh the third degree, so I said, "My house—how bad?"

"It's an absolute shambles," said Mom, still ogling Josh. No doubt she was sizing him up as future son-in-law material. He seemed unaware of her narrow-eyed appraisal. "The walls will need sheet rocking, paint. Probably some electrical work."

"Expensive," I said.

"That's what your insurance is for," said Pop. "Don't worry about that now. I'll get everything lined up. I want you to concentrate on recovering."

My headache was building momentum in spite of the pain meds. "More apple juice, please?"

"I'll go," said Josh. At the room entrance, he stopped. "Detective Murphy is down the hall at the nurse's station. Are you up to talking to her?"

"Oh, that awful, cold woman," said Mom. "She treated Katy like a common criminal. Practically accused her of shooting Chad. Completely heartless."

"The detective was only doing her job," said Josh. "Spouses or ex-spouses are usually the first ones on the suspect list, and it didn't help that Katy was at the scene when her ex was shot."

That comment did not sit well with Mom. She crossed her arms and said in her fiercest mama-bear tone, "As a victim, *Josh*." She virtually spat out his name.

He held his hands up in defense before she charged him. "I was only explaining how it goes. I'm sorry."

Pop draped his arm around Mom's stiff shoulders. "She knows that, Josh. She's just very upset."

Mom shook Pop's arm away. "You don't have to make excuses for me." Then she noticed his hurt look and softened. "I'm sorry. It seems that every time we turn around, something bad is happening to Katy." She expelled a labored sigh. "When I saw you next to her in the attic." She pressed a hand to her lips, shaking her head. "I thought my baby was dead." She snatched a tissue from the box by my bed and dabbed her eyes. "You can put that arm back now, Kurt."

He pulled her close, and she whimpered into his chest, "I don't know how much more I can take."

Pop said to Josh, "Can you put the detective off until tomorrow?"

"She won't get past me."

I became aware of a ghastly aroma in the room. "It really stinks in here."

Mom's grim countenance broke into a grin. "Sweetie. That stink would be you, my dear."

CHAPTER THIRTY

TUESDAY • FEBRUARY 24
Posted by Katy McKenna

Still catching up, but before I dive back into it, I need to get this off my chest. As my body and mind gradually mend, I'm getting more and more pissed off about the money. Super pissed. And I hate the word "pissed." But it's the only word that comes close to describing my feelings.

I used the thesaurus to find another word to describe my feelings and came up with words like:

- Annoyed—doesn't even begin to cover it.
- Bitter—oh yeah, I'm bitter.
- Furious, outraged, seething, fuming, and hopping mad.
  I'm all that and totally pissed off, too.

I had planned to pay off my parents' mortgage. Set up college trust funds for Sam's kids. Start a college scholarship for kids who aren't super athletes or straight-A students. Kids who try hard all the time, are good citizens at school and in the community, always get an A for effort, and want to go to college but will never win a scholarship. Kids like I was.

I was also going to have fun with it, too. New clothes, house renovations, new paint job and seat covers for Veronica. I have to laugh at the things I'd been dreaming about doing. They wouldn't have made even a dent in the money.

Tuesday, February 17

I woke at dawn, freezing cold thanks to Daisy who'd rolled over on her back and taken the covers with her. I got up and peeked out the window. A police car was parked out front, watching the house. I knew for a fact that Erin was off the radar, living the good life in Costa Rica with my money. There wasn't one good reason for her to stick around and risk getting caught, so why did I need protection? Plus, I was staying at my folks' house and Pop's a retired cop. With a gun. And an alarm system.

The police department had held back on sharing information with the press, so the media had already lost interest. As far as they were concerned, the ambulance and cop cars at my house the day before were a non-story.

Pop told me the cops want Erin to believe I'm dead for two reasons. The first is my safety. If she knows I'm alive she might decide to come back and finish the job. Like I already said—why would she risk getting caught? The other reason makes a lot of sense: I'm the only one who knows it was Erin. If she thinks I'm dead, she might get careless. Maybe even think it's safe to stay in the States.

I wondered what she'd think when there was no big news story. Wouldn't that make her suspicious? How could a crime of this magnitude not make national headlines? But if the police had released a phony story about my death in order to fool Erin into a false sense of security, I'd have to go into hiding, and all my friends would think I was dead. That would be like going into the witness protection program. I'm extremely grateful that the coin theft is being kept under wraps, too. If the public knew about that, you can bet there'd be fortune hunters digging up my yard.

I covered Daisy and hobbled to the kitchen to make coffee. Pop was sitting at the table, wrapped in his ancient wool plaid robe, working a crossword with Tabitha curled on his lap.

"Hey, Katy-did. What're you doing up?" He set the puzzle aside. "I thought for sure you'd sleep 'til noon."

"Can't. Too many bad dreams."

"I couldn't sleep either. Too many bad dreams, too." He stood, placing the cat on the rattan settee by the window. "Sit, and I'll get you a cup of coffee. Two sugars and half-and-half?"

"Better make it four."

He chuckled. "Why even bother with the coffee?"

Like I haven't heard that before.

He set the steamy cup on a placemat and sat again. "I imagine the police will be dropping by at some point today to ask questions."

Can't wait. "Pop?"

"Yes?"

"Don't you ever get tired of putting up with me? This is the third time in the last year that I've wound up back home because of the stupid decisions I keep making." I cupped the hot mug in my icy hands but found I couldn't lift it.

"Let me get you a straw." He opened a couple of cabinets. "Where does your mother keep the straws? Oh, never mind. Found them."

He plunked one in my coffee and sat. "First off, I'll never get tired of putting up with you. Don't tell your mother, but you're the reason I married her. You were the cutest little two-year-old. You stole my heart, pumpkin." He reached across the table and stole my nose, making me grin. "Still works. What exactly are these stupid decisions you've made?" He shrugged his shoulders with a wry smile. "One. You found a treasure trove in your attic, and you tried to find the rightful owner because you're a good person. Boy, was that stupid." Pop ticked off the recent events on his fingers. "Two. You befriended a long-lost cousin and then tried to help her. Wow. How stupid was that? Three—"

"I told Erin about the money."

"I'll give you that, but we all liked Erin. She seemed genuinely nice. And she led us to believe she was wealthy, so you never would've thought she'd steal it."

"Not in my wildest dreams. But the trip to Belize. That was so unlike me."

"You're right about that, Miss Un-Spontaneity."

"I know. Usually, I research everything to death. If I'd done that, I wouldn't have wound up being left for dead in the attic. And I'd still have the money."

"Erin was determined to take it, and she used her boyfriend just like she used you. Except she murdered him in cold blood."

"Oh, Pop. I thought for sure she was going to shoot me. And then the gun went off, and...he fell on me." I hadn't told my parents any of this yet, and now the whole awfulness of it was tumbling out of me. "Pop, he...I ...couldn't breathe, and...and."

My father held out his arms, and I sat on his lap, bawling into his shoulder while he patted my back, murmuring, "It'll be all right, honey. You're safe now."

"And when the rats started...eating...him, I was relieved because at least they weren't crawling on me anymore and...." I stopped, feeling my father's body stiffen. I pulled back and saw the horror on his face.

"Oh my poor baby," said Mom from the doorway. She came to us, wrapping her arms around me.

I set my cheek back on Pop's shoulder, tears running freely as the terrible memories surged.

After a while, he whispered, "Katy-did? You need to get off my lap." He gasped. "My knee."

I lifted my head and saw him trying to maintain a stoic face, and for some odd reason, I giggled. Not maniacally, like I was slipping off the deep end, but more like a tension release. Like, in spite of everything awful that happens, normal, everyday life still goes on.

"Sorry, Pop. I forgot about your knee." I stood, stifling my giggles because I think it was scaring the folks.

"Are you all right?" asked Mom, using a quiet, measured tone. Probably wondering if she needed to call the people with the straitjacket.

"No, and yes. I realize that I have a lot to work through, but I was laughing because here I am, sitting on poor old Pop's lap like a three-year-old, forgetting that I weigh at least one-hundred pounds more than a toddler."

She half-smiled and sat at the table next to me, not looking reassured. "I'm sure you're holding back a lot to spare us, but you may need some therapy."

"You may be right, but the thought of spilling my guts to a total stranger does not sound comforting. Who knows what they'd dredge up?" Then I tried a little humor. "Probably find out that everything's my parents' fault."

She ignored my hilarity. "Well, I can't force you to do something you don't want to do, but," she swung her eyes onto Pop, "it's time to schedule your knee replacement. You've put it off long enough."

"I know. Just hate the idea of being out of commission for several weeks."

"Everyone I know who's done it says it's worth it." She stood, heaving an annoyed sigh aimed at both of us. "And now I'll make us all some breakfast." She opened the refrigerator and removed eggs and orange juice, then looked out the kitchen window. "I wonder if the officer out there would like some breakfast."

The phone rang, verbally announcing, "Santa Lucia Police Department."

———

Detective Kailyn Murphy arrived on the dot of ten a.m., accompanied by the police chief, Angela Yaeger. The chief hugged me, then drew back to take a long look at my puffy, scraped face. "Good grief, girl. How do you keep getting into so much trouble?"

"Just lucky, I guess." Murphy held out her no-nonsense manicured hand and shook mine, and I winced. "Sorry. Really sore."

"I'm sorry. I didn't think," said the detective. "I hate to intrude like this, but I have to ask you some questions."

Was that a hint of warmth in her tone? I wasn't sure, but she didn't seem as nasty as I remembered.

"I understand," I said. "Let's go sit in the living room."

Angela took off her tweed coat and settled next to me on the sofa. The detective sat across the coffee table in an armchair. Pop offered coffee, which both declined.

"We won't be here that long." Angela shot a glance at Murphy, as if to say, *right?* "So, please don't trouble yourself."

"Well, maybe half-a-cup for me, please." Murphy opened her notebook on her lap. "Just getting over a bug and I'm dragging a bit."

About ten minutes into it, Angela accepted a cup, too.

It was grueling going over every dreadful detail, and I broke down several times. At other times, I found myself shaking my head in awestruck wonder at my naiveté. "How could I have been so trusting?"

Murphy looked up from her notes, "Because you're a good person."

What the what? She thinks I'm a good person?

"You look surprised I said that."

"Well, yeah."

She leaned back in the chair. "I deal with a lot of bad people, and sometimes that overshadows all the good, decent people out there."

"Most people are good," said Angela. "Or this job wouldn't be worth doing."

Now I felt like a jerk. "I thought you didn't like me, Detective Murphy."

The slim brunette's smile warmed her face. "That was just me, doing my job."

I started to say, *You accused me of shooting my ex-husband, arrested me, and threw me in jail.* But the truth was, she was just doing her job. So I didn't.

The interview turned out to be cathartic (there's that darned word again) for me. I had to organize my thoughts and tell the entire sordid story, in minute detail, from beginning to end. Angela and Murphy patiently guided me through the process, and when I finished, I felt lighter. Relieved, if that makes any sense.

CHAPTER THIRTY-ONE

WEDNESDAY · FEBRUARY 25
Posted by Katy McKenna

Friday, February 20

That morning, with profound relief, I peeked out the living room window and saw the police car was no longer parked in front of the house. I took that to mean that it was safe to get on with my life.

———

Ruby called in the a.m. to check on me. "Hey, hon. How're ya doing?"

"Oh. You know. One minute I'm feeling pretty good, and then the next, I kind of crash and burn."

"You need to give it some time. What you've been through was very traumatic. Devastating. I can't even imagine what it must've been like." She paused. "You lost the money, but you didn't lose your life. And you already have everything that truly matters. Your family and a nice, hunky boyfriend."

"Who's busy taking care of his ex-wife."

"Does that bother you?" she asked. "Because it sure would bother me."

"No. I know it's the right thing to do."

"You do realize that the situation that broke them up is no longer a situation now."

My back muscles seized up at this point. "Well, he's no longer an undercover narcotics cop, if that's what you mean. But I'm sure there was more to the breakup than just that."

"I'd be a little worried is all I'm sayin'."

"There's nothing I can do about it. We talk a few times a day—"

"On the phone?" she said.

"And he's come over to visit me, too." I tried to keep my tone from becoming defensive, but she was pushing my buttons.

"Okay, I'll keep my mouth shut. You know what I think?"

"What?" I blew out an exasperated sigh, not caring if Ruby heard or not.

"You need to get out of the house and blow off some steam. The gals are going to Applebob's "four by four" happy hour. Four dollar Long Island iced teas and four dollar all-you-can-eat buffet snacks, starting at four. It'll be a hoot. You up for it?"

"Jeez, Granny. That's a little early to start drinking. You better count me out. Four is coffee time, not booze time. If I start drinking that early, I'll be in bed by six-thirty."

"Oh, don't be such a party pooper. How about we push it to four-thirty? How's that sound?"

Like I'll be in bed at seven. "Who's driving?" *'Cause I'm not.*

"We'll take the dial-a-ride bus, of course. None of us are willing to lose our driver's license like poor Iris did the last time we partied. I could've sworn she only had one Long Island. Maybe two. Anyhoo, Iris lost her wheels, and she was a damned good driver, given her age and all. She's the only one who doesn't have night blindness."

"Isn't she ninety-two?" I remembered her telling me her age when she told me she was planning a birthday bash for Granny.

"Yes, but these days, ninety-two is the new eighty-two, or maybe it's seventy-two."

"That would make her younger than you. Oh wait, seventy-four is the new fifty-four, right?"

"You got it."

Which would make me, at thirty-two—too young to drive. Makes sense to me. "Is the bus driver going to be that Duke guy? I know you told him I'd go out with him, but I have a boyfriend now—so it would be embarrassing."

"Oh, didn't I tell you? Duke went back to jolly old England. Turns out he really is a duke. Get this—his family lives in that Dunton house. You know. The one that TV show was all about."

"*Downton Abbey?*"

"Yeah, that's the one. Guess I'll have to watch it now, especially since he invited me to visit if I'm ever in the area."

"You're telling me that Duke—the Dial-A-Ride guy is a real duke and he lives in a freaking castle in England? Come on, Granny. You're kidding me, right?"

"I was pretty flabbergasted about it, too. I'm trying to remember the real name of the castle. I know it's not Downton."

"Does Highclere Castle ring any bells?"

"Bingo. That's it."

"Why on earth would a duke be driving a senior bus in Santa Lucia?" I may have been screeching at this point.

"He was learning how real people live—all over the world. We were part of his quest. Anyhoo, he's back in the bosom of his family and running the estate."

Oh. My. God. I could've been a princess. Princess Katy. Oh wait—he's a Duke. Duchess Katy. We would've had adorable English children. Penelope and Peter. And they would have called me Mummy. And we would have gone to Buckingham Palace to have tea with the queen. And I would've become besties with Princess Kate. And I would've lived in Downton Abbey! Downton freaking Abbey! And maybe, if enough people died first, I could have been queen. Queen Katy!

"Sweetie, you still there?"

"*Yeeessss*. I'm still here." *In Santa Lucia. All my money is gone. My house is a shambles. My boyfriend lives with his ex, and I could've been queen of the British Empire. But instead, I'm going to happy hour at Applebob's with a bunch of grandmas. My life sucks!*

The forensics team had finished at my house, so it was time to go see the damage. After I parked in the driveway, it took me a good five minutes to muster up the courage to go inside.

Mom and Pop had described the havoc that Tyler and Erin had wrought upon my home, but the reality was so much worse. My cozy bungalow had been trashed. Piles of broken plaster were strewn everywhere. A thick coat of chalky dust coated the furniture, the wood floors, drapes, shutters, windows.

Every square inch of the hallway walls had been stripped down to the quarter-inch wood lath. The family pictures that had lined the hall, dating all the way back to Ruby's childhood, lay smashed on the floor. The original ornate cast iron wall grate was battered beyond repair.

Tears threatened as I bent to touch the dusty grate. I recalled how its uniqueness had caught my eye the first time I had looked at the house. Even if I could find a similar replacement, that's what it would always be. A replacement. I sat on the floor, legs crossed, clutching the metal cover to my chest.

"I hope you rot in hell," I screamed at Erin and Tyler.

"Katy?" Josh bent down behind me and folded his strong arms around me. "You really shouldn't leave your door wide open. No telling who might walk in."

I leaned back into his safe embrace. "It's all too much." I held up the grate and blubbered, "Look what they did."

"I know, cupcake." He set the grate on the floor, then helped me up. "Let me get you a tissue."

I dried my eyes and blew my nose.

"Things are going to get better." He kissed me tenderly, mindful of my healing chin, then grabbed a brown lunch bag from the entry table. "Nicole made you chocolate chip cookies. They're still warm."

"How's she doing?"

"Most days, pretty good, considering. But she's having some trouble today. The oncologist put her on a new medication, and it's kicking her butt. On top of that, she's losing her hair. She seems more upset about that than the cancer."

I get that. "And still, she thought of me and made cookies. That's so sweet."

"It's typical Nicole. Always thinking of others."

"And here I am crying over my messed up house. Compared to what Nicole's going through...." I gestured at the chaos surrounding us. "This is nothing. It can all be fixed."

"Katy. This is a lot more than just a mess. Your cousin put you through hell and left you for dead, so you don't have to make light of it. It was a very traumatic experience and most people wouldn't be handling it as well as you are."

I didn't want to tear up again, so I asked, "Why'd the doctor change Nicole's medicine?"

"Her white count isn't where she'd like it to be." He sighed. "I guess it's a lot of trial and error. It's an uphill battle, but Nicole's a fighter." He glanced around. "So, what's the plan here?"

"Pop had a claims adjuster inspect the house, and he said there'd be no problems, other than I have to cough up the $1,800 deductible."

"Do you have it? If not, I do."

"That's sweet of you, but I'm fine. I have it in savings."

Josh set his hands on my shoulders, looking grim. "I can't get over the fact that you were over here, trapped and close to dying." His voice broke, and he cleared his throat. "I was home, dammit. Right next door. Probably watching a game. And you could've died." He ran his hands down my arms and took my hands.

"Don't feel bad, Josh. You had no way of knowing."

He sighed a ragged breath. "Hey, how about tomorrow morning I help you clear out the mess? I can borrow my friend's truck and haul this stuff to the dump."

"Won't the insurance company take care of that?" I said.

"Probably, but I feel like I need to do something physical."

Hmmm. He wants to get physical. "You wanna see the holes in my bedroom walls?"

Girls Night Out

When the Dial-A-Ride bus picked me up in front of my parents' house, the atmosphere on board was a tad cool. A woman wearing a red satin turban, matching caftan, and huge black-rimmed round glasses, said, "I hope we can get a good table. We usually don't go this late."

"Oh, put a lid on it, Betty." Ruby leaned close to me and whispered, "Don't tell her, but we already have a table. Ben's holding it."

"Ben? I thought this was ladies night."

"Believe me, he has no intention of staying. But the dear man knew I'd never hear the end of it if we didn't get our favorite table, so he offered."

"Wow, he's a keeper."

"Don't I know it," said Ruby.

Ten minutes later, we exited the bus and made our grand entrance into Applebob's. Ben stood to greet the seven of us and made a big show of helping the flirty ladies get seated.

"And now, dear ladies," he said with a swashbuckler bow. "I bid you adieu."

"Oh, Ben, darling," said Betty, twiddling her jeweled acrylics at him. "You don't have to leave on our account." She patted the empty seat next to her. "Come. Sit. Stay."

He cast fretful eyes at Ruby, that screamed, *Save me!*

"Ben's playing pool with the boys," she said flatly.

"You mean this lovely man came here just to save a table for little old us?" said Betty, fluttering her false lashes at him. "You shouldn't have."

"He did it for me." Ruby gave Ben a passionate peck on the lips. "*Arrivederci, mi amore.*"

Betty looked like she wanted to whip off her turban and beat my granny to death with it. Ben snatched his leather bomber jacket from the back of Ruby's chair and hightailed it to the exit.

I could see why our table was their favorite. It was the closest one to the happy hour buffet—a tempting array of nachos, buffalo wings, meatball sliders, greasy french fries, greasy onion rings, and greasy jalapeño poppers. Being a pescatarian since high school, I couldn't eat the meaty items, so I overindulged on the greasy stuff to get my four bucks worth. And you had to move fast because the place was already jumping. I piled my tiny plate high, because who knew if there would be anything left by five?

The "four-by-four" happy hour special included a Long Island iced tea. You're going to find this hard to believe, but I'd never had one before. One taste and I slurped that tasty drink down like I'd been crawling through the Sahara Desert for days.

Ruby anted up for the next round. As the server set our cock-tails on the table, a tall, lanky woman in a black velvet palazzo jumpsuit swooshed her big-boned body over to our table. "Well, well. If it isn't the Shady Acres gals," she said, in a low, whiskey and cigs voice.

"Who's she?" I whispered to Ruby.

"That's *Frankie.*" Granny wink-winked. "If you get my drift. She's (wink-wink) from the Whispering Pines Senior resort."

"Why're you winking?" I whispered. "Something in your eye?"

"Shush," muttered Ruby.

Frankie held out a large veiny, hand to me, "Hello, darlin'. I don't believe we've met. When did you move to Shady Acres? And *who's* your plastic surgeon, sweetheart? You look at least twenty years younger than everyone else at this table."

Twenty years younger? She thinks I look like I'm in my.... I glanced around the table at my dinner companions, remembering that Iris is ninety-two.

"You really need to have that cataract surgery, Frankie," said Ruby. "Or at least wear your damned bifocals. Katy's my grand-daughter."

Frankie slipped on rhinestone studded specs and peered down her long beak at me. "Oh, yes. You're a very pretty girl. Lovely neck." She unconsciously ran a hand over her bulbous adam's apple. "But I really don't see the family resemblance."

"Looks like your posse is signaling at you to come back, Frankie," said Ruby. "Don't let us keep you."

She turned and waved at her table. "Are you gals entering the poker fundraiser at the senior center?"

"We'll all be there. Right, ladies?" said Iris.

"Wouldn't miss it for the world," said perky Judy, talking through a full mouth of jalapeño popper. "Been practicing online."

"Bring it on," said Susan, furrowing her perfect tattooed eyebrows.

"What's the fundraiser for?" I asked.

"Homeless Chihuahuas," said Janet. "I volunteer at the humane society, and it breaks my heart to see so many abandoned because their owners didn't realize that they're real dogs, not purse bling." She waved her hands as she spoke, and her bracelet lined wrists clinked with every move. "The shelters are full of them, and we're raising money to help seniors adopt them."

"The winner's jackpot is $1,500," said Frankie. "I've got a *gor-ge-ous* gold silk caftan picked out for the trip to Vegas I'm planning with my winnings."

"You mean, *if* you win. If I win, I'm donating the money to the cause," said snarky Ruby.

"If I win," Judy flicked back her long silver braid, "I'm going on a mad shopping spree." Her eyes zeroed in on Frankie's. "For Toys For Tots. Think of the joy I could bring to underprivileged kids next Christmas." She sighed, fanning threatening tears away. "Well, you know."

Dammit. Another wonderful thing I could have done with all that money. I could've been Santa Claus.

"Too bad that's not happening." Frankie looked unfazed by our table of do-gooders. "Ta-ta ladies."

When she was out of earshot, I whispered to Ruby, "What was up with those winks earlier?"

"Sweetie, Frankie's a transgender."

"You mean she's a man?"

"Not anymore." She patted my hand. "Honey, the girl's a bitch, but it's mostly an act, to cover her insecurities about transitioning so late in life. She had to wait until she retired. Then she waited a few years more so her grandkids would be old enough to understand. Then moved out here from Oklahoma to begin the next phase of her life. Hormones, several surgeries. It had to be miserable."

I watched Frankie sit down with her group across the room. "Talk about following your dream."

"Or never giving up on your dreams. We could all learn something from her."

Saturday, February 21

I woke up with the all-time worst hangover of my entire life, bar none. Worse than any hangover during college, and believe me, I've had some doozies. Worse than my college spring break hangover(s) in Palm Springs. Worse than the hangover from my ski trip to Tahoe where I met my "wasband," Chad-the-Cad. Worse than...okay, you get the point. I've had a lot of hangovers, but this was the Guinness-World-Record worst!

I sat up, which annoyed Tabitha, who'd been sleeping wrapped around my noggin. She bopped me on the head to let me know she didn't appreciate being disturbed.

"Tabitha, have pity on me. I'm sick."

She wasn't buying it until I barfed on her. New all-time low.

I had plans to meet Josh at the house at eleven, but that wasn't happening, so I called to put it off until one. Or two. Or never.

"Katy, you don't sound so good," said Josh.

I told him about my wild early-bird wingding. Geez Louise, I'm starting to talk like the Shady Acres gals.

"You say you drank four Long Island iced teas?"

"Oh, God. Don't even say the word." I urped a burp, then nibbled a soda cracker.

"Maybe we should forget about today, and you get some rest, party-girl. My friend has offered to help, so let us take care of it."

"No-no. I can do it." Huge belch, and then my stomach lurched a tsunami warning. "Nope. Can't do it."

Much later in the day, I was snoozing on the chaise lounge under the oak tree when the screen door slammed. A moment later Daisy burrowed her head under my arm for a neck massage. As I gave her a good scratching, it dawned on me that I still had that coin listed on Amazon.

"Sorry, Daisy. Gotta go." Barefooting to the kitchen, I grabbed my laptop, a granola bar, and a bubbly water. Back under the shady tree, I logged into my account. There was a message from an interested buyer offering $5,800 for my 1888 S Liberty Head ten dollar coin.

Oliver Kershaw, the British numismatics expert, had said it was worth at least seven thousand and not to take less than $6,200.

This crook was trying to steal it from me! "Ya think I just fell off the turnip truck, buddy?"

Alas, I was no longer in possession of the coin, but "Sixpence" didn't know it, so I answered, "Sorry. Too low."

I chomped into the granola bar, then washed it down with a swig of soda water and immediately erupted in hiccups. As I held my breath to squelch them, I recalled telling Erin how easy it had been to set up the Amazon coin account. "Do you think she'd—*hic* —have the nerve to do that?"

I held my breath and swallowed five times. "Ahhh—*hic*—rats."

I held my breath again and clicked on the "collectible coins" department, then narrowed my search to something that reflected several of the coins in my hoard: the San Francisco Mint, dollar denomination, 1860 to 1880.

Hiccups gone, I refined my coin search. Price: $1,500 to $8,000. Most of the coins hovered in the $3,500 to $4,000 range. None of them matched the condition of mine until the third page, where I found a shiny 1871 Liberty Head in "like new" condition. The asking price was $7,300. Under seller information, it said, Unique Coins—recently launched. Could this be her? My pulse amped as I clicked on "Seller Profile."

Unique Coins is located in Boise, Idaho, and specializes in United States Rare Coins. We have bought and sold over a billion dollars in rare and unique coins, and have engaged in the purchase or sale of 43 of the "100 Greatest U.S. Coins." Our team of educated numismatists is devoted to providing our patrons with the highest quality coins.

Erin could have made all that up. Although it sure sounded legit. I clicked on the Unique Coins storefront, and thirty-six pages of rare coins came up. Obviously not Erin's shop, but so interesting. There was a 1797 "Draped Bust" dollar for $420,000 and another from 1802 going for $1.5 million.

I resumed scrolling through pages of gold coins, looking for something that might lead me to Erin, and then it dawned on me. This was exactly what a private investigator would be doing. Perhaps this is my career calling, and this is my first official case— not counting the cold cases I've accidentally solved.

"Erin Cranston. I'm going to hunt you down and make you pay for what you did. And then I'll get my private investigators license and rid the world of scum like you."

Feeling righteous, I went into my Facebook friends list and clicked on Erin's profile. There she was, smiling coyly at me. Her last post, dated January 22, was about how excited she was to meet me. I had commented, *looking forward to it!*

I slammed the laptop closed, feeling a flood of hot resolve course through my body. The stupor I'd been drowning in for days had washed away, and I felt energized and in control of my life again.

———

Note to self: Never, ever drink another Long Island iced tea. I looked up the recipe and it's a deadly concoction of vodka, rum, gin, triple sec, sweet and sour mix, and a splash of cola for color. Some recipes even call for tequila. Just typing this is making me sick again.

CHAPTER THIRTY-TWO

THURSDAY · FEBRUARY 26
Posted by Katy McKenna

Monday, February 23

After a stop at the Verizon store for a new phone, since Erin stole mine, I headed to the police station to begin my search for my cousin. I checked in at the front desk and asked for Detective Kailyn Murphy. The ruddy-cheeked woman shook her head. "Sorry, she's not on duty today."

"I don't suppose I could see the chief?"

"Hold on and I'll check."

While I waited, I thumbed through a pamphlet about volunteer programs in Santa Lucia County. The clerk hung up the phone. "She has a few minutes. You know the way?"

"I do."

She buzzed me through the door, and I marched down the hall to the chief's office and found Angela waiting in her doorway. We shared a hug, and she waved me to the seat opposite her tidy desk.

"I love that color on you," I said. "Usually you wear dark colors."

The peach blouse flattered Angela's warm brown complexion and close-cropped silver hair.

"My sister gave me this blouse for Christmas, and this is the first time I've worn it. She says I dress too somber."

"I've never thought that, but I do think you look younger wearing a pretty pastel color."

"You just said the magic words. Guess I'm going shopping." She closed a folder and set it aside. "I imagine you're here to see if there's any news on Erin Cranston."

"I am. I've got my energy back, and I'm anxious to track her down and see justice done."

"I wish I had something to tell you, Katy." She folded her hands on the desk, shaking her head. "But so far we don't have any leads other than what you told us."

"How could she just vanish?"

"It's easier than you think. Remember, Erin had plenty of time to get out of the country before we started looking for her."

"What about her phone? Can't they track that?"

Angela shook her head. "She hasn't used it since she texted your friend that she was going home. Probably was the first thing she got rid of."

"What about my phone? She used it to text everyone so they wouldn't worry about me. Sam told me the message said I was having so much fun that I may never come home."

"We traced that text. Erin was in the Henderson, Nevada area when she sent it. When Detective Murphy and I spoke to you the day after you were found, you said they had planned to go to Las Vegas."

"Yes. Erin said she could sell some coins there and then they would charter a private plane, a Lear jet, to fly to Costa Rica."

"She wasn't on any of the flights out of Las Vegas. Of course, a sketchy private pilot may not have listed her name on the flight manifest. We have the police in Costa Rica watching for her, although she's probably changed her appearance. Hair color and style, glasses."

"We're not going to find her, are we?" I was feeling defeated already.

Her expression looked doubtful. "I wish we had a complete inventory of the coins. Then we could have put out a bulletin, and if she tried to sell to an honest collector or dealer, then perhaps—" She shook her head.

"If only I had done that. How stupid."

"Katy, don't beat yourself up over this. I doubt that anyone she sells to would be the type to question where the coins came from, anyway."

Angela stood and stretched. "I need a coffee. How about you?"

"I'm dragging, so I could use one."

We sat on the worn leather sofa passed down through the years from chief to chief. Angela set a file on the coffee table.

I sipped my steamy beverage. "Mmm. Good coffee." After another swallow, I said, "Erin said her parents died in a car crash. Do you know when that happened?"

Angela wrinkled her brow. "I was about to get to that. According to her parents—"

"Her parents? You mean they're not dead?"

She shook her head. "They're both very much alive and well in the Bay Area."

"Atherton?"

"Close. Redwood City. A few miles north. Detective Murphy spoke to them at length on the phone. Her father teaches high school world history, and her mom is a kindergarten teacher. Erin was an only child, and according to them, a sweet girl until she won a scholarship to a nearby college prep school. Her new friends came from wealthy families who lived in big, fancy mansions. When her folks encouraged her to invite her new friends over, she told them she was ashamed of her home."

"That had to hurt," I said.

"Teenaged girls can be cruel," said Angela. "I raised one, and for a while there, I considered locking her in the basement until she turned thirty-five." She chuckled. "I can't tell you how many times I called my parents during that phase and apologized for whatever hell I put them through as a kid."

"I probably should do that, too."

"When Erin's parents suggested inviting her old friends over, you know, the ones she'd grown up with, she refused that, too. Said she no longer had anything in common with them."

"What a bitchy little snob," I said.

"It got worse. When her rich friends turned sixteen, they all got pricey new cars for their birthdays. Beamers, Mercedes, Jags. Erin got a shiny new key to the family car: a Ford Taurus station wagon."

"I got a key to our Volvo station wagon for my sixteenth birthday."

"And I bet you were over the moon when they gave it to you."

"I sure was. For the first few months, I constantly offered to go to the grocery store so I could drive by myself. Mom loved that."

"My daughter did the same thing. Anyway, Erin's clothes were another painful issue. Her mother had always made them. They would look at teen magazines together and then her mother replicated the outfits."

"Oh, how sweet. I would have killed to have cute clothes like that."

"Me too. But that was no longer good enough. Erin wanted to shop at Nordstrom's and Neiman Marcus like all her friends did. Her mother offered to take her to Macy's instead. Not good enough."

"I've been to the Macy's up at the Stanford Shopping Center, and it's a nice store." I drained my cup and set it on the coffee table.

"But Erin's friends didn't shop there. And that's when she started shoplifting. Would you like more coffee?"

"I better not."

Angela continued talking as she refilled her cup. "Her parents asked her where she was getting the new outfits, and she told them her friends gave them to her. They got suspicious and searched her room. In the back of her closet, they found a pile of clothes with the tags still on." Angela glanced at the file on the table. "That was in her junior year."

"Those poor parents."

"They didn't know what to do. If they forced her to return the clothes, she would've wound up going to a juvenile detention center. They couldn't bear the thought of their girl imprisoned with gang members and the like."

"I don't blame them."

"So, they made her donate all her stolen clothes to Goodwill. And they pulled her out of the prep school and put her back into public school."

"I'm guessing that didn't go well."

"No, it did not," she said. "Erin went completely out of control. Wouldn't go to school, got into drinking and drugs. They tried to get her into counseling, but she refused to cooperate. And then one day, when she was seventeen-and-a-half, she disappeared."

"So, what did they do?"

"They reported it to the police. Hired a private investigator. But never found her."

"And now this."

"Yes, now this. Their daughter is a cold-blooded murderer and a thief." Angela's eyes strayed to the doorway. "Murphy. Isn't this your day off?"

The detective leaned her slim body against the door frame. "I have too many irons in the fire to take a whole day off. At least my laundry's done. May I join you? I have some information that I think you'll both find interesting."

"Care for a coffee?" asked the Chief.

"No, I'm good." She sat in a chair facing the sofa. "I had another conversation with Erin's mother, Molly Cranston. Turns out there's more to the story than we were initially told."

"You mean they withheld information?" I said.

"No. It's more of a tragic family saga. Mrs. Cranston said she'd been thinking about it, and thought it might help the investigation. I could hear in her voice how hard it was for her to tell me."

Angela checked her watch. "Hold on a sec." She stepped to the phone on her desk and pressed a button. "Would you call the city manager and tell him I'm running behind. Tell him I'll be there in thirty–forty minutes, and if that doesn't work, we need to reschedule. Thanks." She returned to the sofa. "All right, continue."

"Sorry, Chief," said Murphy.

"Don't worry about it."

Murphy looked at me. "Katy, you know how Erin told you she grew up in a mansion in Atherton?"

"Yes. But it was all a lie to impress me."

"Well, the truth is her father, William Cranston, actually did grow up in an Atherton mansion. The Cranston Mansion on Cranston Lane. William was all set to go to his father's alma mater —Harvard—when he announced to the family he was in love with the housekeeper's daughter."

"I bet they weren't thrilled about that," I said.

"You got that right. Especially when William told them the girl was pregnant, and he was going to marry her."

"I assume this is unborn Erin we're talking about?" said Angela. Murphy nodded. "It is."

"So what'd the parents do?" I asked.

"Gave him two options. Abortion or adoption. William refused both. He begged them to accept his decision and welcome Molly into the family, but they would have none of it. Told him he would be cut out of the family if he married her."

Murphy snatched a pencil off the coffee table and twisted her dark hair into a bun. "That feels better. I owe you a pencil, Chief."

"Duly noted," said Angela. "I feel like I'm listening to a soap opera."

The detective continued. "The parents stayed true to their word and cut him off without a penny. William and Molly got married, and while raising little Erin, they both worked and got their educations at local colleges."

"What about William's parents?" I said. "Did they ever forgive their son?"

She shook her head. "No. In fact, shortly after Erin was born they sold the family mansion and moved to Greenwich, Connecticut."

"About as far away as you can get and still be in the U.S.," said Angela.

Murphy shook her head with a rueful smile. "They never even met their granddaughter."

"Perhaps if they had, maybe none of this would have happened," I said.

———

My cell chirped in my purse when I parked in front of my parents' house. By the time I fished it out, it had gone to voicemail. It was Josh. He was in a cooking mood and wanted me to come over for dinner.

I texted, *Watt tome?* I sent it, then read it, and sent a follow-up: *What time?* Everyone's been on my case to read my texts before I send them, and evidently for good reason.

He answered as I was letting myself in the front door: *7. Nicole thinks she'll feel like eating by then.*

I have to admit, that deflated me a bit. Then I instantly felt guilty for being petty.

The house was quiet. Mom was at the beauty salon, and Pop had declared it "take your grand-dog" to work day. Tabitha was unresponsive in a sunny puddle on the kitchen floor. I tip-toed past her and grabbed my laptop from the kitchen table and headed outside to the chaise lounge.

I signed into Facebook and went to Erin's profile. Checking her friends list, I was surprised she had fewer than me. Seventeen to be exact. Why hadn't I noticed that before? Most Millennials have hundreds.

I clicked on the first person in Erin's friend list. Crystal Adams. 1,778 friends. Crystal was a partier. Lots of group selfies with her pierced tongue hanging out.

I moved on to the next friend: Brent Haskins. 3,122 friends. He was into rock climbing and body building.

Then boring me: Katy McKenna. 36 friends.

Bambi Randall. Pole dance teacher at a fitness club. 5,312 friends.

Saul Ramirez. Shirtless with a flowing ebony mane. He could have been on the cover of one of those bodice-ripper romance novels that Sam reads. 2,347 friends.

Amelia Wright looked like a nice, normal person in my age range. Lots of photos of cute kids. 142 friends.

Everyone in the Friends list, except Amelia and me, were connected to each other. But what I didn't see was exactly how any of these people were related to Erin.

I looked at her timeline past posts. There were only eight—the first one dated from when we first connected through Pedigree-Tree.com. A photo of a generic mansion that could have been anywhere, with a post that said: The Old Homestead. Another of a house on a tropical island—the same one she'd shown me. A group wedding photo with no Erin in it captioned: What a great day!

I sent a friend request to all of Erin's friends. Within minutes,

Mia Lang accepted. Then I messaged her: *Hi Mia. Have you heard from Erin Cranston lately?*

The chat box opened and she responded: *Who's that?*

———

At seven, I tapped on Josh's door and waited to get swooped into his strong arms. Instead, Nicole answered. We shared a hug, and I felt her frail body through her thin cotton dress.

"Josh is in the kitchen begging his asparagus soufflé not to collapse. I think he really wants to impress you," she said.

"Plain old steamed asparagus would've impressed me."

She laughed. "I love how down-to-earth you are, Katy."

In the kitchen, Josh whispered, "Tiptoe. This is my first soufflé."

I pecked him on the cheek and glanced at the dish resting on the counter. "Uh-oh."

He spun around to witness the soufflé's deflation, then collapsed on a chair looking as deflated as his creation. "It's also my last soufflé."

"I'm sure it'll still taste delicious." I patted his shoulder. "Would you like a glass of wine?"

"You sit, Katy," said Nicole. "You're our guest. I'll get you both a glass."

She was only being cordial, so why had that innocent little line —*you're our guest*—rub me the wrong way?

Nicole squeezed Josh's bicep as she handed him a glass of wine. "Poor baby. Don't forget the rolls in the oven."

"The rolls!" He dashed to the stove and yanked open the oven door. "Phew! They're okay."

Nicole removed a green salad from the refrigerator and put it on the formally set table in the dining room.

I gazed at the folded linen napkins and pretty flower arrangement. "Everything looks lovely, but you didn't have to go to so much trouble. It's just me."

"Nonsense. You're company," she said.

No, I'm not. I'm Josh's almost-someday-future-fiancée.

"You two sit," called Josh from the kitchen. He came out and topped off my wine and set a tumbler of ice water in front of Nicole.

She wrinkled her nose. "I can't wait to have a glass of wine. But I have to get through this darn chemo first. My hair is falling out in wads"—she touched the paisley scarf wrapped around her head —"hence, the scarf. Tomorrow, Josh is going to shave my head."

"I could do that for you." To be honest, the idea of Josh shaving her head seemed so personal. Almost intimate.

"Oh, that's sweet of you, but there's no need for you to go to the trouble."

Josh ladled the sloppy soufflé on our plates, and we helped ourselves to salad and rolls.

After my first bite, I said, "This is delectable, Josh. Truly the best asparagus soufflé I've ever tasted, and I'm not just saying that to make you feel better. It's true."

His face brightened adorably. "You mean it?"

"I really mean it." It was also the first asparagus soufflé I'd ever tasted, so what did I know?

"Josh, I need to pick your private investigator brain," I said, as I buttered a warm French roll.

"Is this about...you know?"

Nicole set down her fork. "Would you rather discuss it in private?"

"No, it's okay. But it must stay just between us."

Her eyes grew wide as I narrated the incredible tale of the Santa Lucia Hoard.

"That's an amazing story," she said. "Remember that old HGTV show, *If These Walls Could Talk?*"

"I used to watch it all the time," I said.

"Boy, what stories your walls could tell," she said.

"Every old house in this neighborhood has a history," I said. "I just hope mine won't be haunted by the ghost of Tyler." I watched their reaction as I said that last line, but neither one gave me a "you're crazy" look.

"Don't get Nicole going on ghosts," said Josh.

"Do you believe in them?" I said.

"I've had several close encounters. Josh knows this from personal experience."

"More like, *bitter* experience," he said with a chuckle. "She used to wake me up whenever one was visiting our bedroom."

So do not want to hear about their bedroom experiences.

"And you always told me I was dreaming." She playfully socked his arm. "But I knew I wasn't."

Josh rubbed his arm with a mock-pained expression while I battled my inner green-eyed monster. Then he turned his attention to needy me. "So what did you want to ask me about?"

It took me a moment to refocus. "I learned some new facts about Erin's background today and was wondering if you might have any ideas about how to find her. The police don't seem to be making much headway, and I've heard that P.I.'s can do things that cops can't."

I relayed Detective Murphy's story about Erin's family. "So, what do you think?"

"Katy, I want to help, but I honestly don't know what I can do that the police haven't already done. Believe me, I want to catch that woman and see her spend the rest of her life behind bars. Or better yet, six feet under."

Nicole jumped up and excused herself from the table. Moments later she vomited in the downstairs guest bathroom.

"Should we help her, Josh?"

"No. This happens a lot. We need to leave her alone."

After several minutes of Nicole's violent retching echoing

through the house, I shoved back my chair and stood. "I can't stand this. I'm going to check on her."

"Katy, there's nothing we can do. I've been through this several times with her." He followed me to the bathroom. "And she always gets mad when I try to help."

"Nicole?" I opened the bathroom door and found her sprawled on the floor clinging to the toilet bowl. "Can I get you anything? A cold cloth for your head?"

I moved closer and saw blood in the toilet. "Oh, my God, Nicole!"

She looked up at me with hollow, woebegone eyes. "It's nothing. My throat gets raw, that's all."

I turned to Josh who was hanging back in the doorway. "That doesn't look like nothing to me."

Nicole lurched and a flume of crimson blood splashed the back of the toilet seat and splattered the floor.

"There's no way that's normal." I crouched beside her holding her trembling shoulders.

Josh looked grim. "It's not. We need to get her to the hospital. I'll call them and tell them we're coming."

Josh's BMW is a two-seater, so we went in my car. Nicole sat in the passenger seat, clutching a bucket in her lap. Josh sat behind her, holding her erect. I turned on the hazard lights and honked at everyone in our path. A few people honked and flipped me off, but everyone gave me plenty of leeway. Nobody wanted their plastic cars crunched by Veronica's bad-ass chrome bumpers.

I squealed into the ER entrance and beeped the horn several times. Two attendants dashed out with a wheelchair and rushed her to a bed in a curtained cubicle. Within minutes they had her hooked up to a saline drip. Ten minutes later, her oncologist arrived.

Feeling like an intruder, I stepped out while Josh spoke with the doctor. In the waiting area, I poured a styrofoam cup of vile coffee and sat staring at the silent TV on the wall. I'd had no idea it was this bad for her, and remorse was eating me up for feeling envious of her history with Josh.

Two hours later, Nicole was allowed to go home.

"Her doctor put her on a new anti-nausea medication." Josh shrugged his sagging shoulders. "Hopefully, this one will work."

———

After Nicole had been tucked in bed, she apologized for ruining our evening.

"Don't be silly," I said. "This was out of your control. Try and rest now."

"You too." She closed her eyes, and for a frightening moment, I thought she'd passed. I watched her chest until it rose and fell several times.

We left the room, and in the hall, I said to Josh, "I should leave. You need your rest, too."

"Katy, I need you. Please stay."

It felt good to be needed.

CHAPTER THIRTY-THREE

THURSDAY · FEBRUARY 26
Posted by Katy McKenna

Tuesday, February 24

I returned to my folks' house in the early a.m. After I showered and dressed, I brewed a cup of my favorite Murchie's #10 tea and settled on the comfy old sofa in the family room. Daisy planted a paw on the couch, ready to get cozy with me.

"Sorry, girl. Your mean old grandparents don't want dog hair on the furniture."

She gave me a dumbfounded look.

"I know. Crazy, huh? But you know the rules. If you don't like it, then talk to them."

Moving slower than a sloth, she withdrew her paw, then slinked into a corner, spun around a few times, and collapsed. Every few seconds, she'd sigh like it was the end of the world, no doubt waiting for me to break down.

"Give it up, Drama Queen. I'm not breaking the rules. Not even for you."

We had a "stare-down" until she dozed off. I opened my laptop and checked Facebook for replies from Erin's so-called friends. Everyone except Amelia had responded, and no one had a clue who Erin was.

Next, I searched her name, Erin Beth Cranston. Top of the list was Erin Beth in Cranston, Rhode Island. Then Bryon Cranston, the actor—loved him in *Breaking Bad*.

"Okay, I'll try refining my search."

I typed Erin Beth Cranston, age 34. And I got the Moosetooth Run results in 2011—**Erin**Bingham, 27, 1:01.33. **Beth**any **Cranston**, 37, 53:26.23

"If at first, you don't succeed."

I searched: Erin Beth Cranston, born in Redwood City, CA, age 34. And I got IMDb: Most famous people born in Redwood City/California...

You may be wondering why I was doing this, since I already knew where she's from, her age, her parents' names, etc. But I thought something current might pop up. Addresses, jobs, arrests. After scrolling through ten pages of nothing that had anything to do with her, I gave up and shut down the computer, muttering, "Maybe I'm not cut out to be a private investigator."

———

I checked in with Josh at noon. He said Nicole was worn out but doing all right. He didn't suggest getting together, and neither did I. The night before had terrified me, and I wasn't ready for a repeat.

I'd been neglecting Sam, so I gave her a call. "Hey. It's me. Watcha doing?"

"I just got back from a mommy meet-up at the animal shelter. Big, fat, friggin mistake."

"Uh-oh. Did you bring home a new furry family member?"

"No. But Casey had a meltdown when it was time to leave. Seems he'd bonded with an elderly mini-dachshund."

"Why on earth, would an old dachshund be at the shelter?"

"Her owner died, and no one in the family wanted Francine. So the sweet girl will probably live out her golden years in that noisy, stressful place. It was hard leaving her there, let me tell you."

"That's heartbreaking," I said.

"Tell me about it. Someday soon, we'll get a dog, but it's going to be a young Daisy-clone. That old girl is too fragile for a crazy four-and-a-half-year-old."

"So what else is going on?"

"Spencer's out of town, as usual."

"When's he going to quit flying?" I nibbled an annoying emerging pinky fingernail.

"Are you biting your nails?" she asked.

I jammed my hand into my jean pocket. "Nope."

"Yeah, right. Stop it! Okay, back to your question. There aren't a lot of good paying jobs around here that fit his education and training. We may have to move to a state where more jobs are available, and the cost of living is reasonable. Luckily for me, nurses are in demand everywhere."

My heart belly-flopped. "Like where?"

"Like Austin, Texas."

"Texas? But that's so far away."

"I know. But there are job opportunities there. I hear it's nice," she said. "Their motto is Keep Austin Weird. That's kinda cool, don't ya think?"

"I've heard it's expensive there."

"It's cheaper than here."

"What about the weather? I hear it floods there. And gets super hot and humid in the summer. And the bugs are humongous. And there are bats everywhere. Millions of them. And tornadoes too. Blizzards. Monsoons."

"Just about anywhere we move will have real weather. Unlike here."

"What about your parents? Have you told them?"

"Yeah. Mom cried. They're so attached to the kids. It'll kill them."

It'll kill me too.

———

Pop told me the insurance agent called to say the contractors would be at my house the next morning at eight.

"He said it'll only take a few days. That means, if all goes according to plan, you can be back in your own bed by the weekend. But the more I think about it, scratch that time estimate. The area rugs and upholstered furniture have to be cleaned. The floors will need sanding and refinishing and then they'll need to dry. You can't be breathing those fumes, so it may be more like Monday or Tuesday before you're back in the house. They're also going to patch the hole under the eaves so the rodents can't get in anymore."

Part of me couldn't wait to go home—to get back to normal. Whatever that is. But I also felt apprehensive about being alone in my house. Not because I thought Erin would sneak in and finish me off, but what if (please don't laugh) the house was now haunted by Tyler? Aren't ghosts usually someone who met with a violent, sudden end and aren't ready to cross over?

I used to watch *The Ghost Whisperer*. The show was based on an actual person who communicates with the dead and helps them cross into the light. What if Tyler's spirit is stuck in my home?

Maybe I should put the house on the market. Sell it and start fresh. Oh, who am I kidding? Nobody's going to buy a haunted house.

CHAPTER THIRTY-FOUR

FRIDAY · FEBRUARY 27
Posted by Katy McKenna

Wednesday, February 25

I wanted to give myself at least an hour at my house before the contractors showed up. When I pulled into the driveway shortly after seven, Josh was sitting on the porch steps waving a blue mug of steamy coffee. "Latte for my lady."

I sipped the sweet ambrosia peering over the brim at my hot Viking, thinking, *He can't get any better because he's already perfect.*

"A buddy of mine is coming over to help. I don't want you straining your back, and I know your arms and shoulders are still pretty sore." He glanced down the street. "That's him coming around the corner. I think you'll like this guy."

A yellow VW convertible cruised toward us, and guess who was waving from the driver's seat: Justin Fargate, from the Jane Austen Book Club.

"Surprise!" Justin hopped out and grabbed me in a bear hug, then stepped back and gave me a boo-hoo face. "You poor thing.

Chloe sends her love. We miss you at the book club. You made it so lively."

If you've been following my blog for a while, then you know why I'm no longer a member, but Justin doesn't know why and I can never tell him.

"Love your new look," I said.

He raked his fingers through his trendy dandy-hipster do. "It was Chloe's idea."

"How is she?"

Justin clasped his hands in mock prayer, eyes to the sky. "Preggers. Can you believe it?"

When I met Justin, I thought for sure he was a gay man, and I could not fathom his relationship with his girlfriend—a cute Audrey-Hepburn-clone. But I was wrong. He's simply a dear man who's in touch with his feminine side. Very in touch.

"When's the baby due?" I asked.

"Our little girl is due on Father's Day. Is that a hoot or what?"

"Ohhh. You're having a girl."

"Yes. And we're having so much fun decorating for our little princess. Pink, pink, and more pink." He waggled his left ring finger at me. "Notice anything?"

"Oh, my God!" I said. "Did you two tie the knot?"

"We did. We slipped away to Zephyr Cove in Lake Tahoe and got hitched. It was so romantic."

"How do you and Josh know each other?" I asked.

"We used to be on a bowling team," said Josh. "Justin was our ace in the hole."

The barrel-chested man rolled his eyes. "Oh please. You exaggerate."

"Seriously. This guy's average was around two-fifty." Josh punched the big man in the arm.

"More like two-sixty-five, but who's counting," said Justin, checking his watch. "If the contractors are due here at eight, we need to get this show on the road."

In the hallway, Justin glanced at the ceiling, shaking his head. "Oh, sweetie. Josh told me what happened. What an awful, awful ordeal. I'm surprised I didn't see it on the news."

"The police are afraid that if my cousin knows I'm still alive, she might try to harm me."

"Nobody's going to hear it from me." Justin ran his fingers over his mouth. "My lips are sealed."

Josh scrubbed his hands together. "We better get to it."

I opened the French doors to the patio. "I thought we could put everything out there. There's no rain in the forecast, so it should be safe."

"Girl, there's never any rain in the forecast," said Justin. "Until I wash my car, that is."

"Or put indoor furniture outside," I said.

The men headed to my favorite overstuffed chair, and I began removing the seat cushions from the couch. I sniffed the cushion I'd been sitting on when Erin had threatened to shoot my toe and caught the rank odor of dried urine. Josh noticed and gave me a questioning look.

"Smells like one of the pets had an accident. Thank goodness everything's going to be cleaned." I carried it outside and set it on the patio table. Back inside, I picked up the third cushion, and something clanked on the floor. It was the coin I'd tried to sell on Amazon.

"I can't believe it. I must not have put it back in the safe." I slipped it into my pocket, praying that the person who'd contacted me on Amazon was still interested.

Within twenty minutes, the living and dining rooms were empty. We didn't need to clear out my bedroom. There were only a few holes in the wall, and they could be patched easily.

"Anything else I can help with before I go?" said Justin. "My shift at the hospital doesn't start until eleven."

"Nothing I can think of. I appreciate you coming over to help," I said. "I owe you."

He tapped his chin, surveying the gutted walls. "What a shame. Do you think they were looking for something?"

"Who knows?" said Josh. "But I discovered something interesting inside one of the walls." We followed him to the kitchen table. "These old newspapers were tucked behind the wood lath for insulation."

I read the date on one. "October 5, 1931. Well, now I know my house's birthday. And this explains why my house runs hot and cold. Lousy insulation."

"Other than a little yellowed, the papers are in good shape," said Justin. "Might be fun to frame some."

"I love that idea," I said.

"What about wall color?" said Justin. "You know wallpaper is very popular again. Maybe something bold and splashy to jazz up the place."

"Actually, I'm thinking of going with white. I've always had a lot of color, but I need it to be completely different now."

"*Ooo*. I'm seeing *everything* white. It's fresh. Very cottage." Justin waved his arms at the furniture on the patio. "Slipcover the sofa and chairs. And you could milk-paint all the oak furniture."

"They're all flea market finds, and I love them, but not crazy about oak. Maybe I'll do that."

"I'd love to help," said Justin. "Now, I'm going to scoot." He gave me squeeze. "Seriously, girl. Call me. I know Chloe would love to see you."

We escorted Justin to his car, and after he had driven away, I showed Josh the gold coin.

"Oh, honey, I'm so happy for you," he said. "What a lucky find."

He kissed my forehead, and one of my rowdy neighbors across the street shouted through a window, "Get a room!"

I yelled, "Get a life!" Then back to Josh, "I'm dying to know if the buyer is still interested. I left my laptop at my folks, and I don't want to do it on my phone."

"You can use my computer, and I'll wait for the contractors."

"What about Nicole? I don't want to bother her."

"Don't worry about it. She's probably still asleep, anyway." He gave me an amorous leer. "How about we give our neighbors something to shout about?"

After a smooshy Hollywood kiss that elicited lots of hoots and hollers, I staggered to Josh's house and tiptoed inside. He has an antique Arts and Crafts era desk tucked in the corner of the living room, with an iMac on it. As I was pulling out the chair, Nicole peeked out from the kitchen.

"I thought I heard a little mouse sneaking around out here."

I told her about finding the coin.

"That's wonderful," she said.

"How're you doing? You gave us quite a fright the other night."

"I've never felt that awful before. I thought I was going to die. Gives me chills just thinking about it now, and yet at the time, I wanted to let go and be done with it." She tugged her cardigan sweater tighter and crossed her arms. "This has been much harder than I anticipated."

"It'll be worth it. I mean, you have a good prognosis, right?"

Nicole took my hand and led me to the couch. She hung her head, wringing her hands in her lap. "I told Josh I had an eighty to ninety percent five-year recovery prognosis."

My heart sank. "So what's the real prognosis?"

She clasped a hand over her mouth, looking away. "More like twenty-to-thirty percent. They say they got it all, but, you know, when cancer metastasizes…. Anyway, that's why I'm doing the radiation, too."

"Oh, Nicole. I don't know what to say." Then I began filling the air with nonsense platitudes that no one in her shoes wants to hear. "Well, thirty percent is doable. I mean it's not like you're ninety-five years old. You're young and in good health, except for the damned cancer. You can win this. And hell, what do doctors know, anyway?"

She gave me a wan smile. "You're right. But it's so damned hard. I felt fine. Absolutely fine, other than sore from the surgery, until I started the chemotherapy and radiation. Just the thought of going back for another round makes me feel sick."

I took her icy hand and warmed it between mine. "We're here for you. We'll help you get through this. But Nicole, you need to tell Josh the truth. He needs to know."

"Josh is so lucky to have found you. I hate the fact that I'm taking so much of his time away from you."

"It's okay. We have our whole future ahead of us." As soon as I said that, I wanted to rip my tongue out. So thoughtless.

"Yes, you do." She set her other hand over mine. "And you're right. I need to tell him."

———

The contractors didn't show up until after nine. A phone call would've been nice. Josh went home, and after I had gone over everything with the foreman, I drove to my folks' house to grab my laptop. Turns out, Sixpence had countered with an offer of $6,150. That was close enough for me. Sold!

I called Ruby, Mom, and Pop and invited them to dinner at The Green Door, a fancy, upscale restaurant downtown. Pop begged off—his knee was killing him, but the ladies were on board. I would have asked Josh, but after my conversation with Nicole, I thought he should stay with her.

I returned to my house, and in the early afternoon, the floor refurbishing guys showed up. I wasn't looking forward to having the wood floors sanded, re-stained, then polyurethaned. Thankfully, they said the floors would look good as new with a thorough cleaning and polish.

———

Mom and I drove in my car to pick up Ruby for our dinner date. As we approached the Shady Acres security booth, the skinny guard stepped out. "Hold it. Hold it." George held up a hand like he was stopping a line of traffic.

"Oh brother. Here we go again," I muttered.

"Try to be patient, honey. He means well. He just takes his responsibilities very seriously."

"I know. But he's worse than ever these days." I rolled down my window. "Hi, George. We're here to pick up my grandma."

He stepped to my window clutching his clipboard. "Gonna need to see some identification."

"Seriously, George? You know who I am. I come here all the time. So does my mom."

"Just doing my job, ma'am." He hoisted up his belt and patted his pepper spray holster with an arrogant sniff. "These days, can't take any chances. You never know who might be a terrorist or a crazy lunatic."

I sifted through my bag for my wallet. "This is ridiculous. I am *not* a terrorist." I held out the open wallet. "See? It's still me."

He shined his flashlight on it. "And the nature of your business?"

"Like I said, I'm picking up my grandmother."

He waited, eyebrow cocked.

"Ruby Armstrong."

"Is she expecting you?"

"Oh, for God's sakes, George," said Mom. "It's none of your business. But if you must know, Katy is taking us to dinner."

"No need to get huffy, ma'am." He scanned his clipboard. "I don't see your names on here. I'm going to have to call Mrs. Armstrong to confirm." He stepped inside his booth.

"George," I said. "I'm going through now."

"I haven't called your grandmother yet."

"Too bad." I stomped on the gas and we peeled out, breaking the fifteen-mile-per-hour speed limit by five more.

"Well, now you've gone and done it," said Mom. "You do realize we have to drive back through?"

"Yeah, but it felt so good."

"Kinda like Thelma and Louise, huh?"

Granny was standing on her porch, talking on her cellphone when I pulled up. "Yes, George. You're right. My granddaughter is a juvenile delinquent." She got in the backseat, still on the phone, and after she buckled up, we headed back to Checkpoint George.

As we closed in on the booth, Ruby held her hand over the cellphone. "Don't stop." She returned to her conversation. "Yes, George. I agree. Kids these days have no respect for authority."

I watched his narrow back through the booth window, arms gesturing wildly as I rolled by, waving and honking. In my rearview mirror, I saw him run out, flapping his arms. I'm such a bad-ass juvie.

———

I was up half that night, partly because I indulged in dessert at The Green Door. Flambéed peaches and bananas with sea salt caramel ice cream and Grand Marnier whipped cream. Who could say no to that? But maybe I should have shared.

The other reason I couldn't nod off was that something was niggling my brain. I read somewhere that your brain is functioning at its best during slow, deep breathing. I inhaled, thinking, *Is it something I should remember about Erin? The money? What?*

I exhaled, straining my pea-brain. *If I were Erin, what would I do?*

I sat up and switched on the bedside lamp, disturbing Daisy and Tabitha. "Sorry, kiddos. Mama thought of something, and I need to check it out."

I piled the pillows behind me, flipped open my laptop, went to Google Maps, and typed in Cranston Lane in Atherton, CA. I zoomed in with the satellite view. The homes were large, and the lots looked to be at least one or more acres.

"I wonder which one was her grandparents' home."

I clicked on *street view* and strolled along, admiring the charming tree-lined lane. Couldn't see much of the houses with them set behind walls, hedges, and security gates. I typed in "Houses for sale in Atherton, CA" and got Twillow, one of those sites that lists houses.

"Holy cow. Here's a two-bedroom, one and a half bath house for 2.5 million bucks."

It was built in 1938 on a quarter acre lot and was storybook enchanting in a charming shady neighborhood, but over two million? Good grief. My house was built in 1931 and has three bedrooms, two full baths, and a creepy attic. I paid a mere fraction of that price, and thought it was too much.

I scrolled down the listing. "Oh, well, here's the reason." The price per square foot was nearly $1,400. Guess I won't be buying a house up there. Who can afford that?

I could have if Erin hadn't stolen my money. That thought led me to a crazy idea. "No. She wouldn't dare do that. Would she?"

I searched recent home sales in the area, and Twillow came up again. This time at least one hundred yellow circles indicated recent sales with prices ranging from 2.2 million to the-sky's-the-limit.

There were photos in the right sidebar of the page, and most of the homes were ranchers and two-stories, not mega-mansions. No sales showed up on Cranston Lane. I was relieved that my crazy idea had been just that. Crazy.

CHAPTER THIRTY-FIVE

MONDAY · MARCH 2
Posted by Katy McKenna

This morning was moving-back-in-day! Josh and Justin Fargate did the heavy lifting, while my folks and I did the directing. I'd intended to put the furniture back in its original positions, but Mom and Pop had different ideas. Good ideas. Things I never would have thought of that made the space feel more open and yet cozier.

After everyone left, I spent the day nesting. Mom had offered to help, but I needed to do it by myself. I took my time filling the china cabinet, hanging some art, but only my absolute favorites. While staying at my parents I had read a book about decluttering. The essence of the book was—if something doesn't give you joy, get rid of it. That's a little oversimplified, but you get the drift. So I've decided if I don't love a piece of art or furniture, then it doesn't belong in my home. Same goes for my clothes.

Josh brought takeout Thai food for dinner, and we ate in my living room. It was the first alone-time we've had since Nicole told me the truth about her cancer.

After several spicy bites, I asked, "Has Nicole said anything more to you about her prognosis?"

"Yes. She has. Just this afternoon, she told me about her talk with you." He leaned toward me, taking my hand, absently twiddling my fingers. "Thank you, Katy. I should've been told what I was letting myself in for. I think she needs to tell her father to come home and...."

He let that last line hang in the air, so I finished it. "And take care of her?"

"Yes." Josh shook his head, looking desolate. "I'm not her husband." He dropped my hand. "God, Katy. I don't know what to do. I care about her. Always will. But we're divorced. I'm not the one who should be doing this."

"Did you tell her?"

"No. How can I?" He paused, staring at the fireplace. "I owe her for what I did to our marriage."

"Josh, I have to ask." I pulled a deep breath while my inner voice screamed, *Don't do it!* "Do you still love her?"

Josh vehemently shook his head. "No. Absolutely not." He paused a moment and sighed. "All right, yes, but only as a friend. A good friend. God, we go way back, so how could I not? And to be honest, I feel a deep obligation to her. Maybe it's guilt."

I felt horrible pressing him like this, but I had to know where we stood. "When she said she was leaving you, what did you do?"

He shifted to the edge of the sofa cushion, leaning his forearms on his knees and hanging his head.

I wanted to take him in my arms and say, *It's okay, baby. Forget I asked.* Instead, I moved closer, touching his arm. "You can tell me, Josh. And you need to be honest about this. For both our sakes."

He leaned back, raking his hands through his scruffy blond hair. "I begged her not to go."

"Because you loved her." I took his hand, pressing it between mine, feeling like I might throw up. "It would be understandable if you're still *in* love with her, you know."

Josh looked me square in the eyes. "Katy. It took a long time, but I got over her. What I feel for her now is not that kind of love. Not like I feel for you."

"I think I love you too, Josh," I whispered, feeling my heart swell.

He reached for me and I shook my head, weighing my next words. "Do you think she's still in love with you?"

"Yes. I do." His eyes shimmered, and a tear slipped down his cheek.

That tear did me in. I love my Viking. Oh, how I did not want to say my next words. "Josh? I don't want to say this, but I think we need to put us on hold—"

"No!" He flicked the tear away.

"Just for a little while so you can concentrate on helping Nicole get well."

"I don't want to take a goddamned break." He turned away from me and groaned. "I've ruined everything. Again."

"No, you haven't, honey." I placed my hand on his shoulder. "You're a good man trying to do the right thing, and I get that. But right now you have enough on your plate without worrying about my feelings."

A shroud of silence dropped over us, and I could barely breathe from the weight of it.

Finally, Josh said, "I guess it's time for me to go. Nicole wasn't feeling too good when I left." He stood, bending to pick up the food cartons.

"Don't worry about that. I'll clean up later."

"You sure?"

No, dammit! I'm not sure about anything. "It's no problem. In fact, maybe I'll have a little more wine and nibble a bit." I was talking like a hyper cheerleader. "The food is great. Thanks for bringing it over. Oh! Do you want to take some home with you?"

"No. Nicole can't stand the smell of food, so I better not."

I walked Josh to the door, and we shared an awkward, lack-luster kiss. I was so torn. I wanted him in my bed, and I wanted him out the door.

CHAPTER THIRTY-SIX

TUESDAY · MARCH 3
Posted by Katy McKenna

Needless to say—no sleep last night. At least I wasn't fixated on Erin for a change. It's funny how everything else moves to the back burner when your heart is breaking.

I have to know if Nicole is still in love with Josh. Then I'll know what I'm dealing with instead of my imagination running amuck with all the what-ifs.

———

I was nursing a cup of tea on my porch swing when Josh's sports car growled into life. I waited until he drove by, then walked to his house and knocked on the door.

Nicole called, "Who's there?"

"It's me. Katy. Got a minute?"

"Sure. Come on in."

I found her resting on the living room sofa, bundled in a fuzzy blanket. A *Sunset Magazine* lay open on her lap.

"How're you doing?" *Oh, God. Stupid question.*

"Pretty good today, although I know I look like hell." She shivered and drew the blanket closer. "Josh won't be back for a while. He went to the office to meet a client."

"Actually, I came to talk to you." I sat across from her in a leather recliner. "I have a serious question to ask, and I want this conversation to remain between you and me."

She set the magazine on the coffee table and tugged the brown blanket to her chin. "Now you've got me worried."

I clenched my hands in my lap praying this wasn't a terrible mistake. "It's something that I need to know. I mean, maybe I'm being paranoid, but I need to know if...." I took a deep breath, forcing the words out. "Are you still in love with Josh?"

Her eyes shifted away from mine and she nodded. "Yes."

"Oh."

"I'm sorry, Katy. I know that's the wrong answer, but it's the truth. I thought I was over him a long time ago, but when I got the cancer diagnosis, all I could think about was how much I needed Josh."

"Have you told him?"

She shook her head. "I want to, but spending time with you has made it difficult. I really like you, and Josh says he loves you, so it would make things very awkward around here if he knew how I feel."

"I think he deserves to know."

"Why?"

I stood. "I just do. Even if it means I lose him." I went to the door, then turned to her. "And if I lose him, then I never really had him, did I?"

———

After a long, hysterical cry on my bed, I drifted to sleep, cuddled next to Daisy. The doorbell woke me at 11:45.

Oh, crap. What if it's Josh? I checked the doorbell app on my cellphone and saw a UPS truck out front. I set the phone back on the nightstand and closed my eyes. Then I remembered the porch pirates that have been stealing boxes in the neighborhood and got up.

In the kitchen, I slit the box open and found a pretty, flowered toilet plunger nestled in bubble wrap. I had completely forgotten that I'd ordered it, so it was like getting a present. After setting it behind the hall bathroom toilet, I stepped back to admire it. Who knew a toilet plunger could lift my spirits?

I brewed a strong cup of dark roast, and Daisy made me go outside to soak up some vitamin D. The bird feeder hanging in the pepper tree was empty so I filled it. After I had hung it up, a blue jay landed on it and screeched, "What took you so long, Food Lady?"

"Sorry, buddy. Been a little distracted lately."

He gave me the stink eye, then selected a sunflower seed and flew away.

Daisy and I sat under the tree, and I sipped my coffee, waiting for Jay to return. I finally gave up and went to the front porch to see if Josh's car was in the driveway. It wasn't, so that meant Nicole hadn't spoken to him yet.

What if she breaks her promise not to tell him? I imagined him banging on my door to have it out with me for butting into their personal business.

"Even if I don't answer the door, he'll know I'm home. Unless...I'm not." Mind made up, I dashed inside and threw some things into a suitcase.

I called Mom and told her I was heading up the coast to Cambria to spend a few nights.

"Honey, this is so unlike you. You never used to be spontaneous about anything. I remember when you were seven or eight, I gave away your baby wading pool and got you a bigger one, thinking you'd love it. But instead—"

"I remember. I had a major meltdown."

"Did you ever."

"I've never liked change, and yet everything keeps changing, so I'm trying to be more carefree and go with the flow, plus, I think I need a timeout from Josh."

After I told Mom what was going on, she said, "Well, now your sudden spontaneity makes more sense. You going to drop Daisy off here?"

"I'm going to take her with. I have a travel app that lists all the dog-friendly hotels in California, and it'll be an adventure. But could you check on Tabitha?"

"Of course, sweetie. Don't forget to take dog food for Daisy."

The first two hotels I called had no vacancies, then I tried an Airbnb and got a room. The owner said the room is booked tomorrow, so I'd need to check out by eleven, but I took it anyway. I'll worry about tomorrow, tomorrow.

CHAPTER THIRTY-SEVEN

WEDNESDAY · MARCH 4

Posted by Katy McKenna

After a leisurely beach stroll with Daisy, I ate breakfast at an outdoor cafe while my girl snoozed under the table. I splurged on Eggs Benedict with smoked salmon on a homemade English muffin. Amazing. Afterward, I made calls to book a room for the night.

Several calls later, it became apparent there were no rooms at the inns. I didn't want to go home, so I headed up the coast toward Big Sur.

Fifteen minutes out of Cambria, we passed by the Hearst Castle perched high on a hill overlooking the Pacific. I stopped to photograph a herd of zebras grazing in the field along the two-lane highway. When William Randolph Hearst built the castle in the early 1900's, he imported exotic animals from around the world. At one time there had been camels, yaks, bison, giraffes, lions, tigers, and bears. Now only zebras and cattle roam the ranch.

Further up Highway One, we climbed into the Santa Lucia Mountain Range that runs along the coast of central California.

I'd forgotten how scary those hairpin turns can be, especially when a mega-huge RV was heading in my direction. After several mini-heart attacks, I pulled off at a view point to take a breather and give Daisy a potty break. I crawled out of the car, unclenched my stiff muscles, then opened the back door, expecting her to go nuts. Instead, my girl lay sprawled on the seat with a thick stream of drool hanging from her lips.

"Baby? What's the matter?"

She gave me a bleary look, raised a paw as if to say, "Farewell, cruel world," and heaved her breakfast onto the floor mat.

I helped my feeble girl hobble out of the car, and the breezy ocean air instantly revived her.

"Are you all right now, baby?"

Tail wagging, she lobbed me an air kiss.

"I'll take that as a yes." I lifted the floor mat out to drain her spew. "Thank you for hitting the rubber mat instead of the seat." I threw a few handfuls of dirt on the mat, rubbed it in with tissues, then shook it off. "There. Good as new. You ready to get going again?"

I rolled down the back window so she could hang her head out, and we resumed our journey. Along the way, we passed a couple of small hotels with the No Vacancy signs lit up.

At last! A place with rooms available. The Mantra Motel. I parked and checked their rating on Trip Advisor. Only one review from a Melvin Schwartz. One star.

On the lobby porch, an aging hippie dude sat in a willow twig rocking chair, strumming a beat-up guitar. "Greetings, sister. You gotta a reservation?"

"No."

He nodded a moment, stroking his long gray beard. "Cool."

"Do you have any rooms available?"

"Let me check our reservations." The man set the guitar aside, and I followed him inside to the lobby desk. He flipped open a leather binder and scanned the page with his finger. "Looks like you're in luck."

"Do you allow dogs?" I said.

"Depends."

"On what?"

"If I like it."

"*It* is a girl. A very sweet, well-behaved, quiet girl. You wanna meet her?"

"Groovy."

At the car, I opened the backseat door, and Daisy leaped out to greet Mr. Hippie.

"Nice pooch." He crouched to pet the wiggle-worm.

"So, what's the verdict?" I asked.

"Tell you what. You two can have our deluxe suite. It's sweet."

Daisy and I followed him back to the desk. "I doubt I can afford the suite. A regular room will do."

"Not for my new friend, Miss Daisy. You get the suite, no extra charge. Here's the key." He handed me a real metal key attached to a leather peace symbol. "Down at the end and around the corner. If you're hungry, there's a vending machine. The restaurant across the road," he pointed at a ramshackle building, "is closed for the winter. Bummer. Awesome organic vegan fare."

"Thanks. Don't I need to do some paperwork?"

"Naw. First names are good enough." He held out his hand, and we shook. "Name's Mel, as in mellow, although that wasn't my mother's intention at the time." He chuckled. "Melvin. Can you dig it?"

"I'm Katy. Do you need a credit card number?"

"Nah. Don't take cards."

"Uh, oh. I don't have much cash on me."

"No worries. You can send a check when you get home."

"Seriously? Don't you have problems with that?"

"Not often. I figure if someone doesn't pay, they must need the bread more than I do."

"I promise to send you a check as soon as I get home. What time's checkout?"

"Anytime before noon, but if that's too early, no worries. Sleep tight and don't let the bedbugs bite."

I expected the room to be shabby and full of bedbugs. Instead, it was charming and well appointed. King-size brass bed, stone fireplace, claw-foot tub in the bathroom, and a wide screen TV with an impressive collection of DVD movies. To top it all off was the vending machine. I had anticipated candy bars and stale corn chips, but instead, got a nice selection of fresh, organic delights.

Final catch-up on today's blog

Halfway through a good movie I'd never heard of: *Red Rock West*—an offbeat mystery with Nicolas Cage and Dennis Hopper, I realized I'd had my phone off all day. Should have left it that way.

There were three texts from Josh.

- First one: *Hey, cupcake, where are you?*
- Thirty minutes later: *Everything all right?*
- Then a couple hours later: *We need to talk*

"Oh crud. I knew that was coming. Thank goodness I'm not home."

- A text from Mom: *Josh called asking if you're all right. Are you?*
- One from Samantha: *Road trip helping?*
- And Ruby: *Where the hell are u?*

Now that reality had shattered my mellow mood, I replied to everyone. I won't bore you with the silly auto-correct misspellings.

- To Josh: *I'll be back soon. In Big Sur with Daisy. I needed a little "me" time with my girl.*
- To Mom, Sam, and Ruby: *I'm fine. Daisy and I are staying at a great place in Big Sur. The Mantra Motel. More later.*

I admit it was pretty chicken of me, running away like I did. But I wasn't ready for Josh's knock on the door and the, "We need to talk," conversation.

Yes, it'll happen, for better or worse, but we both need time to think. I do not want a man whose heart still belongs to someone else. Even if it's just a little piece of it. For me, it's one hundred percent or nothing. I'm selfish that way.

CHAPTER THIRTY-EIGHT

THURSDAY · MARCH 5
Posted by Katy McKenna

This morning, after coffee and a cranberry muffin, I headed to the lobby to fetch my bill. Mel was sitting in his rocker, reading a book. I peeked at the title. *A Dog's Purpose.*

"Oh, I love that book. It's one of my all-time favorites."

Mel glanced up, teary-eyed, then blew his nose on a red bandana. Daisy licked his hand, and his tears welled up again.

"The story has a happy ending, Mel."

"I hope so. I don't know how much more I can take." His gravelly voice broke, and he cleared his throat.

"Hang in there. Trust me, it's worth it." I waited for him to compose himself. "I'm here for my bill. I enjoyed my stay, and I'm going to post a glowing five-star review on Trip Advisor, Yelp, Google, and anywhere else I can think of."

"Whoa, girl. I appreciate the sentiment, but please don't. Word of mouth works fine for me and the missus."

"I just think that—"

"I know. Everyone always thinks that, but we make enough to

get by, and we're content. All we need is a roof over our heads, enough bread to pay the bills, and good vibes from kind folks like you. So please, no reviews."

"Okay, but I'll be back.

"I look forward to when we meet again. Happy trails."

———

At the southern boundary of Carmel, I stopped for gas. In the minimart, I purchased a few bottles of water, a bag of Sun Chips, and a giant chocolate chip cookie.

Back in the car, I swigged some water and nibbled on the cookie wondering where the hell I was going and why. I recalled the line, "You can run, but you can't hide," and thought how true that is. Sooner or later, I would have to deal with the Josh dilemma.

I headed north through Carmel on Highway One, and in a few miles, it dumped me onto the 101 freeway. I passed through Salinas, "The salad bowl of the world," Gilroy, "The garlic capital of the world," and San Jose, "The capital of Silicon Valley."

In Mountain View, I exited the freeway and turned north onto El Camino Real in search of sustenance. I found an In-N-Out Burger and went through the drive-through, then parked under a tree to eat my fries and figure out where I was going. After checking Google maps, I realized we were close to the former home of Erin's grandparents. I asked my phone, "Siri? How far to Atherton, California?"

"Thirty minutes on U.S. 101 North. Twenty-five minutes via Alma Street."

I typed in Cranston Lane, Atherton into the GPS app, and chose the quickest route.

Siri hadn't taken traffic into account. I suppose at three in the morning it's only twenty-five minutes, but it wound up taking more like forty-five.

Since I'd traversed Cranston Lane via Google Street View at

home, I thought I knew what it looked like. But the reality was way beyond the virtual. At the end of the road, I did a U-turn and ogled the other side of the lane, wondering which palatial estate had been the Cranston home.

I stopped and checked on my phone for pet-friendly hotels in the area. The Comfort Plaza in Palo Alto had semi-affordable rooms available, so I called and booked one. It was too early to check in, so I thought it would be fun to do some window shopping at the Stanford Shopping Center. I hadn't been there in years, but it's my favorite mall.

I parked near The Pottery Barn, and then we strolled into the center of the outdoor mall. Daisy was patient with me while I drooled over the cute clothes in the windows. A saleslady in the Coach shop saw me ogling a fabulous yellow bag and beckoned me in. But the only store Daisy frequents is PetSmart, where she can act like an idiot and no one cares, so I shook my head. I couldn't afford to buy anything in that shop, anyway.

We continued on toward the west end of the mall where Neiman Marcus loomed ahead. At the entrance, a stout fiftyish female was sweet-talking her obese brown Labradoodle through the doors.

"Mommy wants to shop for shoesies, Freddy," she said in a baby voice, tugging his leash. "Please, baby? For Mommy?"

Fred plunked his rear end down, and the woman growled, "Move it or lose it, Fred."

"Come on, Daisy. Let's watch poor old Fred through the window, and see how he's doing."

The miserable dog shuffled toward footwear and then my attention shifted to a slender, well-dressed brunette at one of the cosmetic counters. I could only see her back, but there was something familiar about her perfect posture and the way she gestured with her slim hands as she spoke.

"No. It can't be. No way. She's in Costa Rica. But that woman's hair looks just like Erin's. And her height and build and mannerisms—no, I'm imagining things."

The woman on the other side of the window was at least twenty feet away, so I had to be mistaken—or hallucinating. But I could not tear my eyes away. "Come on. Turn around so I can see you're not her."

She shoved her credit card into the payment terminal, and I waited, tapping my foot while butterflies dive-bombed in my tummy. The transaction ended, and the woman walked around the counter to the middle aisle, going deeper into the store.

"Dammit. I need to see her face."

I stepped to the entrance. As the automatic doors whooshed open, Daisy skittered back and yawned several times. She always does that when she's nervous.

"Honey. The doors won't hurt you. It's just like the pet store, remember?"

She looked at me like I was nuts but followed me with her tail tucked between her legs. The woman was nearing the escalator, but Daisy had her heart set on catching up with Fred in the shoe department and tugged to the left.

"No, baby. We have to go this way." I towed her along, watching the woman stop and read the store directory at the foot of the escalator. "Please don't go up," I muttered.

She set a gold stiletto sandal on the first step and began her ascent.

Daisy had panicked at the automatic sliding glass doors, so how was I going to coax her onto the escalator? And what if her toenails got stuck in the metal step grooves? Would she jerk away and send us both tumbling down the moving stairs? I couldn't risk it, so we hung back, hiding behind an anorexic mannequin, hoping the woman would glance around and give me a view of her face. The mystery woman stepped off on the second floor and turned left.

Dammit. I squatted next to Daisy, rubbing her neck. "Hey, girl. Are you up for a super fun, new experience?"

Her tail wagged limply, and she yawned three times.

"Oh yeah. That's my girl. Let's go have some fun."

Her leash stretched taut as I dragged her across the shiny, terrazzo floor toward the escalator. A few people threw me nasty looks, and I couldn't have agreed with them more. But what if, for some insane reason, that woman was Erin and I let her get away?

"Young lady," snapped an elderly redhead in a teal, satin jacket. "There's an elevator at the other end of the store. Perhaps your dog would be more comfortable using that."

"I know, but her trainer, um, Cesar Millan, said I have to do this to get her over her fears."

She arched a copper penciled brow. "Oh, really? Well, I have no idea who that is, but I have half-a-mind to call canine social services and report you. You know, you could lose custody."

I needed to see if that woman was my cousin, but I also knew I was probably letting my overactive imagination get the best of me at my puppy's expense. The odds of that woman being Erin had to be less than my chance of winning the lottery. And I never play the lottery.

I crouched and pulled Daisy close. "Screw Cesar."

"Thata girl," said the matron and tottered away.

I returned to the mannequin, hoping the woman would come back down the escalator and confirm that I was losing my mind.

"May I help you?" called a Lancôme salesperson from a glass counter across the aisle. Her perfect airbrushed makeup and stenciled brows would have made a drag queen jealous.

"No, I'm good. Just waiting for a friend."

The woman smiled a chilly smile that said, *You are obviously not our kind in your Ross clearance attire, so I'm keeping my eye on you.*

"I'm sure she'll be along any second." I made a big show of checking the time on my phone, muttering, "Where are you?" I glanced at the woman to see if she was buying my performance and saw she had been joined by a Marilyn Monroe wannabe sales-person. "She's late." I scowled. "So typical. I'm going to text her."

As I pretend-texted, Daisy whined and lifted one back leg, then the other. Her sign language for, *Gotta go potty*.

"Seriously, Daisy? Now?"

Her pink tongue dangled out the side of her mouth, and she wagged a yes.

"No. You have to wait."

With a noisy groan, she sat down and yawned. I finished my phony texting and glanced up to see three women watching me. I waved my phone, shrugging, *Watcha gonna do?* I was so busy trying to fool them that I almost missed the lady in question stroll by, heading to the exit. She passed through the glass doors and turned left.

Daisy was thrilled we were leaving until she realized she'd have to go through the "doors of death" again. About three feet from the exit she froze.

"Come on. She's getting away." I tugged her leash and she jerked back, piddling on the shiny floor. "Daisy, we need to go. She's getting away." The cosmetic ladies were glaring at me and a store security guard was rushing toward me. And then I remem-bered the magic words that always get her moving. "Let's go get a snack." Tail wagging, she hauled me out of the store and we hurried to catch up to the woman.

Midway through the mall, the woman turned into Sephora's. I caught up and peeked in the window but didn't see her. "This is getting ridiculous, Daisy. Clearly, I've lost it. There's no way in hell that woman is my cousin."

And yet, I couldn't walk away without getting a good look at her face. I knew that if I didn't, I would always wonder if I'd let Erin slip through my fingers. "Okay, Daisy. I promise to get you a treat—but first we're going in the store."

"Treat" is another favorite word, so she was game. She trotted in like she shops at Sephora's all the time. Inside the entrance, I looked around but didn't see the woman, so I walked to the center of the store and did a three-sixty scan.

She was perched on a stool, her back to me. A beauty consultant was cleansing her face. Acting nonchalant, I slipped down the Bobbi Brown aisle, approaching the woman's back. The tall, muscular makeup artist noticed me and smiled. "May I help you?"

I shook my head and stepped backward, grinding my heel into Daisy's paw. She yelped and scuttled her rear-end into a low shelf of open blusher cases, knocking the entire display of thirty-two dollar compacts to the floor. I turned toward Daisy and bent to pick up the compacts.

"*Achtung!*" yelled the lady on the stool. "*Dein hund, ich meine* your dog is about to knock over *dass* kiosk."

Distracted by the woman's strong German accent, I was slow to react to her warning and the display tipped over, spilling its contents onto the floor. Poor Daisy stood amongst the mascara boxes and eyebrow pencils, trembling and yawning nonstop.

"I'm so sorry," I said.

"No problem. Happens all the time." The makeup man set down the jar of gunk he'd been using to cleanse the middle-aged German woman's face and came to my assistance.

"I seriously doubt that." *How could I have thought that woman was Erin?*

Two sales associates joined us. One of them took a dog cookie out of her apron pocket and asked if she could give it to my dog. "I always keep a few in my pocket for our doggy friends."

Daisy joyfully accepted her well-earned treat. Too bad the saleswoman didn't have a valium in her pocket for me.

We left the shop and dashed to the car. On the way, I felt like every security camera in the mall was focused on me—the loony, stalker lady. After tethering Daisy in the backseat, I spent several minutes apologizing to her. She gave me several reassuring kisses and then settled down for a snooze. Thank goodness dogs don't hold grudges.

After hearing the woman's voice and seeing her face, it was hard to wrap my brain around the fact that I'd actually thought she could be Erin—to the point of stalking her. However the episode left me wondering if my cousin really had gone to Costa Rica. *The cops don't want her to know I'm alive, in the hopes that she might think it's safe to stay in the U.S.. What if they're right?* I pondered that thought for a moment. *No. It's too risky. But what if?*

It was after three so we could have gone to our hotel, but I was too restless to call it a day, so I decided to check out Erin's hometown. I drove out of the parking lot and turned left onto El Camino Real. We passed through Menlo Park, which merged into Atherton. The next town was Redwood City.

I passed an old high school on the left. Mature redwoods and eucalyptus shaded the park-like campus. I wondered if that was where Erin's father taught. When I reached a sign that read: Welcome to San Carlos, I made a U-turn and pulled into Kimmy's Nail Spa parking lot. I wanted to find Erin's parents' house and do a drive-by to satisfy my curiosity.

I dug my phone out of my purse and searched William Cranston in Redwood City, CA. The top listing was William Cranston in CA/Whitepages. I clicked on it, and several names popped up. One in Bakersfield, 103 years old. One in Camarillo, 27 years old. And two in Redwood City. A 45-year-old and:

William Cranston
Age: 62-64
Lives in: Redwood City, CA
Prior: Atherton, CA
Possible Relatives: Molly Cranston, Erin Cranston, Evelyn Cra...

On the next page was his address. 3742 Ranch Hill Road.

I typed the address into my GPS and set the phone in the plastic holder suction-cupped to the dashboard. The directions led me west off of El Camino. I drove for a few miles past middle-class neighborhoods built in the 1920's to 1950's.

The road continued into a long-established housing development. A couple of stop signs later, GPS said to turn right, then left, then right again. I climbed halfway up a steep hill, before hearing, "Your destination is ahead on the right." And then, "You have arrived at your destination."

"Yeah, but which house is it?" I couldn't remember the house number, so I drove further up the hill, parked, and took a look at what I'd typed into the GPS. 3742. The house across from me was 3755. I did a U-turn and inched down the street until I was looking at 3742. Two stories, gray with black shutters and a fire-engine-red front door. Double garage under the upstairs bedroom windows. Big magnolia tree in the front yard. Black and white cat perched on the faded cedar fence gate, giving me the stink-eye.

I killed the engine and Daisy got antsy in the backseat.

"Daisy, just give me a little while, then we'll check into our hotel, and you can relax on the bed. Maybe take a dip in the pool —kidding!"

A few houses down, three subteen boys were doing their damnedest to break their necks skateboarding on a wooden half-pipe in the driveway. Two teenaged girls were walking up the hill, both texting. The closer the oblivious girls got to the future studs, the more daring their stunts became.

"Oh, come on, girls. At least favor them with a glance before they kill themselves."

They did not, and the boys' scrawny chests deflated the moment the girls passed by.

After my ridiculous Neiman Marcus fiasco, it was crazy to think that Erin might be at her parents' house, but I decided to stick around for a while. Just to make sure. Besides, it was either hang out there or hang out at the hotel.

"We can pretend we're on a stakeout, Daisy. Like real private investigators." I turned to my slumbering backseat companion. "I'll take the first shift while you nap."

To kill time I looked up the Cranston house on Twillow. Four bedrooms, two-and-a-half baths, built in 1959. Valued at 1.5 million. Last sold in 1988 for $102,500.

It occurred to me that if Erin showed up, she might recognize my orange Volvo, so I rolled down the hill, turned right and drove to the next block. I put on the raggedy red baseball cap I wear at the dog park and tucked my hair inside. Sunglasses completed my sleuthing disguise. "Hey, girl. How about a little stroll?"

Daisy was all about that and struggled to leap out her half-open window. I released the nutcase and got pulled to a bark-chipped mound where she took a long leak.

We headed back to Ranch Farm Road and sauntered up the hill—sniffing every bush, flower, and rock along the way. As we dawdled past the Cranston home, Daisy noticed the kitty gate-keeper and dragged me across the lawn to the dog-eared fence.

"Daisy! Stop barking! What's your problem? Your best friend's a cat. Geez!"

The cat seemed to be enjoying the spectacle, meowing just enough to keep my dog agitated. Talk about a power trip. Then the cat got bored and nonchalantly licked his paw.

"Sorry about that," said a male voice on the other side of the fence.

The gate opened, and I was pretty sure I was face-to-face with William Cranston. 62–64 years old. Thick wavy salt and pepper hair, and he had his daughter's nose.

"It's Bob's hobby. He sits there all day long waiting for inno-cent, unsuspecting dogs to torment." He patted Daisy on the head.

"She'd never hurt Bob. She lives with a cat. They sleep cuddled up."

"I hear you. But a cat sitting on a fence is like seeing a squirrel. Ya just gotta bark and go nuts."

"You ever see the movie, *Up*?" I asked.

"I have."

We both shouted, "Squirrel!"

I laughed, thinking, *What a nice man. I bet his students love him.*

"Do you live in the neighborhood?" he said.

Oh, crap. Now what do I say? "No. I'm visiting some friends."

"Oh? Who? I know just about everyone around here. My wife and I have lived here for years."

Samantha popped into my head. "The Drummonds, a few blocks over."

He pondered a moment, puckering his brow. "Nope, don't know them."

I wanted to get a picture of him, so I said, "I love your house colors. I've wanted to paint mine for quite a while now, so whenever I see a combination I like, I take a picture. Would you mind?"

"Be my guest and thank you for the compliment. My wife, Molly, will be thrilled. I wanted yellow, but she won the coin toss."

Feeling like a bonafide private investigator, I snapped several photos, including two of Mr. Cranston with snooty Bob peering over his shoulder.

"I've been thinking yellow, too," I said. "But this color palette would go better with my roof."

"That's what Molly said."

Hoping not to sound nosy—but when you're investigating, you have to ask tough questions. "This seems like a family-friendly neighborhood. Do you have any kids?"

His smile sagged, and I felt like a jerk for asking.

He sighed. "We did. A daughter."

"Oh my God, I'm so sorry. I shouldn't have asked."

"No, no. It's okay." He shook his head, lips pressed into a tight line. "She's alive. But we haven't heard from her in years." He stroked Daisy's back, not looking at me. "She wants nothing to do with us. And now, I guess that's for the best." He straightened, rubbing the side of his neck.

"I shouldn't have pried. I didn't mean to dredge up pain."

"Not your fault. Your question was a normal one to ask. And to prove that point, do you have kids?"

"Just the furry kind."

His wife stepped out onto the front porch, and he said, "Hey, hon, this young lady...I'm sorry, I didn't catch your name."

"Samantha." The lies just kept rolling off my tongue.

He extended his hand. "Bill Cranston and that's my wife, Molly."

"Hi." We waved at each other.

"Samantha likes our house colors and wants to do the same on hers," said Bill.

Molly moved to the edge of the porch. "Thanks for the compliment. Do you want to take some pictures?"

"I already did. But maybe one more." I snapped one of the porch and Molly. "I love the red door. And don't worry. I don't live around here so you won't have a copycat house in the neighborhood."

"Then I won't tell you that we already do. Ours." A timer jingled through the kitchen window. "The cake is calling me. Nice meeting you, Samantha."

It was time for me to move on before I blew my cover.

———

Our hotel room was on the ground floor facing a grassy fenced courtyard. I fed Daisy, then went to the hotel restaurant to get some takeout. After ordering the salad and grilled cheese combo to go, I sat at the bar, sipping a glass of draft house white. A tubby, balding fellow with a droopy mustache was sitting a few seats down nursing a beer. He caught my eye and smiled, looking lonely. I returned a polite half-smile, looking unavailable. Next thing I knew, he was settling his tush on the stool next to me.

Oh, crud. Why didn't I call room service?

"You alone?" he asked.

"Nope."

"So, has anyone ever told you...."

That I look like Anne Hathaway?

"That you have soulful eyes?"

Oh, good grief. "That's probably the crow's feet you're seeing."

"No. You have beautiful hazel-green eyes like my wife." He paused, swallowing hard. "Did."

"Oh, I'm so sorry." I unconsciously placed my hand on his. "When did she...."

"A year ago." He sniffed, shaking his head. "Today would have been...our...anniversary."

I patted his hand. "This must be such a hard day for you."

He placed his hand over mine. "It...." His voice broke and he pulled a quivery breath. "...Is."

The melancholy man's glass was empty, and mine was getting close, so I gently withdrew my hand from his and said to the bartender, "May I have another glass of wine and a beer for the gentleman?" I wanted to get out of there, but I had to wait for my food, so I figured it didn't hurt to be compassionate.

"You're so kind," he whispered.

"It's nothing. I only wish I could do more."

His sad eyes brightened. "Maybe you can." He hung his head. "No, it's too much."

"What?" I asked.

Our drinks were set on the bar, and my seatmate chugged a few gulps of his beer, then hunched over it, and blew out a dejected sigh. "It's been so long since...."

"Since what?" I foolishly asked.

He took my hand again, giving me puppy dog eyes. "Since I've had...sex. You, beautiful lady, could ease some of my grief on my...anniversary."

The bartender plunked my plastic bagged food order on the counter and jovially said, "Happy anniversary, Steve." He grinned at my shocked expression. "Steve's wife dumped him a year ago. Can't imagine why."

I yanked my hand free from Steve's clammy claw, slipped off my chair, and snatched my order off the bar while trying to think of something blistering to say. I picked up my wine and considered tossing the contents in his face but didn't want to waste eight bucks. I'd have a million brilliant zingers later, but at that moment I came up with zip, so I gathered my dignity and turned to stomp out.

Instead, Steve had the last line. "So I take it a blow job's out of the question?"

CHAPTER THIRTY-NINE

Posted by Katy McKenna

After Daisy's morning tinkle-tour, I poured water into the coffeemaker and inspected my coffee choices. Decaf crud or caffeinated crud and not enough powdered creamer crud or real sugar. "Daisy, I've a feeling we're not at the Mantra Motel anymore."

I sat on the mini-patio and thought about what I should do today. Go home was probably the right answer, but I was still curious about which house on Cranston Lane had been the family mansion. With that decided, I booked the room for another night and then called room service and ordered my usual coffee shop breakfast: scrambled eggs, crispy hash browns, rye toast.

While I waited, I group texted Mom, Pop, Sam, and Ruby: *All good. Daisy is an awesome road warrior. Not sure what I'm doing today, but staying in Palo Alto another night. Maybe two. XOX.* I typed slow and carefully, then reread the message before sending and was proud to see no spelling errors.

After that, I went online to find the Cranston address but had no luck. Not a surprise considering how many years ago the grand-parents left the area.

I recalled that when I was tracking down info about my bigamist great-great-grandfather on PedigreeTree.com, I had access to all sorts of public records: marriage and divorce certificates, death certificates and census records. The census records had addresses listed.

I logged into my account and clicked on census and voter lists. The search filters were: town, state, year—1790 through the 1900's. I clicked on the 1960's when Erin's father would have been a kid living in the house. Then edited my search to:

William Cranston
Location: Atherton, San Mateo County, CA.
Gender: Male.
Collection focus: United States.

Then I hit Search, and a little pop-up told me there is a rule that keeps census data private for seventy-two years.

My meal arrived, and one look told me I should have said, "Extra-extra crispy hash browns. Please don't dry up the eggs. And let the toast actually get toasty."

After breakfast, I called the library and asked if they had phone books from the 1960's and 1970's.

"Excuse me?" said the fellow on the other end. "I didn't quite catch all that."

I asked again, speaking slowly and concisely.

"I thought that's what you said but wanted to be sure. I'm sorry, but the answer is no. We don't have room to store old phone books. Sorry, I can't help you."

"That's okay. Thanks anyway."

"Oh, wait!" said Library Man. "Check the Library of Congress online. They might have a database of old phone books. Anyway, it's worth a try."

It turned out to be a good idea—if you live in Washington D.C. and can walk into the building and ask to see the records.

I checked the time and was surprised I'd frittered away the entire morning. After a shower and makeup, I thought of another way to find the address.

My killer cousin and I had connected through our family trees. Maybe I would find something in hers that would give me the answer. I logged onto the site, then found her tree. Above her photo were her parents. I clicked on her father's photo and lo and behold, it expanded into a box with his address at birth. I did a seated happy-dance, congratulating myself on my super sleuthing skills.

I Google-mapped the address, then went to *street view*. I remembered the ornate wrought iron gates from my cruise down the street the day before. In street view, I couldn't see much, but in satellite view, I could see everything.

The Cranston lot was the largest on the block. The huge house had a back lawn large enough to host a soccer tournament. Beyond that, an Olympic-sized pool and cabaña, a tennis court, and a building that looked like a small home. The patio area off the main house was resort size. The ultimate staycation home.

―――――

On Cranston Lane, I drove by number 322 and continued to the end of the block and parked around the corner. The sun was tilting to the west, and a gentle breeze made it feel like the low sixties, so I slipped on my navy cardigan.

"Watson? Let's get snoopy."

We sauntered along the side of the road until we reached the address. As I stepped onto the wide driveway of 322, I slowed my pace and peered through the gates at the property, but could see only a sliver of the stately gray stone house. I didn't dawdle because there was a video camera watching me.

Back at the car, I gave Daisy a drink of water, then searched 322 Cranston Lane's current status on my cellphone.

- Off-market.
- Built in 1888.
- 22,000 square feet. *Whoa!*
- 2.4 acres. *You can bet it was a lot more land when it was originally built.*
- Twelve bedrooms
- Nine bathrooms
- Pool
- Pool house
- Putting green
- Tennis court
- 1,200 square foot guest house
- Last sold: March 2002.

I turned on Cranston Lane for one final drive-by. Next door to the Cranston home, a large empty lot had a temporary-looking chain link fence across the front, as if someone was getting ready for construction. The property was choked with tall weeds and shrubs, and the fence leaned flat to the ground in a couple of places. I thought about walking through the lot to see if I could get a look at the Cranston estate's backyard. But would I get in trouble for trespassing?

I parked down the street and Google-mapped the area. I found 322 Cranston and the empty lot next door, 320. Then I looked up the address on Twillow. 1.98 acres. Built in 1921. Six bedrooms, four baths. Last sold in February 2007.

There was no house there now, so whoever bought it must have torn it down and then had to walk away from the project. Probably when the economy slumped.

I turned to Daisy in the backseat. "Change of plans, kid."

We hustled back to the empty lot and edged the fence line to a spot where a panel was flat on the ground, and stepped across.

If anyone asks what I'm doing, I'll say I'm interested in the property. I caught sight of my ratty cross trainers and wrinkled jeans. *I'll say I'm looking at some properties for my...my aunt, uh, Aunt Martha Stewart. Yeah, that's it. She's sick of the snow and thinking about building a home out here.*

We tramped through the tall weeds to the back of the lot. On the Cranston side, I saw the peak of a building beyond the high stone wall and figured it must be the guest house. A sprawling oak with low slung branches grew close to the wall. I climbed aboard to take a peek while Daisy did sentry duty.

Yup. It was the guest house. A flagstone path from the front door led to a sitting area with a white pillared pergola draped in purple wisteria.

"HGTV should do a series on guest houses," I whispered down to Daisy. "*Guest House Hunters.*" I snapped a few photos to send to Sam.

A twig snapped, and I froze. Daisy growled, low and menacing.

Scrambling off the tree limb, I grabbed her leash and tried to pull her behind the oak tree, but she was rooted to the spot, her back hair puffed like a porcupine.

"Seth? Is that you?" called a male voice. "Come on, dude. Quit screwin' around. Did you score anything?

Oh crud. Have I stumbled into a den of drug dealers or burglars? Daisy's rumbling growl intensified and I crouched, holding her close. Footsteps crunched on dead leaves as the thug moved closer.

"Shhh," I whispered in her ear. She struggled against my arms and wrenched free, toppling me over on my rear-end.

"What're you doing?" asked a gruff voice. He was holding Daisy's leash and petting her.

I scrambled to my feet and snatched the leash from his hand, trying to look bold—and not feeling it. "I'm walking my dog, and she wanted to explore back here. That's all."

He looked mid-twenties, tall, nice-looking in a scruffy kind of way, dressed in a red plaid flannel and jeans. Not what I would call your typical criminal—as if I'd know. "Did *she* send you to spy on us?"

"Who're you talking about?" I asked.

"The woman who's been prowling around here lately. Have you seen her?"

"No."

"Well, if you do, my advice is to steer clear." He tapped his temple. "There's something not-quite-right about her."

"What do you mean?"

"She yells at my friend and me to get off her property. Shit, this isn't her property. This is free land, and we have squatter's rights. That woman is disturbing the sanctity of our home."

"Does she live around here?"

"She's staying over there." He pointed at the estate on the other side of the vacant lot that was not the Cranston property.

He thrust out a hand. "I should introduce myself. I'm Jessie."

"Katy." We shook hands. "Tell me more about the crazy lady."

"Not much to tell, really. She just showed up one day. The family that lives there seems to have vanished. They have little kids who're usually running around in the yard. Even the dog's not barking. I kind of miss all the commotion. One of the problems with squatting is you spend most of your time hiding from the neighbors, so I have no idea where they've gone."

"What does she look like?"

"Like money, you know? Classy, slim. In her twenties, I guess. Short blonde hair. If she wasn't such a bitch, I'd even say she's good-looking."

Darn it. Definitely not her. Although she could have bleached her hair, and I suppose she could pass for in her twenties. Late twenties.

"There's a slight chance I may know who she is. And if it *is* her, the police are looking for her."

Jessie crossed his arms, looking impressed. "Really? You a cop or something?"

I laughed, stalling to think up an excuse. "No. No. I'm a private investigator."

That wasn't a total lie. I was investigating if asking questions counts, and I'm a private citizen. Plus, I did that stakeout with Josh and got paid for my services. Ergo, I'm a professional private investigator.

"A P.I. That is so cool. The trail led you here?"

"Yes. Well, almost. I actually thought she might be at that house over there." I pointed behind me at the Cranston mansion.

He rubbed his hands together with a grin. "So what's your next move?"

"I need to get a look at her to confirm her identity." I knew it wasn't her, but I didn't want to disappoint my new friend. "Wouldn't want to call the police on an innocent person." It was time to change the subject before I told any more fibs. I glanced around. "So where do you live?"

Jessie nodded at a grove of trees. "We got a sweet setup back there. Nice tent under the trees. Even got Wi-Fi. It's surprising how many people don't lock down their internet access."

"I can't see it."

"That's the beauty of it. We're totally concealed by all the trees and shrubbery. We've been living there for almost a year now, not bothering anyone. Until that bitch, excuse my language, that woman showed up and started prowling around." Jessie looked beyond me, toward the street. "Ah. Here comes my compadre."

A stubby, bushy-bearded man in gray sweats was pushing a rusty ten-speed and toting a bulging grocery bag. His steps slowed as he drew near.

"It's all right, Seth. This is Katy. She's a private investigator, and she's looking for a woman who may be our new neighbor."

"Is she in some kind of trouble?" asked Seth. "Please say yes."

"If it's her, then the answer is yes. But it's highly unlikely. The person I'm looking for is probably out of the country."

Ernie set his bike down and handed the cloth bag to Jessie.

"What'd you score?" asked Jessie, jiggling it.

"Homemade tamales."

He peeked in the sack. "Did Grandma Rosita make them?"

"Yeah. I stopped by to give her some money on the way home, and she'd just made a batch."

Give his grandma money? But he's homeless.

"How was work today?" asked Jessie.

He works?

"Scored some good tips," said Seth, then glanced at me. "Jessie and I work at a carwash."

"You have jobs, but you live in a tent?" I said. "Sorry, that was kind of rude."

"Don't worry about it," said Jessie. "Sometimes, if we're lucky, we have two or three jobs. The rents are ridiculous around here, and ever since the economy slumped, it's been impossible to find jobs in our field."

"What did you used to do?" I asked.

"I was an Applications Development Manager for a start-up company that went under."

"And you, Seth?"

"Software development at the same company. That's where I met Jessie. Wanna see our humble abode?"

They led me through the bushes to a clearing where the spacious tent was staked. High in a tree, they had rigged up solar panels. Inside the tent were two neatly made inflatable beds, two vintage recliners, and a folding table and chair set.

"This is great." I glanced around. "So, uh, what about a…."

Ernie grinned. "Bathroom? Follow me."

Behind the tent were a portable camping toilet and shower.

"This is our biggest crime, right here." Jessie pointed at a hose.

"It's connected to a hose bib in the back of the property line. I doubt anyone over there even knows of its existence."

"Well, I gotta say, I'm impressed with you guys," I said. "And now I need to get going."

My new pals escorted Daisy and me to the chain link fence. "So what's your next move?" said Jessie.

"Since it's getting close to dark now, I'll come back in the morning and try to catch a glimpse of her."

"We both got an early shift at the carwash," said Jessie, "but we want to know what happens. Let me put my number in your phone."

———

I stopped at a wine shop and purchased a bottle of Syrah and some snacks for later. Back at the hotel, I poured a glass, then checked my messages. There was a voicemail from Josh.

"Hey, cupcake. How long is this road trip going to be? I miss you. Call me."

I miss him, too. Oh, how I miss him. However I don't want to talk to him. But I didn't want to hurt his feelings, so I called. After two rings, I disconnected with relief and texted: *I called, but you didn't pick up. Hope everything's okay with Nicole. Really tired and going to bed early.* Then I realized it was only a little past five-thirty, so I added: *Grubbing dinner first.* I meant to type *grabbing*, but oh well.

I called Sam with an update on what I'd learned that day. She got upset about my plan to try and verify if the woman that was harassing the tent-boys was Erin.

"I think you should call that Detective what's-her-name."

"It's Murphy."

"Whatever. Let her decide what to do, instead of putting yourself in danger," said Sam.

"And tell her what? That there's a bitchy woman who doesn't

like the tent-boys? I don't want to risk getting Jessie and Seth in trouble for nothing."

"I still think you should call her," she said, sounding grumpy. "That guy said she looked classy and rich. Erin looked classy and rich, too. She sure had me fooled."

"I think a lot of people look like that in this town."

"The thing is, Katy. If that woman's so upset about those guys living in the tent, why hasn't she called the police? Isn't that what most people would do? Unless they're wanted by the police."

CHAPTER FORTY

WEDNESDAY • MARCH 11
Posted by Katy McKenna

Saturday, March 7
Part One

My phone hollered, "Time to get up, Sleepy Head. NOW!" I thought it was hilarious when I downloaded the alarm app, but it's not that funny at six-thirty in the morning. After getting dressed and slapping on a little makeup, I fed Daisy and turned on *Animal Planet* so she wouldn't get lonely while I was gone. When she saw me sling my purse over my shoulder, she pranced around the door, ready for action.

"Sorry, kiddo, but Mama can't take you this time. I need to be real sneaky, and that's not one of your strong suits."

She disagreed, but I slipped out the door while she was distracted by a dog cookie.

I parked at the end of Cranston Lane and donned my sleuthing disguise—baseball cap and sunglasses, then zipped my phone and keys into my black windbreaker pocket. The overcast morning was a damp and chilly 53, so I zipped to my chin, wishing I'd layered with a sweater.

Staying in the shadows, I crept down the street. Before crossing the bitchy lady's cobblestone driveway, I peeked around the entrance pillar to make sure no one was in the front yard.

At the far end of the vacant property, I hunted for something to stand on so I could look over the stone wall. I remembered a picnic bench outside the tent and lugged it to the wall.

The estate's native drought-tolerant landscaping had spacious areas for lounging and entertaining. On the far side of the yard, a whimsical tree house clung to a sprawling oak tree, and was surrounded by a play area and a bike path. I snapped a few photos, focusing mainly on the guest home, thinking if the woman the boys had complained about truly was Erin, maybe she was renting it. It was single level, with a courtyard sitting area. I texted the pictures to Samantha, then decided to give her a quick call.

"Hey! I wasn't sure if you were at work or not, but I had to call. Check your texts, I just sent some photos."

"Okay. Checking. Oh, wow. Casey would go nuts over that tree house. Do people really live like this?"

"They do here," I said. "I doubt there are any homes like this in Santa Lucia. It's all the techie money up here. Bill Gates—"

"Pretty sure he lives in the Seattle area. On Lake Washington in a mega-house," said Sam.

"Jeff Bezos—"

"Him, too. I think."

"Okay. The Google people," I said.

Suddenly, something sharp dug into my back. I dropped my phone and almost tumbled off the bench. Clutching the mossy stone wall, I turned to see Erin pressing a shushing finger over her smiling lips. Her other hand held a gun. She handed my phone to me and whispered, "Time to say bye-bye, Katy."

"Uh, Sa-man-tha?" I said.

"What happened?" said Sam.

"I dropped the phone. Got to go now. Love you."

Sam hollered. "Wait! Do you see—"

Staring down at my nemesis, I ended the call.

"Heard you visiting the squatters yesterday. I couldn't believe it when I heard your voice," said Erin, shaking her bleached blonde head. "You're supposed to be dead. At first I thought I'd have to kill all of you, right then and there, but then you said you'd be back this morning and those losers said they'd be at work." She laughed. "Sure would've been difficult dealing with so many dead bodies. Guess where I've been hiding?"

"I have no idea." I tried to sound bold, but was terrified that my luck had run out.

"In the tent. I watched you get the bench. Could have stopped you right then but wanted to see what you'd do." She expelled an exasperated sigh. "Get down."

I was trembling so hard I had to crouch and grip the edge of the bench to step off. "What're you going to do?"

She shook her head like I was a petulant child. "I already spared you once and look how that turned out."

"You left me to die. How was that sparing me?"

Erin regarded me with cold eyes. "Point taken. But you being alive has really screwed things up for me." She snorted a laugh. "Enough with the chit-chat. Let's go, cousin."

"Where?"

She gnawed her lower lip—a habit I'd found endearing before all the bad stuff happened. "To the house. For now." She waved the black automatic. "Just walk along like we're besties. If we see someone and you do anything to get their attention, you'll both be dead. I'm already wanted for one murder, so what's a couple more?"

She had a point, and the gun sealed the deal. As I stumbled through the weeds, panic gripped my heart, and I could barely catch my breath. "Hold on a sec." I bent over, hands on knees, trying to breathe.

"Wow. Talk about out of shape."

I glanced up at her. "I'm not out of shape, Erin. I'm scared."

"Too bad you're so goddamn greedy. You just had to try and get the money back, didn't you? Big mistake."

"I know you won't believe this, but I was on a road trip, and you're the last person I expected to see."

"And yet, here you are." She waved her gun-free hand, taking in her family's former home on one side of the vacant lot, and the house on the other side that she was staying in. "Snooping around. So no, I don't believe you."

"I heard the story about your parents and wanted to see what your father walked away from so he could marry your mother and raise you. By the way, they miss you." I was stalling, hoping I'd see someone pass by on the street that I could scream "call the police" to.

"How would you know?"

"I met them. Nice people. You know, they're my relatives, too."

"Did you tell my parents what I did?"

"No. But I know the police have."

Her shoulders sagged, but the gun aimed at me never wavered. "You really shouldn't have come here, Katy."

"I thought you were in Costa Rica."

"That's what you were supposed to think."

"What about Tyler? He sure sounded like that was the plan."

"It was never the plan. He just didn't know it." Erin stepped behind me and jabbed the gun in my ribs. "You're breathing fine now, so let's go."

At the home's driveway entrance, Erin poked a code into the security keypad, and the double gates swung open. All business now, she picked up the pace, directing me toward the main house's front entrance. She used a code to open the double door, and ushered me into an expansive two-story foyer where we were greeted by a tiny, cheerful Yorkie.

"Hey, there's my little Lulu." She scooped up the dog with one hand while still keeping the damned gun on me. She nuzzled the dog's head. "Have you been a good girl?"

"Is that your dog?"

"Yes. Remember I told you I had a Yorkie."

"I figured that was a lie, too. Don't the people who own this house have a dog?" The tent-boys had mentioned a barking dog.

"They do. But he was big and too rough with Lulu, so I—"

"Oh my God. You didn't kill it, did you?"

"No. What do you take me for? I would never hurt an animal. I'm boarding him at a kennel. A nice one. I even paid for daily walks."

She pointed down a hallway. "There's a huge closet in the hall that locks. More like a room, actually. Don't try anything funny with me, because I swear I'll use the gun." She laughed, kissing Lulu's nose. "Mommy sounds like some cheesy thug on a cop show, doesn't she?"

I led the way through the art-lined passage to a wood plank arched door. She set Lulu down and inserted an old skeleton key into the lock. "Pretty cool, huh? They got this antique door at a salvage yard."

As she pulled the door open and turned on the light, I said, "Whose house is this?" I was playing for time, hoping I could get the upper hand and snatch the gun.

"Funny story." She leaned against the doorjamb, directing the gun at my soft belly. "Around the same time I connected with you, I hooked up with an old high school friend on Facebook. Turns out she'd always wondered what had happened to me way back when. I wasn't about to tell her the truth, so I said my father died suddenly, and my brokenhearted mother had taken me to live with relatives in France. This house belongs to her, and I'm housesitting while she and her family are on an extended trip in Europe. And you want to know the funny part?"

No. "What?"

"Amelia was so, so grateful that I would do this huge favor for her." She laughed, shaking her head. "What she doesn't know is I knew she lived on Cranston Lane and that's the reason I Facebooked her. Then right before they were scheduled to leave, she posted that she was in a panic because their housesitter had been hit by a car—a hit and run." Erin shook her head. "I tell you, people shouldn't post so much about their personal life. I mean, I never would've known about Amelia's trip or who her housesitter was if they hadn't been commenting back and forth. Everything they posted was coming through my newsfeed. Luckily, Sara, the housesitter, will survive, but she's in pretty bad shape. So I stepped up and offered to housesit."

"You mean you hit the housesitter with your car?"

"In my defense, I didn't mean to hit her *that* hard. Just enough to put her out of commission for a while, but it's hard to judge these things. Plus, she was walking her dog, and I had to swerve so I wouldn't hit it." She shrugged with a wry smile. "It's kind of like kismet, don't you think? Everything is finally going my way. I'm living on Cranston Lane, and thanks to you, it won't be long before I own the family mansion."

"You do realize the police are looking for you, right?" I said. "The minute you try to buy that house, they'll arrest you."

"The cops think I'm in Costa Rica, remember? And it's not like I'll use my real name. I've already sold a few coins in Las Vegas to keep me in cash. Going to Vegas was the one good idea that Tyler had. It was incredibly easy to find a buyer who didn't ask questions there. When I get them all sold, I'll set up a dummy off-shore corporation to buy the house. When the time is right, I'll make them an offer they can't refuse."

"What if they won't sell?"

"You know what they say, everyone has a price."

"Where are you keeping the coins?" I asked.

"Katy. Get real. Do you really think I would tell you that? Trust me, they're hidden where no one will ever find them." She pushed away from the doorjamb. "It was fun having this little catch-up, but I've got things to do, so in you go."

I stepped into the spacious linen closet, and just as she was closing the door, my phone chirped a text alert in my pocket.

She held out her hand. "I'll take that."

The illuminated face said the text was from Samantha.

Erin glanced at the phone. "What's your password? I'll answer Sam's text for you, so she won't worry."

I kept my mouth shut.

Erin glanced at my shoes, making her point loud and clear. "Remember when I almost shot your toe off?"

"1776."

"How patriotic." She slammed the door in my face and locked it.

I tied my windbreaker around my waist and slumped against the wall on the tile floor. I knew there wouldn't be any last-minute reprieves this time.

"Oh, God. Daisy. She's going to be so scared." I thought about her trapped and frightened in the hotel room, not knowing where her mama was. I ripped the baseball cap off my head and flung it. "How could I be so damned stupid?" I sobbed, gasping convulsively. "Why did I do this? Why? Why? Why?"

I was close to hyperventilating and had to get control of myself, or I didn't stand a chance. I stood and leaned over, forcing myself to breathe slow, deep breaths. Gradually, I regained control.

The roughly eight-by-ten closet was neatly organized with labeled places for everything. Turkish towels, Egyptian cotton sheets, cashmere blankets, down pillows, toilet paper, French milled soap.

I tossed the shelves, and dumped every bin looking for something I could use as a weapon. I found a label maker and typed:

Erin Cranston killed Katy McKenna. When the machine expelled the tape, I stuck it on a wall where someone would see it when they cleaned up this mess. Then I realized Erin would be the one putting the linens back, so I refolded a stack of towels and stuck the label on the last one, then set the pile on the proper shelf. Someday, someone would see it and tell the police what happened to me.

I hid the label maker, in case I got more information about my fate. Then a niggle of hope bubbled up. Erin couldn't kill me in the closet. She would have to take me somewhere else. That meant I still had a chance.

CHAPTER FORTY-ONE

THURSDAY • MARCH 12
Posted by Katy McKenna

Saturday, March 7
Part Two

After ransacking the linen room, I sat on a pile of snowy-white blankets to figure out an escape plan. It had been about thirty minutes since Erin had locked me in, so time was running out.

The only exit was the sturdy wood door. It opened outward—a good idea because it left more wall space for storage. But bad for me because I couldn't hide behind the door when Erin opened it.

My first idea was to stand flat against the wall nearest to the door handle. That way she wouldn't immediately see me when the door opened out into the hall. Then as she stepped in, I would jump her and shove her into the wall, then grab the gun and run. And probably get shot before I could wrestle the weapon out of her hand.

I closed my eyes, forcing myself to think and not let fear overwhelm me again.

When she comes through the door, I could fling a sheet over her head, and while she's flailing around, I'll run out and lock her in the closet. Except she'll have the damned key, so I can't lock the door. Then she'll chase me through the house and shoot me.

I inhaled a deep breath, willing the oxygen to rev up my sluggish gray matter.

I could twist a sheet into a rope and fling it around her neck and strangle her. And probably get shot during the struggle. Really like the strangling part, though.

I...could.... My eyes darted around the room for inspiration. *I could stuff a sheet into a pillowcase and wallop her with it. Then when she doubles over, bash her in the head—knocking her to the floor, then snatch the gun. Then lock her in the closet.*

"That might work!" I grabbed a king pillowcase, and jammed a sheet into it and swung it around.

"Shit! This won't do anything. It needs to be heavier."

I crammed another sheet inside the pillowcase, but it still wasn't heavy enough to knock her off her feet.

"So much for that brilliant idea." I dropped the sack, feeling desperate. "God, I'm running out of time."

A blue plastic five-gallon water jug sat in the corner. I raised it a few inches off the floor. It must have weighed forty or fifty pounds, so hitting Erin with it wasn't happening.

"Think, Katy. She's gonna be back any minute."

Maybe if the jug was empty, I could hit her with it. But what do I do with all the water? I can't pour it on the floor. It'll flow under the door and Erin will see it before she opens it. I dragged the jug to the middle of the room, pried off the cap, and poured the water on the pillowcase until the sheets inside had soaked up about two gallons. Now the jug weight was manageable. I did a few experimental swings with it, but I couldn't get a good grip on the short neck or the inset handle. It was too cumbersome with the water whooshing back and forth inside and I doubted I could inflict any damage with it. I set the jug in the corner and looked at the drenched sack of sheets. I swung the cotton bag back and forth a few times, spraying water on the walls and floor. It was heavy but manageable.

"I can definitely do some damage with this."

Now surging with a fresh rush of adrenaline, I felt proud for not giving up. "Just call me Katy MacGyver."

I leaned against the wall and waited. Finally, I heard Erin's shoes tapping in the hall. Feet spread wide for good balance, I held my hefty, dripping weapon, ready to wallop the bitch to kingdom come.

"Katy!" She slipped the key into the lock. "Sorry, it took so long. I needed to make some, uh, arrangements."

Ready.

The key turned.

Set.

The door swung open. "Time to come out," said Erin from the hall.

I held my breath, willing her to step inside.

"Not funny, Katy. Did you forget I have a gun? Get out here. Now!"

I was terrified, but I knew this might be my only chance to get the upper hand, so I waited.

"Okay, have it your way. But don't say I didn't warn you." Erin's designer-shod foot stepped over the threshold.

GO!

I swung the sack with everything I had, aiming for her belly, but slamming her in the kneecaps. She pitched forward, slipping on the wet tiles and went down with an "Ooof." Her forehead smashed into the floor, and she was out cold.

I raised the bag high, prepared to drop it and crush her pretty face into the floor, then hesitated. Hitting her the first time had been easy—knowing it was my only chance to save myself. But looking down at her defenseless body, I had second thoughts. I'd never hurt anyone on purpose before. I can't even kill spiders. Was I ready to be a cold-blooded murderer? I was not.

When Erin went down, the gun had skittered out of her hand. I scanned the floor, not seeing it. I thought maybe it had slid under the shelves. I stepped one foot over Erin, and as my other foot followed, she grabbed my ankle and jerked me off balance. I tried to catch myself but went down hard. On my butt. On her head.

I scrambled away, ready to battle, but she lay still. Blood oozed from her face, pooling around her head. I've seen how bloody a broken nose can be, so I assumed that was the source. She was definitely unconscious this time, but I gave her a hard poke in the ribs with my foot to be sure.

Keeping an eye on Erin, I crawled around searching for the gun, and saw its muzzle peeking out from under the pile of blankets. I cautiously turned it so I could grab the handle. Once I had a firm grip on it, I stood, aiming the weapon at my cousin as I edged my way around her. I backed out of the room, then remembered I needed the key to lock the door. It wasn't on the floor, so it had to be in her hand. The hand I could see wasn't holding the key, and her other hand was wedged under her body. At that moment, I was winning the war, but the tables could turn quickly if I moved her and she woke up. It wasn't worth the risk.

In the hallway, a hideous marble-topped Victorian sideboard sat about three feet from the door. I shoved the heavy piece across the tiled floor, screeching a trail of scratches until it was planted in front of the linen door. In her condition, I didn't think Erin would be able to push the door open, but if she tried, I'd hear the cabinet moving.

I dashed to the kitchen, set the gun on the counter, and did a three-sixty, taking in the French country all-white kitchen and great room. Lulu was whining in a pink dog crate under a rustic harvest table.

"Hey, sweetheart." I slipped a finger through the wire door and touched her nose. "It'll be okay."

Private

Some things can't be shared with anyone.

I went back to looking for a phone. "I must really be behind the times. I thought every kitchen had a phone."

I spotted Erin's handbag on a kitchen chair. My phone was inside, and as I was about to press 911, I remembered the coins. I assumed they had to be somewhere in the house so she'd have easy access. I knew I should call the police immediately, but once they showed up, the place would turn into a circus. If my coins were in the house, they'd become evidence, and who knew if I'd ever get them back.

I tucked the cellphone in my pocket, grabbed the gun, and ran back to the linen closet. "Erin! Where'd you hide the money?"

No answer.

"You're going to prison. Probably for life. So you might as well tell me."

Still no answer.

I figured the logical place to search would be the bedroom she was using. I rushed down the hall checking every room I passed with no luck.

Back in the foyer, I raced up the stairs and turned right at the top. First door was a fairytale nursery. Next, a princess bedroom and bath. Then a toy room, and after that, a Star Wars bedroom and bathroom. I spun around and headed in the other direction. The first room was a luxurious master bedroom suite. Beyond that the hall turned to the left, leading to three more bedrooms—one with an unmade bed and clothes strewn on the floor.

"Gotcha!"

I set the gun on the dresser. Top drawer: undies, socks. Second: nighties. Third: t-shirts and such. Fourth: Jeans. Then I had an alarming thought—my fingerprints. If the cops dusted for prints in her bedroom, they'd want to know why I'd rifled through her things before I called them. I slipped a pair of socks on my hands, wiped down everything I'd touched, then continued.

There was nothing under the bed. The closet was crammed with trendy clothes, most still sporting tags. I flipped through the expensive garments. "Been having some fun at my expense, haven't you, Erin?" A shoebox caught my eye—or rather the label did. Christian Louboutin $945. I moved on to the bathroom. When I finished, I was still coin-less, and the suite looked like a crime scene.

I sat on the bed, seething with rage and frustration. Then I remembered Erin's words, "Trust me, they're hidden where nobody will ever find them."

I stood and kicked at the pile of size four designer jeans on the floor, screaming, "You win, Erin. Hope you enjoy never getting to spend another penny of it while you rot in prison."

Halfway down the hall, I halted, trying to capture an impression tickling the periphery of my brain. I glanced around, shaking my head. "What?"

I returned to the bedroom and stood in the doorway, scanning the area for a clue. I opened the spacious closet and stepped back, taking in the contents. The tickle shouted, *You're getting warm.*

I scrolled through the outfits again, slowly this time. The tickle said, *Keep going, you're getting warmer.* I came to a classic taupe sheath dress and matching jacket. As I slid it aside, the hanger stalled on the metal rod. I lifted it, and it was unusually heavy for a summery linen outfit.

The little tickle screamed, *Watch out for third degree burns!*

I peeked down the neck of the dress. A rectangle nylon bag resembling a long, flat fanny pack dangled from the hanger. I unclipped the tan bag and placed it on the bed.

Two zippered pockets ran the length of the foot long bag. Inside one were six slots meant for credit cards and ID. I poked a finger in a slot and discovered four gold coins tucked inside. My fingers shook as I searched each slot. Twenty-four coins in all. The other compartment held three rubber-banded stacks of cash. I slipped one out, fanning through it. Every single one was a hundred dollar bill.

I counted the bundle. "One, two, three, four, five, six." I stopped. "What was that noise?" I put the cash back in the money belt, then grabbed the gun from the dresser and sneaked down the curved staircase. At the bottom, I peeked around the corner. The sideboard looked slightly askew.

I tiptoed to the buffet. It had been moved a couple inches. Just enough to make the screechy sound. The door was ajar, and through the crack I could make out the crown of Erin's head on the floor, her face mashed against the travertine tiles. The bloody fingers of one hand were wedged in the open door so I couldn't close it.

"Erin? Move your hand." She didn't move. Not even a twitch. "Dammit. Now, what do I do?"

I thought about slamming the door and crushing her fingers, but the mere thought gave me the willies. Then I remembered the pool cues in the game room I'd passed by while hunting for Erin's room. I fetched one and used it to shove her limp hand out of the doorway, then closed the door and snugged the table back in place.

Returning to Erin's bedroom, I removed the black windbreaker tied around my waist and strapped on the money belt. I slipped my jacket over it, zipped it halfway, and checked my image in the full-length mirror on the wall.

"Sure hope the cops don't frisk me, or the jig is up." At the doorway, I scanned the messy room and decided I had no idea what happened up here.

Downstairs, I listened for signs of life in the linen closet and heard nothing. It was time to call the police. I went to the kitchen, set the gun on the counter and pulled out my cellphone. I pressed 9, and then was sidetracked by shouts in the backyard. I gazed out the paned-glass windows facing the yard and saw the tent-boys banging on the guesthouse door.

I opened the French doors and hollered, "Hey, guys!" I wasn't sure if they could hear me over the chop-chop of a helicopter passing. "Up here!"

They saw me waving and sprinted to the flagstone patio steps.

"What's going on?" yelled Jessie.

"Get inside." I gestured them through the door. "Can't hear you with that noisy helicopter."

"We saw the bench against the wall and got worried." Seth glanced around the kitchen. "What're you doing inside this house?"

"Is she here?" whispered Jessie. "And is she the woman you're looking for?"

"Yes to both questions," I said.

"Where is she?" asked Seth.

"I've got her barricaded in a closet. I was about to call the police when I saw you guys out there."

Concern pinched Seth's shaggy eyebrows "Your forehead's bleeding. You've got a pretty big goose egg."

I touched it and came away with sticky blood on my fingers. "Didn't even realize it. Must've happened during my scuffle with Erin."

"You better put some ice on that," said Jessie.

"I need to call the cops, first."

"You're trembling." Seth pulled a barstool out from the counter, took my arm and eased me into it. "I'll call. You sit."

"Thanks. I guess the adrenaline rush is over."

Jessie wrapped a handful of ice in a blue dish towel and handed it to me. He returned to the refrigerator and removed a beer. "After what you've been through, I think you could use this. It's on the house," he said with a wink.

I sipped the cold microbrew and listened to Seth make the phone call. Then it hit me. My friends were squatters on private property! "You guys need to get out of here. If the cops find out where you're living, they'll kick you out."

"We know. But it's all good." Jessie glanced at Seth. "We've been saving to go backpacking in Europe, and we've got more than enough now, so it's time for us to get out there and see the world."

"Yeah, this is the kick-in-the-butt we needed." Seth shoved his phone back into his jeans pocket.

Less than a minute later, someone pounded on the front door. "Police!"

"Whoa! That was fast." I slipped off the barstool and then I noticed the freaked-out look on Seth's face. I turned and saw three cops on the patio, guns aimed at us. They opened the French doors and stepped inside.

An officer yelled, "Down on the floor. Hands behind your head!"

Hands in the air, I screamed, "Please don't shoot. We're the good guys!"

Those first minutes were terrifying. The cops had a photo of me, but it wasn't until I vouched for Jessie and Seth that the diligent officers finally holstered their weapons.

One of the cops, a fierce looking bald man, showed me a picture of Erin. "Is this the woman, ma'am?"

"Yes, that's her. Erin Cranston. I have her locked in a closet in the hallway."

"Is she armed?" he said, all business.

"No, sir. I got the gun away from her and put it on the counter by the fridge." I pointed. "Over there."

I expected the officer to be impressed that an untrained civilian had apprehended a murderer and had her secured in a closet, but he acted like it was no big deal.

He picked up the gun. "All right, I want all of you outside. Officer Carpelli will escort you."

"Wait a sec," I said. "How'd you guys get here so fast?"

"We got a call from the Santa Lucia police department. A detective there had reason to believe you were in danger."

Samantha must have called Detective Murphy. I felt a surge of sisterly love hug my heart. *Thank you, dear friend.*

The street was blocked on both sides by squad cars with lights flashing. A fire truck and a paramedics van idled at the curb. Beyond the police cars were a crowd of curious neighbors and two local TV station news vans. A reporter shouted, "Can you tell us what's happening in there?"

"Justice!" I yelled with a fist pump.

———

*Quick note here: Wouldn't you think that a police helicopter would be black and white with "Police" in bold letters on the sides? The one that had been hovering overhead was cobalt blue, and I didn't see any police insignia on it. For all I knew it was someone buzzing the neighborhood.

CHAPTER FORTY-TWO

THURSDAY • MARCH 12
Guest Posted by Samantha Drummond

Katy asked me to post about what happened
on my end after Erin caught her.

———

Anybody who knows my best friend knows she's never been a spontaneous person. For example: I couldn't get Katy to try another flavor of ice cream besides vanilla until she was fourteen. That's when she discovered mint chip. So this sudden road trip of hers was totally out of character. But I understood her need to get away.

When Katy called me while spying on the house she thought Erin might be staying in, and then abruptly hung up, I got concerned. However, the more I thought about it, the more I realized it was highly unlikely that Erin was still in the country, so I quit worrying.

About twenty minutes later, the high school called and told me Chelsea wasn't feeling well.

On the way home, I told Chelsea what Katy was doing.

"Do me a favor. Get my phone out of my purse and text Katy. Tell her I want to know what's going on."

Chelsea sent the text, and a few minutes later, she said, "Katy answered your text. It says, 'Sorry I hung up. I thought I saw Erin. But it wasn't her. LOL. Planning on staying up here for a few more days.'"

"That's a relief."

For the next few minutes, Chelsea stared out the car window, not talking or texting, so I grew concerned. "How bad do you feel, honey? Do we need to go to the doctor?"

"No, I'm thinking about Aunt Katy's text." She glanced at my phone. "You know she's the worst speller on the planet. Like, whenever she texts me, I have trouble trying to figure out what she's saying 'cause she always lets the stupid auto-corrector screw it up. But this text is like perfect."

My heart flip-flopped, and I pulled to the curb and read the text. "That's it. I'm calling the police. But which police? The ones here or up there?"

"I think here," said Chelsea. "They know her."

"You're right about that. They know her all too well." I looked up the police department number, then tried to remember the name of the detective Katy had been working with but drew a blank. "I'll ask for the chief. I hope she's in." It was already over an hour since I'd texted Katy. "If anything has happened to her, I'll never forgive myself."

"Mom, this is so not your fault. And we could be wrong you know."

"I don't think we are. You know what? Let's just go to the police station." I swept her pink-streaked blonde hair back and felt her forehead. "You feel a little warm. Are you up to it?"

"Yeah. It's Aunt Katy."

———

"We need to see the chief. It's an emergency."

"I'm sorry," said the desk clerk. "She's in a meeting. With the mayor. I can't disturb her. Her orders." Then she whispered, "Budget cuts."

"This is going to sound weird, but I think my friend, Katy McKenna, is in danger."

"I know about Ms. McKenna's case. The detective handling it is in. Detective Murphy. I'll call her now."

She had barely hung up when Murphy sprinted down the hallway, clutching a pair of shoes against her chest. "What's going on?" She winced as she slipped on the sensible black leather shoes. "New shoes giving me blisters."

I showed Murphy the photos that Katy had sent me. "She thinks Erin might be staying in this house. It's on the same street that Erin Cranston's grandparents lived on. She was looking over the wall hoping to see her when she snapped these pictures."

The detective took the phone and scrolled through the photos. "Nice house."

"She called me right after she sent those pictures, and then right in the middle of our conversation, she abruptly ended the call."

"You need to see this." Chelsea snatched the phone out of Murphy's hand and showed her Katy's last text message. "Here's why we think Aunt Katy is in trouble. No way did she send this. It's too perfect. Her spelling usually sucks."

"That's not much to go on. A well-spelled text message. Doubt the police up there will be willing to go to the house on something as flimsy as that."

Then Chelsea scrolled through Katy's text message history, and that did it.

"I'm sending those photos to my phone," said Murphy. "Then forward them to the police up there. Got an address?"

"No. But it's on Cranston Avenue."

"No, Mom. Cranston *Lane*," said Chelsea. "At least, that's what you said before."

"Yes, you're right. God, I'm so upset I can't think straight. Cranston Lane."

"I want you to text her now," said Murphy.

"What should I say?"

"Something that she'll know is wrong."

Chelsea tugged my sleeve. "I know, Mom. Tell her I broke up with my boyfriend."

"You don't have a... Oh. Very good, Chelsea."

Chelsea is so bummed. Her boyfriend dumped her.

"I'm going to go contact the Atherton police right now," said the detective. "If you hear back from her, tell the desk clerk to ring me."

When she was halfway down the hall, my phone chirped a text message notification. "Detective Murphy?" I waved my cell at her. "She answered my text."

She limped back to us. "That was fast. Let me see."

It said, *So sorry about that. Poor kid.*

"That seals the deal," said Murphy.

———

Katy, you have no idea how hard it was to know you were with that psycho. For all I knew, my best friend was already dead.

CHAPTER FORTY-THREE

THURSDAY • MARCH 12
Posted by Katy McKenna

Saturday, March 7
Part Three

Jessie, Seth, and I sat on cold, butt-numbing boulders in the front yard of the Cranston mansion waiting to be questioned by the cops. I was starving and had a monster headache.

I still held the dishtowel of ice to my forehead and was trembling so hard my teeth chattered. Jessie took off his hoody and helped me slip it over my windbreaker. He draped his arm over my shoulders and gave me a gentle squeeze. His compassionate gesture brought me close to breaking down.

A hunky paramedic approached with his medical kit to check my injury. When he was satisfied that it was just a nasty bump on my noggin, he cleaned and bandaged it.

Out on the street, a scrawny reporter in a slinky red dress was talking to a video camera. She gestured at the front door of the home, and then over at the boys and me. We all turned away, not wanting our faces plastered on the news, although it was probably too late to avoid that.

I said to Jessie and Seth, "When they haul Erin out in cuffs, then she'll really have something to talk about."

But that didn't happen because Erin was pronounced dead at the scene.

———

A couple hours later, I pulled my phone from my jacket pocket, and Officer Carpelli said, "Who're you calling?"

"My hotel. I left my dog there early this morning thinking I'd only be gone an hour or two."

She glanced at her watch. "What kind of dog do you have?"

"A yellow Lab. Her name's Daisy."

"Hope she hasn't destroyed the room. Go ahead and make your call."

The hotel receptionist immediately put the manager on the line. "Ms. McKenna."

Uh-oh. She sounds mad.

"Your dog..."

There goes my deposit.

"...Has been barking for the last few hours. We've called you several times, but you've ignored our calls, so we had no choice but to call the SPCA."

My poor baby! "Have they taken her away already?" *Please say no.*

"They should be arriving any minute now."

"Please, please don't let them take Daisy. I have a very good excuse."

———

"How much longer do you think they'll keep us here, Katy?" asked Jessie.

"Who knows? I've been stuck at crime scenes before, and we could wind up sitting here all day. I'm sorry you got dragged into this."

"Nah. Don't feel bad." Seth stood and stretched. "Besides, Jessie will undoubtedly incorporate this into one of his books."

"You're an author?"

He shrugged, looking embarrassed. "Fledgling."

"What type of books do you write, Jessie?" I asked.

"True crime."

"Anything published? I'd love to read one."

"No takers as of yet," he said. "I've written three so far. Thinking of going indie. Pretty hard to get a publisher interested when you don't have a book on the bestseller list. It's like trying to get your first job with no job experience, but a heck of a lot harder."

"We should stay in touch," I said. "I have lots of life experience in the true crime genre."

"Being a private investigator, I bet you do," said Seth.

Really need to stop telling so many tall tales. "Well, I haven't been doing it for very long, and it's all pretty boring. But my personal life is a whole different story. The last couple years have been utter chaos. I think I should get one of those coffee mugs with the slogan —*shit happens*, because boy does it ever."

"You're a fascinating person, Katy," said Jessie. "I'm glad we met. I'll definitely take you up on that offer."

"Good. You've got my number." Then I raised my voice so Carpelli could hear me. "I really need to take care of my dog. The manager said if I don't get back to the hotel soon, the SPCA is taking her to the pound. My poor Daisy will think I've abandoned her, just like her first owner did." Another tall tale. The truth was, after the hotel manager heard my story, the kindhearted lady told me not to worry about Daisy.

"If it was up to me, you could go right now," said Carpelli. "Let me see what I can do."

Ten minutes later, we were released with appointments at the police station the next morning.

I inserted the plastic card into the hotel room key slot, and the little red light flashed. Daisy's tail banged a steady beat against the wall on the other side of the hotel room door.

"Hang on, baby. Mama's coming."

I turned the key over and still got the red light. Then I realized I'd been poking in the wrong end. The green light flashed, and I opened the door to my joyful pup.

"Whoa, girl. I'm super happy to see you, too. You have no idea how happy."

At first glance, everything looked in order. The bathroom—not so much. There were a couple puddles on the floor, a stinky gift for me to clean up, and she'd had some fun with the toilet paper.

I pottied Daisy, fed her, then ordered room service. By then, it was pushing four-fifty-five and I was ravenous, so I ordered a big meal, plus dessert. While I waited, I checked my phone for messages. Two from Josh, one from Mom, one from Pop, and three from Ruby. Couldn't talk to Josh because I would have broken down completely. Wasn't ready to listen to Grandma. I called Pop.

"Hey, Katy-did. Are you having a good time?"

I struggled to sound upbeat. "I have a little story to tell you. Mom will need to hear this, too."

"Well, now you're making me nervous. Hold on and I'll get her."

When I was done freaking out my parents, I called Ruby.

She answered on the first ring. "Well, it's about damned time you called," she snapped. "What gives, missy?"

When I finished my tale, she said, "I thought raising a teenage girl had aged me. But you, dear granddaughter, are bound and determined to push me into an early grave. I've got a good mind to move in with you and protect you from yourself. Of all the reckless things you've done this really takes the cake. And furthermore, how could you leave that wonderful man—"

There was a knock on my door. "Grammy. I need to hang up now."

"I'm not done talking."

"Room service is at the door." I opened the door to a nerdy-guy wearing horn rims. The nametag on his polo shirt identified him as Brandon. "I'm talking to my grandmother. Sorry."

She heard that. "Oh. Now you're sorry you're talking to me. That hurts."

"Ruby, hold on." She kept talking as I stuffed the phone under a pillow. "She's upset about what happened to me."

"The staff wants you to know we're all thankful you survived your terrible ordeal, and your dinner's on the house."

That did me in. The tears I'd been holding at bay for hours burst the dam. "Oh, oh, oh. That's so, so nice. Thank you."

Brandon's eyes bugged out and he looked like he wanted to make a run for it. Instead, he set down the dinner tray and dashed to the bathroom for tissues.

"I'm sorry. It's just that—" I choked on hiccuppy sobs. "It's been a really cruddy day."

"I totally understand." He opened a bottle of white wine and poured me a hefty glass. "The bartender said this Viognier would pair well with the salmon."

I sipped the wine and sighed. "Maybe I'll live after all."

Brandon arranged my dinner on the table and pulled out the chair for me.

"Let me get you a tip before you leave," I said.

"No, ma'am. No tip." He backed his way to the door and opened it. "Just relax and enjoy your meal."

I guzzled half the glass of wine before retrieving the phone. My dear grammy was still nattering. "Ruby?" I interrupted. "I love you, and you're my favorite grandma in the whole world. I know how much I've upset you, but I'm fine. I really am."

She sighed dramatically. "I can't take much more of this, Katy."

"I know. Neither can I. I'll be home tomorrow, and if you want, you can come over for dinner and yell at me some more."

"Nope. You need to square things with Josh. Now go eat your dinner and get some rest. And for God's sake, drive carefully tomorrow. I can't bear the thought of losing you."

After several bites of the delectable feast, I double bolted the door, locked the slider window, closed the drapes, then spread the money belt on the bed and counted a stack of one-hundred-dollar bills.

"Oh. My. God." I kept counting, feeling my scalp tingle with excitement. "Ninety-eight, ninety-nine, one hundred." I was dumbfounded. "What's one-hundred times one-hundred?"

My weary brain was muzzy, so I swigged my wine—'cause, you know, alcohol always clears your thinking.

"Oh yeah, just add two zeros. Duh." Quivering, I gawked at the bundle of Benjamins. "That's ten thousand bucks. Right here in my hot little hand." I picked up the other two bundles. "Thirty-freaking-thousand smack-a-roos! Holy shit! And who knows how much the coins are worth?"

Daisy got caught up in my excitement, and we danced around the room. "This calls for a celebration!" I refilled my glass and tossed Daisy a handful of doggy treats. "There's going to be plenty more of that in the future, sweet baby girl, because we're stinkin' rich."

———

Even with three glasses of wine and a melatonin, sleep eluded me. I was revved up about the money and apprehensive about my police appointment in the morning. As I lay in the dark, scary scenarios spun through my head....

"Ms. McKenna—after you left Erin Cranston in the linen room, what did you do?" asked my imaginary police detective.

"I looked for a phone so I could call the police."

"We never received a call from you. So what were you *really* doing?"

"Searching for a phone. I swear it. The house had no landlines. And then I finally found my phone, but Seth wound up calling you, because I had a terrible head injury."

"Looks more like a little boo-boo to me." He leaned into my face, and growled, "Ms. McKenna....What did you do with the money?"

"What money? I have no idea what you're talking about. I swear it."

He grabbed my collar and lifted me a foot off my chair, jamming his nose against mine. "Do you know what the penalty is for removing evidence from a crime scene?"

"Oh, God. What have I done?" I switched on the bedside lamp, flipped open my laptop, and searched: What is the penalty for removing evidence from a crime scene?

A criminal defense attorney's website popped up. Here's what it said:

As with most crimes, there are several defenses that a person charged with tampering with evidence may raise. Such as:

1. Lack of knowledge.

"That won't fly. I knew exactly what I was doing."

2. Lack of intent.

"I totally intended to take my money."

The U.S. government takes tampering with evidence very seriously. A person who is convicted of the crime under federal law may face a prison sentence of not more than 20 years, a fine, or both.

"Oh, crap. I could get twenty years for taking what is rightfully mine. How is that fair?" And then once again, I recalled Erin's answer when I asked where the coins were. *Trust me, they're hidden where no one will ever find them.*

"That's my answer. The truth. For the most part. The money I found is a mere fraction of what she stole from me."

I turned on the TV to catch the local eleven o'clock news. After a Viagra commercial, followed by a condom commercial, the news anchor said, "Coming up next, a brutal murder in Atherton."

"Whoa! It was an accident. It's not like I meant to kill her."

As soon as I uttered those words, I stopped cold, stunned to my core. Until that moment, it hadn't fully registered that I had taken a life. Yes, it was an accident brought on by Erin's own actions, but the realization that because of me her life was now over was mind-blowing.

I gazed numbly at the TV while several more commercials hawked their wares, and when the news resumed, I forced myself to pay attention.

"It's been a busy day in the quiet upscale town of Atherton," said the busty anchor with a nasal twang. "Our reporter, Robin Gutierrez was on the scene earlier."

The video panned from the squad cars blocking the lane to the reporter standing in front of yellow crime scene tape strung across the mansion's front yard.

"Today, a young woman's life tragically ended." Robin shook her head, looking woeful. "What led to her untimely death is still unknown." She did a quarter turn and the camera swung over to me—looking guilty as sin. "No charges have been made yet. Back to you, Alicia."

CHAPTER FORTY-FOUR

FRIDAY • MARCH 13

Posted by Katy McKenna

Sunday, March 8

I pushed through the police station doors a few minutes before nine and spotted Detective Murphy chatting with two officers. Her back was to me so I hung out at the entrance while she finished her conversation. One of the cops nodded toward me, and as Murphy turned around, her sunny smile morphed into grim disapproval.

Oh, geez. I'm in trouble. "Hi. I sure didn't expect to see you here." I grinned brightly. "I love your black pantsuit. And the white shirt. Very flattering."

"Katy." Murphy crossed her arms, looking disgusted. "What were you thinking?"

"I was just trying to help."

"Putting yourself in danger doesn't help anyone."

"Yes, but you see—"

"No. I do not see. You could've been killed."

"I know, but—"

I expected her next words to be, *No buts about it, young lady. You're grounded for life.*

Murphy continued. "I hope I can convince them to allow you to go home."

"Why wouldn't they? I didn't do anything wrong. And it isn't even their case. It's yours."

"Theirs too now, since Erin died in their jurisdiction. The department here isn't going to let this go, so we have to cooperate with them." She shook her head at me. "Your friends just left, but they didn't have much to say, so it's your turn now."

———

After we had been seated at a table in a conference room, Detective Ken Fraser and Detective Julie Goldberg introduced themselves and then asked me to tell my story.

"So, you said the last time you saw Erin, she was unconscious on the linen closet floor," said Fraser, while he unbuttoned his snug sport coat.

"Yes." I nodded.

"And during the time after you left her in the closet you were searching for a phone?" he asked.

Yes and no. I was also searching for the money. Oh, God. Do I look guilty? "Yes. I couldn't believe a house like that didn't have any landlines. I mean, what if the power goes out, and your cellphone dies and... and...." I stopped yammering.

"These days, lots of people don't have landlines," said Murphy in a chatty tone. "You're right, Katy, about when the power goes out and you can't charge your phone. I learned the hard way. Now I have a solar charger."

I smiled a "thank you" at her.

Julie Goldberg was tapping a pen against a blood-red fingernail. Really annoying. "Then what happened?" she asked.

"Well, like I already told you, I searched for a phone because

Erin had taken mine. If I'd known the police were searching for me, I would have run out to the street and screamed for help." I shrugged sheepishly. "But I didn't know. And I was afraid to go to a neighbor's house and risk Erin getting away while I was gone. Everything was so crazy. I doubt I was using my best judgment at the time. Anyway, I finally found my cellphone in Erin's purse and was about to dial 911 when Jessie and Seth showed up. They made me sit down and put ice on my forehead." I touched the bandage the EMT had put on my wound. "Then Seth called the cops and a minute later they showed up and practically stormed the place. Really terrifying. I mean, I thought they were going to shoot us." I clasped my hands on the scarred laminate table. "That's pretty much everything."

Detective Fraser leaned forward. His muscular shoulders strained for freedom from his jacket, and I caught a whiff of his minty breath. "Let's go back to when Erin hit her head on the floor." He scanned his notes. "You stepped over her and she grabbed your ankle. You lost your balance and fell on her, and then she appeared to be unconscious."

"That's right. She sure fooled me. I thought she was out cold when I was stepping over her." I swallowed hard, wondering if my interview were about to take a nasty turn. "It all happened so fast. I was in a panic, so the details are kind of blurry. I remember that after I slugged her with the pillowcase—"

"By the way, that was pretty ingenious," said Murphy with a supportive smile.

"I agree," said Goldberg. "You see it on a cop show or something?"

I shook my head. "No. I don't think so."

"Maybe you're a very resourceful person," said Murphy, glancing at her fellow detectives. "I wonder if any of us would have thought of making a weapon out of bed linens."

I saw sincerity in her big brown eyes. "Anyway, when I hit Erin, she went down hard, and I assumed she was out cold. I thought about hitting her again to make sure, but I couldn't. Hitting her the first time was for self-preservation. Hitting her again, well, it could've killed her, and I just couldn't do that."

Goldberg narrowed her cool, gray eyes. "I need some clarification. Exactly *how* did you land on her?"

"Well. Um, I, uh." I exhaled a mortified groan. "I landed on my rear-end. On her head. I rolled off as fast as I could and then I saw the blood and figured she must've broken her nose. And this time, she was definitely unconscious. No doubt about it. I poked her with my foot to make sure."

Fraser took a roll of peppermint Lifesavers out of his pocket and popped one in his mouth, then offered me one.

I shook my head, then realized it might be his subtle way of telling me I needed one since all I'd had for breakfast was crappy hotel room coffee. "On second thought, thanks. I'll take one."

"After you poked her body, what did you do?" he asked.

"I already told you all of this." Feeling warm, I removed my navy cardigan and slung it over the back of my chair.

"Tell us again, please."

Oh, crud. Just like my last police interview. Everyone starts out all nice and friendly and then, next thing I know, I'm in the slammer.

"I searched for the gun and found it under the blankets. Then I went out in the hall and realized I couldn't lock her in because she had the key. No way was I going back in there to try to find it. So I pushed the cabinet in front of the door. It made a lot of noise, scraping the floor when I moved it, so I figured that if she tried to get out, I'd hear her. That's when I started searching for a phone."

"Do you know what time it was at this point?" asked Fraser.

Oh, God. If I blow this question, I am so screwed. When I went into the kitchen the first time and found my phone in Erin's purse, the time on its display was ten-thirteen. That's when I remembered the coins and went looking for them. How long had it taken me to find the money belt? Twenty minutes? Thirty? I had no clue. What time did Seth make the 911 call? Again, no clue. But Detective Fraser knew.

"I really don't know. To tell you the truth, I was pretty freaked out at the time, and my head really hurt." I touched my bandage, hoping for a little sympathy. "The whole morning was a crazy whirl."

Detective Fraser slapped his yellow legal notepad on the table and pushed back his chair. "Well, I think that about covers it." Then he hesitated, frowning. "Except for one thing that's puzzling me." He pulled his chair back to the table. "We found some very expensive clothes in the bedroom Cranston was using. And yet, she only had a couple hundred bucks in her wallet, and no credit cards."

"Yes," said Goldberg. "The shoes alone were worth several thousand dollars. And the room looked like it had been ransacked."

Oh, God. Don't look guilty. "You do know she stole—"

"Millions of dollars' worth of gold coins from you," said Fraser, nodding. "So we have to assume she sold some or all of them." His eyes lasered into mine. "You got any ideas where the coins might be? It would certainly be understandable if you found them and chose not to tell the police. After all, it's your money, so who could blame you?"

I shook my head, keeping my eyes pinned to Fraser's as I thought of the money belt stashed under the driver's seat of my car in the police station parking lot. *He's trying to trick me into a confession. Just stay cool.*

"Erin did some horrible things to you." Goldberg removed her glasses and smiled sympathetically. "I know if I were you and I found—"

"I swear I have no idea what she did with the coins." One of my fingernails snaked its way to my front incisors. "Believe me, I wish I did." I forced my hand to sit in my lap. "In fact, before she locked me in the linen room, I asked her where they were, and I'll never forget what she said."

"What was that?" asked Goldberg.

"Erin said, 'They're hidden where no one will ever find them.'"

And that's the truth, so help me God.

"Okay, I have to say it," said Murphy with a devilish smirk. "Because I know everyone else here is thinking it. Cause of death was a fatal blow to the head, delivered by——" The usually professional woman could barely contain herself. "Katy's...."

———

"Katy's killer booty. That's what Murphy said. Can you believe it?" I was chatting with Samantha on the phone while waiting behind five cars for a latte in a Starbucks drive-through in San Jose—just off the 101 freeway.

"I hope the exact details of Erin's death don't become public knowledge, or you'll be the newest instant media star. The next thing you know, you'll be on every talk show."

"I've always wanted to meet Ellen but not because I squashed my cousin with my derrière."

Sam giggled. "You'd be plastered on every tabloid cover, and you know they won't use a flattering photo, you can bet on that. Paparazzi will be trailing behind you everywhere, snapping photos of your fanny. I can see the *National Enquirer* cover now—Killer Booty Crime Fighter!"

"Yeah, I'll be the butt of every joke—ha, ha. God, that better not happen."

"It won't, and I promise not to tell a soul. Except for Spencer and Chelsea."

"No, not Chelsea! She's a teenager and within minutes the entire universe would know."

"Kidding. Gotta go now. My break's almost over. Oh, wait. I thought of another one! The Tushy Terminator."

"Fun-neee."

"The ASS-sassin. The... The... Oh come on, I know I can think of another one."

"The Keister Killer," I said.

"Oh, good one. Really good one." Her tone slipped into serious mode. "Katy, I'm so thankful we can laugh about this. When I think about what could have happened."

"I know. Me too. Love you. See ya tomorrow."

———

Daisy and I got home shortly after five. The moment we stepped inside the house, she raced to the dog door, and Tabitha laid into me, giving me hell for leaving her. I carried her into my bedroom and plopped her on the bed for a good tummy rub. After a minute of passionate purring, she went into crazy-cat mode and chomped my hand and then streaked out of the room.

I fed the pets, poured a glass of wine, and turned on some soothing music. A mellow coffee house playlist on Spotify.

"Time to quit stalling and call Josh. Really do not want to do this."

With shaky hands and a pounding heart, I was dialing his number when the doorbell rang. Daisy dashed to the front door, ready to pounce on whoever was on the other side. A couple seconds later, the doorbell camera app on my phone ding-donged. I tapped the app and saw Josh. He looked tense, but it's kind of hard to tell with the bubble-vision effect of the tiny camera. He said, "Not going away, so open the damned door, Katy."

Crap. I'm a mess. I cupped my hands, checking my breath, then sniffed my pits. They were less than fresh, but I doubted he'd appreciate waiting at the door while I showered.

I swished my mouth with wine, then checked my face in the entry mirror and pinched my pale cheeks. And then with my heart marching up my throat, I opened the door.

Daisy shoved past me to greet her sweetheart—her tail wagging a three-sixty. Usually, he hunkers down to give her a hug and a good scratch under her collar. But this time, he ignored her and stared at me with an expression that ripped me apart.

For once, I kept my mouth shut. No goofy quips to cover my nerves, not even a smile. Barely able to breathe, I returned his gaze. After several long seconds, he stepped over the threshold, and I moved out of his way, as he slipped by. I closed the door hearing the latch graze the strike plate and click into place. As I pondered whether to turn the dead bolt, his hand reached over my shoulder and locked it.

That move and his intense demeanor unnerved me. I'd never seen him angry before. Guess I'd never given him cause before. I stared at the door, feeling like I might throw up.

"I want to know why you left without telling me," he said. "Oh, and by the way, I saw the news. Do you have any idea how that tore me up?"

"I'm sorry. I texted you."

"You sure did. The day, no, make that the *following night* after you left. And a goddamned text? Kind of cold, don't you think?"

Josh's hand gripped my shoulder, forcing me to turn toward him. "Dammit. Look at me, Katy."

I lifted my eyes to his icy blues, blinking back my tears.

His tone softened. "I thought we had something. Was I wrong?"

"No. I just think, maybe...." I stopped, drawing a shuddering breath, trying to compose myself, but instead getting more rattled by the scent of him.

"Maybe what?"

My thoughts spun at warp speed. *Has Nicole told him she's still in love with him? She said she would, but he isn't acting like she did. Should I ask? If she hasn't, should I tell him?* "Um, how's Nicole?"

Josh shook his head, glancing away. "Not good."

"Is it safe for her to be alone?"

"She has a friend visiting." He stepped closer, his eyes boring into mine. "You didn't answer my question."

I felt his body heat radiating, and I couldn't remember the question.

"Why'd you leave me?" he whispered. "Did I do something wrong?"

"God, no. You're wonderful." *Too wonderful and that's the problem.* "It's just, I thought we were going to take a break because of Nicole and...."

"That was your idea, not mine. I don't want to take a goddamned break."

A tear slipped down my cheek. "I'm sorry. I can't do—"

"Do what?" Josh caught my tear on his fingertip, and his angry look took on a languorous cast as he wrapped his warm hands around my neck. "This?" His lips brushed across mine. "Maybe this?" He nibbled my earlobe, then kissed his way to the crook of my neck. His fingers raked up through my hair, entwining a tight fistful, his breath rough and needy as he propelled me back against the door. "Or this?"

CHAPTER FORTY-FIVE

SATURDAY • MARCH 14
Posted by Katy McKenna

Other than the monumental task of catching up on my blog, the last few days have been a time of quiet reflection. The blogging always helps me to sort things out and get some perspective.

Coming to terms with killing Erin—well, that's going to take time. I know she was her own undoing, but my heart goes out to her parents. I'm sure they know now that it was me in their yard that day and that has to be adding to their burden. I plan to write them a letter to apologize for my intrusion. I don't know if it will help them, but it will help me.

As far as my relationship with Josh? It's hard to think rationally about him. It's like he's too good to be true. Are we truly in love? Or is this simply lusty infatuation? I do think we've been moving way too fast. Right now we're still in the "honeymoon" phase when both parties are on their best behavior. There's been no burping, farting, crankiness, slovenliness, bitchiness (okay, maybe a little on my part), pettiness.... Which in the long term is impossible to maintain 24/7.

From here on out, I'm going to be my natural, organic, genuine, what-you-see-is-what-you-get self. No more sneaking out of bed at the crack of dawn to brush my teeth, fix my hair, and put on lipstick and mascara.

And if I'm PMSing, I'll give him fair warning that his life may be in jeopardy. As far as the burps, farts, and other bodily indiscretions, I'll still try to keep those to myself, because that's just good manners.

Okay. Time to get real. I hate with a capital H the Nicole thing. Yes, I know she can't help being so ill. And she can't help still being in love with Josh. But I'm only human, and I hate it. Josh is one of the good guys, and he'll do the right thing—no matter what it turns out to be.

———

This morning I woke feeling like I needed to do something constructive. I roamed around the house, sipping coffee and looking for a project. My house is clean, tidy, and freshly painted and reorganized—except for the bedroom I use as a storage unit.

In the backyard, I considered planting some veggies and decided to hold off until April or May when it's warmer. And then I thought of the attic and my plans to do something with it. I'd been thinking about making it a light and airy art studio—but that was when I was rich. Now, there's no way I can afford to add bigger windows and skylights. Another idea I liked was a home theater. I called Pop and asked if he could come over and talk about it.

While I waited for him, I decided to spend a little time reimagining the attic of horrors. As I pulled down the steps, I felt proud of myself for facing my fears. Upstairs, I looked at the wall where the plywood had concealed the box for so many years.

"If I hadn't found the money, Erin would still be alive and we'd be friends. I guess it's true what they say. Money is the root of all evil." Yes, I talk to myself. Who doesn't?

There wasn't much I could do on my own, but I could start cleaning. In the laundry room, I half-filled a bucket with warm, sudsy water thinking I'd tackle the bloodstains. And that, if you can believe it, triggered a funny memory.

In middle school, Samantha was playing Lady Macbeth to a packed audience of proud parents. Crazy, huh? Macbeth in eighth grade? Anyway, when she got to the line, "Out, damned spot! Out, I say!" she couldn't bring herself to swear in front of her folks, so she hollered, "Out, darned spot!" and the crowd exploded in laughter. That was the final curtain on Sam's short theatrical career.

I hoisted the plastic pail out of the laundry tub, then realized how nasty the water would become when mixed with Tyler's dried blood. "So what can I do? I know. Sweep up the rat poo. Ooo. Fun."

Private

After watching Pop struggle up the steps, I wasn't sure he'd be able to help with the project, but I couldn't say anything. He would have argued the point anyway.

Up top, he said, "You say you want this to be a home theater?"

"Yeah, I thought it would be fun. You and Mom can come over for movie nights. I know how you hate going to the theater."

"Last time your mother and I went, our one bucket of crappy popcorn and two sodas came to almost twenty-five bucks. That plus the tickets and we were out nearly fifty dollars. Then you have to listen to people yack throughout the movie. On top of that, they shove twenty minutes of TV commercials down your throat. When I was a kid, you got cartoons, and a double feature for—"

"A quarter?"

Pop jammed his hands into his jean pockets and harrumphed like an old codger. "I'm not that ancient. Matinees were a buck."

"Well, my popcorn will be better, and you can have beer."

"Sounds good to me." He glanced around. "You planning on selling tickets to pay for this project?"

I hesitated while I wrestled with my conscience. He's a former cop, and I'm pretty sure I committed a crime. But I couldn't lie to my father.

When I finished telling him about the money belt, I waited for him to lose it, but instead he said, "I'm glad you told me the truth, and although theoretically it was the wrong thing to do, I don't blame you for doing it."

Tears bubbled up and spilled over my cheeks. He held me close and stroked my hair as I sobbed out all my pent-up anguish against his sturdy chest. "Oh, Pop. When Erin locked me in that linen closet, I didn't think I'd ever see you or Mom again. And knowing it was all my fault made it so much worse."

"Sweetheart, it wasn't your fault."

"Yes, it was. I never should've been snooping around like that. What the hell was I thinking?"

"What's important is you're safe now. All the bad stuff is over."

My storm passed, and I drew back, wiping my eyes and snotty nose on my raggedy old Pussycat Dolls t-shirt.

"You used to do that when you were a little girl," said Pop.

"What about Mom? Are you going to tell her what I did?"

"She'll understand." He swept away the hair sticking to my damp cheeks. "But this goes no further, young lady. If anyone asks, just say you found the coins in your closet and that Erin must've dropped them when she was loading the suitcase. No one will question that. And don't put all that cash into the bank in one lump sum. That'll arouse suspicions. Maybe your first investment should be a decent safe. Something big enough to store all your valuables and can't be carried out of the house by a thief. Then put the thirty thousand in it. The less the IRS knows the better. As it is, they'll be making plenty on the coin sales."

"Sounds like a plan, Pop."

He glanced around the attic. "I didn't realize how much room you have up here."

"I guess we could divide the space. But I don't know what I'd do with it."

He walked over to the other end of the room. "How about a pool table? There's plenty of space for one."

"Geez. What's up with you guys? That's what Josh said, too."

"Seems like a good idea to me."

"No pool table. We could partition off part of the space for storage, then I can clear out the bedroom downstairs."

"Or you could get rid of that junk. It's been sitting there for over a year, so maybe you don't need it."

"Well, I might need it at some point."

Pop paced off the room in both directions, then stopped near the chimney and pointed at the floor. "Looks like water stains." He gazed at the ceiling. "Oh, yeah. You definitely have a roof leak."

"More than one. When I was up here, we had that big rainstorm. And water was dripping on my head. I thought I'd lose my mind. I was so thirsty but I couldn't drink it because of the tape over my mouth. I swear I'll never take water for granted again."

"It's a good thing they're both dead, otherwise…." He cleared his throat and patted my back. "I hate to say this, but I think it's time for a new roof."

"Oh. That's no fun. New roofs cost a fortune and I doubt I can afford to do that and still do the home theater, too."

"Maybe you can get away with just some patchwork. Tell you what. Go get a marker or some chalk, and we can circle all the water stains, and that'll give us a better idea."

I fetched two black markers from my desk in the living room, and we went to work marking the spots. A few minutes into it, Pop said, "This is not looking good, Katy. I know you had the house inspected before you bought it. What did they say about the roof?"

"That I would probably need to replace it in five years."

"Well, we haven't had much rain in six or seven years, but that recent downpour seems to have found all the holes. It'd be crazy to spend money up here and then have water pouring in." He leaned against a stud and crossed his arms.

"What's wrong, Pop?"

"I'm looking at the chimney. Something odd about it. I'm going downstairs to check something. You keep circling water stains."

Seven more circles and Pop returned with a tape measure. "For some odd reason, this chimney flue is a lot deeper than it should be."

"Do you think I could add another fireplace to it? Think how cozy that would be up here."

"No. Every fireplace needs a separate path, otherwise you'd have carbon monoxide venting into this room." He pulled out the end of the tape measure. "Help me measure this."

I held the tape on a corner of the chimney. "I was so excited the first time I looked at this house and saw it had a real old fashioned brick fireplace and not a metal insert."

"Too expensive to build these days, not to mention illegal in new construction. Now let's measure the depth." He stepped to the side of the flue. "Honey? I can't see the numbers. Would you get me a flashlight?"

I have little LED flashlights plugged in around the house that go on whenever the power goes out. What I like best about them is that I always have a fully charged flashlight available.

After giving Daisy a hug at the bottom of the stairs, I returned to the attic and shined the light on the tape measure.

"That's strange. I did a rough measure downstairs and this makes no sense." He slipped the tape measure into his pocket. "Give me the flashlight." He aimed the beam behind the chimney, then moved around to the front. "Take a look at this." He again directed the flashlight on the front bricks, then on the back. "Notice anything?"

"They look different. The bricks in the back are dark red and don't have the reclaimed look that the rest of the chimney has. Do you think someone repaired it at some point and figured it didn't have to match since it's in the attic?"

"Maybe." Pop shook his head, looking skeptical. "Whoever did this was no mason, that's for damned sure. Hell, I could do a better job than this."

"Or…" I was getting excited. "Maybe somebody hid something. Maybe there's another—"

"Treasure chest?"

"Why not?" I punched his arm and he laughed. "Why the hell not, Pop? Stranger things have happened."

"Can't argue with that." He swept the light back and forth over the surface of the flue. "I don't think it'll take much to remove this cheap add-on brick. But, Katy, by doing that we run the risk of screwing up a chimney repair."

"When I had that home inspection, the inspector didn't mention this, so I'm not going to worry about it. But we both know we'll never rest until this mystery is solved." I recalled what Emily had said when we were looking at the wood box. *You know, this could be a new Nancy Drew mystery.* "The secret in the old chimney," I whispered.

"What'd you say, honey?"

"Nuthin'." I grinned. "Just thinking out loud."

"Why don't you go down to my truck and grab my toolbox. Guess I should've brought it up when I got the tape measure."

I scrambled down the steps with Pop yelling, "It's heavy, so be careful."

I lugged the red metal box up the steps, banging it against my shins several times. "Great. Just when the old bruises have finally faded away." When I was shoulder-level with the attic floor, Pop leaned down and grabbed the handle.

He set the box by the chimney. "We're going to need more light."

"I have a couple LED lanterns. Be right back."

When I came back with the lanterns, Pop was examining the mortar with the flashlight. "This is going to make a big mess, Katy. Run down to my truck and grab the tarp in the back."

My legs were aching from the previous trips down the stairs, but I didn't want to complain. "I don't care about the mess."

"You will when it's time to clean it up. Oh, and bring up a stepstool."

———

Pop began chiseling out the mortar and handing me the bricks. "The way this mortar is crumbling away, whoever did this should have just stacked the bricks and not even bothered with mortar. Can you hold the lantern a little higher, honey?"

I was holding it over my head with one hand while taking bricks with the other. "No." I set the lantern on the floor and stretched my aching arms. "I'm going to get a chair to stand on."

I was moving slow now. I thought my poor old shins had recovered from when the treasure box landed on them but evidently not. Before I lugged a kitchen chair to the attic, I popped a couple of ibuprofens, did a few stretches, and gave Daisy a treat.

Back in the attic, I stood on the chair next to Pop. "Do you want me to take a turn?"

He handed me the chisel and hammer and took the lantern. "Be my guest."

I slammed into the mortar and sandy granules sprayed into my face.

"Not so hard, Katy. We really should have safety glasses on. I left mine at the shop. Do you have any?"

"No. I'll be more careful. Why do you think it's so crumbly?"

"It has to do with the ratio of cement, sand, and lime. You can buy premixed mortar in different strengths. I'm guessing this was the cheapest available. And now, my dear, you know as much as I do about mortar."

I took another whack and two bricks popped out and landed on the floor near my father's feet. "Sorry, Pop. I didn't realize they were about to fall out."

"Hold on." He lifted the lantern. "Do you see that?"

I raised on tiptoe, craning my neck. "Oh my God. We were right. Something *is* hidden behind these bricks."

He chuckled. "Let's not get too ahead of ourselves."

"Why else would it be hollow back there? This wasn't a patch job." I looked at my father. "Are you thinking what I'm thinking?"

"I'm pretty sure you're thinking there's another box of gold coins back there."

"And this time it's way bigger. So big and so valuable that it had to be hidden behind a brick wall. This is the best day ever!"

Daisy barked at the foot of the steps. "It's okay, baby. Mama's just excited, that's all."

I tapped the next section of mortar a few times, and Pop removed the brick. After a few more were removed, I got overzealous and gave the next section of mortar a hard whack and just as Pop predicted, a few particles flew into my left eye. I dropped the tools, and just as I was about to rub my eye, Pop grabbed my hand.

"No! You'll scratch your cornea."

I cupped my hand over my eye, and he helped me downstairs to the kitchen sink. My eye was gushing tears, my nose was running, and I could feel the grit gouging my eyeball.

"Do you have an eyewash cup?" he asked.

"No."

"Shot glass?"

"No."

"Then I'm going to wash out your eye with the sprayer."

"That does not sound fun."

"Or we can go to the ER. Your choice."

"No! I can't wait that long. Just do it."

He turned on the water and adjusted the temperature. "Okay, this feels pretty good. Now put your head down and tilt so I can get a good aim. Try to keep your eye open."

He aimed the gentle spray at my eye, and I flinched and got a nose full.

"You have to stay still, Katy."

"I'm trying. This is worse than when you used to pull splinters out of my fingers."

After three tries, my eye suddenly felt better. "Okay, you got it." Water was dribbling down my neck, and about two inches into my hairline was soaked. "Can you hand me a dishtowel?"

After I dried off, Pop said, "You want to call it a day?"

"Are you kidding? No way. But you chisel and I'll watch from a safe distance."

———

After we removed another row of bricks, Pop took the lantern and held it in the hollow space.

"Can you see anything?" I asked.

"No, and stop rubbing your eye. Here, take the lantern." He tapped a few spots and removed two bricks. "I sure hope we're not doing all this work for nothing. Now that I can get some leverage, I'm going to slam it a few times from the inside. You better get off the chair and go across the room."

"Be careful," I said. "You don't want any of the grit getting into your eyes. Really hurts."

He slipped on his cheater glasses, then put the hammer on the inside of the wall and gave it a good hit. Nothing happened.

"Try again. Harder."

"It's difficult to get good momentum, but here goes nothing."

Pop hammered the bricks several times and suddenly the entire wall collapsed into a dusty pile.

"Wow, that was like a mini earthquake. Good job, Pop."

"Stay back!" he yelled.

"Why? What's wrong?" I crossed the room. "Oh my God! Oh my God!"

"Dammit, Katy. I told you to stay back!"

My screams had driven Daisy into a frenzy downstairs. The pull-down steps thudded against the floor as she struggled to climb up to save me.

I rushed to the stairs. "No! Off! Mama's all right." I wasn't, but I didn't need her breaking a leg. "Sit!"

She sat trembling at the foot of the ladder, the ridge of her back puffed to high alert.

Pop came to my side. "Go downstairs and call the police."

"Let me catch my breath, first." I placed my hand over my heart. "Wow. Was not expecting that."

"Whoever he is, was, he's been dead a very long time," said Pop. "And now we know why the brick wall was built."

Knowing the man had been dead a long time made it easier for me to look at the withered corpse propped against the back of the chimney. Morbid fascination drew me closer to inspect our archeological find.

The dead man's jaw gaped grotesquely, all the teeth still intact, even two gold crowns. Frizzled brown hair covered his leathery skull. His wide-lapelled pinstriped suit was dusty. A plaid tie dangled from his shriveled neck. Wing-tip shoes were set heels together, toes splayed at ninety degrees to fit inside the narrow space. The head and body were held erect by a rope strung zigzag down his frame and nailed to two-by-four wood boards screwed to the bricks.

"His suit looks like something out of the 1930's or 40's," said Pop. "There's only one reason why a body would be hidden like this."

"He was murdered," I whispered. "But why? And who is he?"

Pop took his phone from his pants pocket. "Time to call the police."

"Why'd you tell me to go downstairs to call if you had your phone?"

He pointed at the dehydrated cadaver. "Because I didn't want you looking at that." He dialed the number. "This is Kurt Melby. This isn't an emergency, but I need to talk to someone about a dead body." After the call he said, "We better wait downstairs."

Ten minutes later, two police officers arrived. When I opened the door, I saw Angela Yaeger parking at the curb. Pop spoke to the officers while I waited on the porch for the chief. She was casually dressed in skinny jeans, boots, and a fuzzy knee-length cardigan.

"My hubby and I were on our way out the door to go to a fundraiser brunch at Le Stella," she said as she climbed the steps, "when I got a call about a dead body at Katy McKenna's house. Well, I certainly couldn't pass that up." She gave me a quick squeeze. "Girl? What is it with you?"

I shrugged, shaking my head. "Just super lucky I guess. The good news is, there's no way anyone can pin the blame on me."

"Yes, I was told that Kurt said it was an old corpse, so I guess I don't have to read you your rights," she said with a grin. "Lead me to it."

Inside, Pop was holding Daisy's collar while talking to the cops. "Katy? Take your dog, and I'll show the officers and the chief what we found."

I put Daisy in my bedroom and shut the door. I had no desire to go back in the attic, so I sat on the sofa and speculated about the dead man.

A few minutes later, Josh walked in, looking rattled. "Katy. I saw the squad cars. What's going on?" He sat beside me, taking my icy hands in his warm grasp. "Are you all right?"

"I'm fine, but the man upstairs? Not so much."

"What are you talking about?"

"We found a corpse in the attic. God, talk about a house of horrors. Even if I wanted to sell this house, no one would buy it. I think I need a glass of water." I stood, took one step, and my knees wobbled. Josh eased me back to the couch.

He went to the kitchen and returned with water. "Now, tell me what happened."

———

My house is once again a crime scene. Can you believe it? And I'm back in the guest/sewing room at my folks until the cops do all their forensic stuff. But I doubt they'll be able to piece together much of a story. Too many years and owners have come and gone since he flat-lined. I hope he deserved what he got.

And now it's lights out for me. I've had enough of this day.

CHAPTER FORTY-SIX

MONDAY · MARCH 16
Posted by Katy McKenna

The mystery corpse has been identified. The murderer made it easy by leaving the victim's driver's license and a confession letter, in the inside breast pocket of his suit. The deceased was...drum-roll...Harold Allan Petersen—Mabel's runaway hubby.

According to Mabel's confession, when Harry told her he'd knocked up his secretary and was running away with her, not only did she feel betrayed but heartbroken, too. She'd lost two babies in childbirth and desperately wanted children. She begged Harry not to leave her and offered to raise the illegitimate child as her own. But Harry ridiculed her, calling her a dried-up old prune. I did the math and she was close to my age at the time. Anyway, it was their last conversation, because the old prune stabbed the cad in the back.

Mabel spread the rumor about Harry running off, and I guess, no one ever questioned the story. I wonder what happened to the expectant secretary? Her baby would be elderly now.

I'll never know how Mabel got the money, but here's my theory based on what my neighbor, Nina Lowen, told me about Mabel Petersen....

Her wealthy grandfather pulled all his money out of the stock market before the big crash of 1929. I think he invested the cash in gold coins, and Mabel inherited them when he died.

I also think that her grandfather passed after Harry's untimely demise, and Mabel couldn't risk the media attention that wealthy heiresses receive, so she squirreled it away in the attic. Get it? Squirreled?

Anyway, if Mabel inherited the money while Harry was still in the picture, I doubt he would've dumped her. Or being the rat that he was, he might have murdered her and run off with his secretary and the money. And it would have been Mabel's body hidden in the attic for all these years instead of his.

Of course, this is all pure conjecture on my part, but it makes sense, don't you think?

After all the bad stuff that's happened in my house, I'd like to sell it and start fresh, but it's unlikely I'd get fair market value given that two murders have occurred in it. No doubt the next thing I'll discover about my home is that it's sitting on top of an ancient burial ground. I love the original *Poltergeist* movie but sure don't want to live it.

EPILOGUE

Posted by Katy McKenna

Last night, during a romantic rendezvous, Josh received a call from Nicole. She was having a rough night and was afraid to be alone.

"I'm sorry, Katy." He kissed my forehead and climbed out of bed.

"It's not your fault. She's sick and she needs you."

He threw on his clothes, and I followed him to the front door. As he leaned in for a goodnight kiss, his phone rang again.

"Let me know if you need help," I called as he rushed down the porch steps.

I bolted the door, turned on the alarm, and got my laptop off the coffee table. In the kitchen, I drained the last of the bottle of wine Josh had brought over and crawled back in bed, feeling grumpy on so many levels.

1. Nicole's timing couldn't have been better, if you get my drift.
2. I don't think she's told Josh how she feels yet.

3. Daisy and Tabitha were cuddled in a heap at the foot of the bed, which meant I couldn't move my feet without disturbing them.

4. I've got PMS. Enough said.

I opened my computer and logged into Facebook to see what the rest of the world was up to. Bio-Dad Bert had posted new photos of my little baby brother, Aiden. My friend, Hannah, had shared a hilarious video about dogs who are afraid to walk past their cranky cat siblings.

Next, I read a story about caring people who adopt senior dogs that have been abandoned at animal shelters because their people died. It got me thinking about the old dachshund at the no-kill shelter.

Sam had said, "Her owner died, and no one in the family wanted Francine. So the sweet old girl will probably live out her golden years in that noisy, stressful place."

I turned out the light and tried to get comfortable but finally had to move the deadweight kids to the side of the bed. I curled into my favorite sleep position, then lay there waiting for Mr. Sandman to do his thing. But I guess he took the night off because sleep wasn't happening. I kept thinking about Daisy and Tabitha winding up in a shelter if I died. I know that won't happen because Mom and Pop would take them, but what if they couldn't? Then Samantha would take them. But what if she moves away? Then she would have to come and get them. I need to talk to her about that.

I wondered if anyone had given Francine a home yet. I switched the lamp back on, flipped open the laptop, and scrolled the photos of dogs up for adoption at the shelter.

"Pitbull. Pitbull. Chihuahua. Boxer. Chihuahua. Chiweenie. Chihuahua. Pitbull. Queensland blue heeler. Dachshund." I clicked on the photo of the black and tan dachshund. "Her muzzle is gray, so it's got to be her." I read her bio.

Francine's Story

Hello there. My name is Francine. I'm a mature sweet lady who is currently in search of my forever home. I enjoy walks and snuggling. I love kids, dogs, cats, and soft, warm laps. Although I'm not young, I'm healthy, and still have a lot of life to live, and I'd love to live it with you.

- Primary Color: Black
- Secondary Color: Tan
- Weight: 12.5
- Age: 12
- Days in Shelter: 92

This morning

I was waiting by the shelter entrance when they unlocked the doors at ten. In the lobby, I asked the snowy-haired volunteer staffing the desk if I could meet Francine.

"Oh, she is such a dear girl," said Nancy. "Did you see her online?"

"I did."

"So you know she's not a youngster."

"Right. She's twelve, which would make her eighty-four in people years."

"Oh, my goodness, no. She's not my age. We don't calculate dog years in a one-size-fits-all number. Dachshunds have a long life span, so Francine is around sixty-five or so. She's in excellent health, although when she first joined us, she was rather obese." She shook her head with a grimace. "Don't get me started on people overfeeding their dogs."

"I could stand to lose a few pounds, but my yellow Lab and cat are in perfect shape."

"Oh, honey. You're beautiful just as you are. You must've been too skinny before."

I love this lady!

Nancy picked up a walkie-talkie. "I need someone to watch the front. A lovely young woman is here to meet Francine."

I heard a "woo-hoo" on the other end.

Nancy grinned. "That's John. He volunteers here and adores Francine, but he already has a houseful. Me too. One of the perils of working in a humane shelter." She pulled a shiny blue walker to her side and stood. "I had a hip replacement recently, so I'm a little slow."

I held the door for her, then followed her past several dog pens. It was difficult passing all those hopeful faces pressing against the chain link barriers, reaching their paws out, eager for a touch.

"Here we are," said Nancy. "Francine, you have a visitor."

The little dog lay in the corner on a blue blanket, cuddling a purple squeaky bone.

Nancy opened the gate. I stepped inside and sat cross-legged on the concrete, a few feet from the dog.

Francine regarded me with her solemn brown eyes, and my heart melted into a puddle of mush. I held out my hands. "Hi there. I'm Katy."

She observed me for a moment. Sizing me up, I guess. Then she picked up her bone, came to me, squeaked it once, and dropped it in my lap.

I scooped her into my arms and snuggled her close. "Time to go home, Francine."

BLOG UPDATES

The Twenty-Four Gold Coins: The coins have been transported to Oliver Kershaw's coin business in Los Angeles. Once they have been evaluated, I can start selling them. I keep seeing those gloom and doom commercials on TV about how precarious our dollar situation is and how we should all be buying gold. Since the coins will continue to increase in value, I will only sell one at a time as needed. However, I am not going to horde them like Mabel did. Life is too short.

Chad: Poor old Chad-the-cad still resides in the memory care clinic. The last time I dropped in for a visit, I was told that it's best I quit doing that. He still thinks we're married and he gets distressed after I leave. I felt bad when they told me that—which is so odd, considering how nasty he was before a dose of poison and a gunshot wound turned him into a sweet, lovable idiot.

Heather: Chad's ex after me, is living in Montana with her mother and doing well. She had a full recovery from her stroke. Her baby, Noah, is healthy and now at seven months he's sitting up and starting to roll around the house. Heather tells me you'd never know he only weighed eleven and a half ounces at birth.

———

If you enjoyed *Coins and Cadavers*,
please leave a review or a rating at Amazon:
Coins and Cadavers

Thank you so much!

Dear Reader,

Like Ruby, I had a bigamist grandfather. As a young woman, my Norwegian grandmother left her small fishing village and came to America. In Boston, she married a man and gave birth to my father. Soon after that, her husband told her he had another family, and then he skipped town.

My bold, determined grandmother then went to work as a housekeeper for a widower with several children in Minneapolis. Eventually they married, and my father grew up in a loving family.

A few years ago, I decided to try and find out what happened to my biological grandfather. Turns out he pulled this trick more than once, and my father had a half-brother who was also abandoned. That search led me to a younger cousin, and several months later we had a meet-up in Malibu. He has a beautiful wife and two incredibly cute, lovable kids.

The wacky brassier lady in the airport was a true story—except it got even funnier. After we were all seated on the plane and ready for takeoff, our flight was delayed because of a pesky little red light flashing in the cockpit. The pilot announced that we had to wait until the mechanics checked out the problem.

That's when Bra Lady decided she desperately needed to go to the bathroom. The attendant told her she would have to wait until we reached cruising altitude.

The woman begged to leave the plane, but that wasn't possible because the plane had already pulled away from the gangway.

"Oh, my *gaawd*!" she wailed in her wonderful southern accent. "I really gotta pee! If I can't use the potty, I'm gonna wet my pants!"

I don't enjoy flying, and that dear, funny woman was a delightful distraction for me.

Respectfully yours,
Pam

My husband, Mike, our two young boys, and I moved from Alaska to the California Central Coast years ago to open restaurants. Now our kids are grown and we have four grandkids! I enjoy gardening, playing guitar, reading, yoga, playing with our four awesome grandkids, and our furry canine kids.

Pamelafrostdennis.com

Learn about my other books on the next pages.
And don't miss the sample of
Was It Murder?

THE MURDER BLOG MYSTERIES
Additional Books in the Series

DEAD GIRLS DON'T BLOG
Book #1 in the Murder Blog Mysteries

Katy McKenna's life takes a dramatic turn when she stumbles upon a newspaper story about the upcoming parole hearing for one of the men who raped and murdered her high school friend, sixteen years ago. Fearing he could soon be set free to prey on other innocent young girls, Katy sets out to make sure this doesn't happen, not realizing she might not survive to blog about it.

BETTER DEAD THAN WED
Book #2 in the Murder Blog Mysteries

Katy McKenna has had enough near-death experiences and heartache to last a lifetime. Now all she wants to do is get her career back on track, find a nice guy, and live happily-ever-after. But when she hears about a man maliciously exposing innocent young women to HIV, she is compelled to put her plans on hold to stop him.

Meanwhile, Katy's mother is forced to reveal a shattering childhood trauma that has come back to haunt her; her obnoxious baby sister is moving in, and her scuzzy was-band is stalking her.

And she's beginning to wonder why every rotten person she has recently heard about has suddenly dropped dead. Is it divine providence? Or is it murder?

WAS IT MURDER?
Book #4 in the Murder Blog Mysteries

In the latest Murder Blog Mysteries novel, Katy finds herself at loose ends. She's jobless, but not penny-less thanks to a recently discovered box of rare coins in her attic. But she's clueless as to what her next career will be. Plus, her sizzling romance with Josh, is doing a fast fizzle since he left town to continue nursing his ex-wife through her cancer battle.

Just as Katy is settling in for an extended pity-party of weepy old movies and tubs of mint-chip ice cream, her mother calls with tragic news. A dear family member has met an untimely end. Now Katy and her grandma must travel to the scenic Cotswolds of England to sort out legal matters. When they arrive, they're overwhelmed by the friendly villagers who offer help and moral support.

However, when Katy and Ruby become the target of vandals, they realize that not everyone in town is pleased about their presence. *Is murder next on the list?*

WHILE SHE SLUMBERED
Book #5 in the Murder Blog Mysteries

With her boyfriend still nursing his dying ex in Los Angeles, heartbroken Katy finds comfort blogging her woes and visiting her elderly neighbor, Nina.

One day, Nina tells Katy that her mystery-writing niece, Donna, is coming for a few days. "I'm looking forward to her visit.

I haven't seen her in years and have always thought of her as a daughter."

However, two days into the stay, Nina has already had enough of her overbearing niece. She confides to Katy, "This visit can't end soon enough for me."

A couple of days later, Katy drops by for a visit. The surly sixty-something author forbids her from seeing Nina with the excuse that her aunt has a cold and is napping.

After many failed attempts to see her neighbor, Katy fears her friend may be in mortal danger, so she doubles down on her efforts to get beyond Nina's front door.

Is Katy's imagination running wild,
or is Donna slowly killing her aunt?

I hope you enjoy the sample of
Was It Murder?
on the following pages.

WAS IT MURDER? PROLOGUE

"Come, Charlie. Time for our walkie." The woman attached a leash to the corgi's collar and opened the front door.

Front paws planted on the threshold, Charlie sniffed the misty late night air and skittered backwards into the house.

"I know it's unseasonably chilly, dear, but nature's calling, and we must answer." She wrapped a red wool dog coat around the boy, kissed his head, then stepped out onto the slate porch and gently tugged the leash. "Come, sweetheart."

The dog plopped his rear on the floor with a beseeching look that seemed to say, *Must we?*

"The sooner we do this, the sooner we can get tucked in snug and watch our shows." She yanked on Charlie's leash, but he didn't budge. "You're not going to win, you know." She ruffled his russet neck. "If you're a good boy, I promise to give you a biscuit."

The Pembroke Welsh Corgi jumped to his feet, grinning and wagging his tail. Now eager to do his business, he scuttled over the doorstep, shoving his muzzle into the laughing woman's slender legs.

"Oh, now you're in a big rush." While Charlie pranced around the porch like a goofy puppy, she zipped her jacket and adjusted her muffler. "Brrr. It's colder than I thought." She removed fuzzy knit gloves from her pocket and pulled them on. "All right, then, Mommy's ready."

As she set her foot on the first step, Charlie scooted down the next three. She gripped the iron handrail and hauled back on the leash. "Charlie! Slow down! The steps are slippery."

The excited dog dashed to the bottom jerking his mistress forward. Her feet slid on the icy stone, and she lost her grip on the railing, plunging headfirst down the steps.

WAS IT MURDER? CHAPTER ONE

WEDNESDAY · APRIL 8

Posted by Katy McKenna

My romance with my next-door neighbor, Josh Draper, secretly A.K.A. "the Viking," (if you saw him, you'd get it—he looks like a Nordic god) has been complicated lately, to say the least.

He's a divorced, former narcotics detective. When I asked him what caused his split-up, he told me, "When you take on an assignment like that, you live and breathe it. I was hanging with lowlife scum, and after a while, the lines got blurred and eventually my wife had enough of it. Said she didn't know who I was anymore. Hell, *I* didn't know who I was anymore. After she left me, I realized I had to get out of it, so I quit. I was broken, and it took a long time to heal."

Nicole and Josh have remained good friends. She's still single and works as a paralegal at a law firm in Los Angeles, three-and-a-half hours south.

Recently, when she was diagnosed with stage four colon cancer, the first person she called was Josh, and being the good guy that he is, he immediately offered his help. She's been staying with him while she does chemo, but since her prognosis is pretty bleak, she wants to move into a nursing home. Of course, Josh won't let her do that. The guilt would kill him.

Yesterday, he had called and said we needed to talk. I'd wanted to shout, "Now's not a good time," because I was pretty sure I wouldn't like what he had to say. Instead, I had invited him over.

As a stall tactic, I offered him coffee which neither of us wanted. I took my time setting a filter in the Chemex glass vessel and filling it with dark roast. I drizzled hot water over the grounds, willing myself not to throw up in the process. Finally, I poured two cups and got the half-and-half out of the fridge.

We leaned against the tile counter clutching our warm mugs, staring at each other, waiting to see who would break the silence.

"Okay. I'm ready," I said. "Tell me what you came to say."

"I don't know how to say this without hurting you."

I tucked a tendril of hair that had escaped my ponytail behind my ear and shrugged. "That's not a good start." One of my fingernails found its way into my mouth and I nervously nibbled.

He gently pulled my hand from my mouth and held it. "I'm moving. Temporarily. To Nicole's condo in L.A. to take care of her. It's too damned hard living next door to you and not being with you every possible moment. But knowing she still loves me..." He shook his head looking so forlorn that I wanted to take him in my arms and tell him everything would be all right. "She told me if she weren't dying, she'd beg me to give our marriage another chance."

Barely able to speak, I removed my hand from his and murmured, "Would you want to do that? I mean, if she was healthy?"

"No. But how can I tell her?" He blew out a long sigh, raking his fingers through his blond hair. "Please know I'm not trying to lead her on. But it was my fault our marriage broke up, and I do still care about her. Always will."

"If she beats the cancer, then what?"

"Then we move on. She lives her life, and I live mine. Hopefully with you." Josh put his coffee on the counter, then set my cup next to his and placed my hands against his heart, gripping them tightly like a lifeline. "Katy. I can't ask you to wait for me. This could drag on for a long time, and that's not fair to you."

"I can wait."

He shook his head with a melancholy half smile. "I want you to have fun. Meet other men. With any luck, they'll make you think I'm worth waiting for."

"I already know that," I whispered.

———

Just after sunrise this morning, I hid behind the trumpet vine that drapes across the eaves on my porch and watched Josh load suitcases into his BMW sports coupe. I'm sure he knew I was there, because he paused, gazing at my porch for a long moment.

After they drove away, I spent the next hour sitting on my porch swing crying buckets. My sweet yellow Labrador, Daisy, did her best to soothe me, but to be honest, deep down inside, I was actually feeling a bit relieved—if that makes any sense.

———

My plan for the next day or two or three was to wallow in self-pity and watch weepy old movies. First pick of the day: *The Way We Were*. Robert Redford was about the same age as Josh when the film was made in 1973, and I was struck by how similar they look, although Josh is taller, his hair is shorter, and I think he's better looking.

When my mother called, I was still in my flannel pajamas moping in the living room with a tub of mint chip ice cream in my lap. Tabitha, my gray tabby, was perched on top of the chair, one paw resting on my shoulder. Francine, my black, tan, and very gray senior dachshund rescue was tucked in next to me, and Daisy was sawing logs in a sun puddle.

I wasn't in the mood for chitchat, but I answered the phone anyway, ready to share my misery with her, but instead she shared hers with me.

"Honey, I have some sad news." Mom sounded stuffed up.

Feeling apprehensive, I set my ice cream on the side table and straightened up. "What's wrong?"

"Aunt Edith has—" She hiccupped a sob. "—passed away."

"When? What happened? She was fine when she was here for Christmas."

"I know. She wasn't sick. She had a bad fall." Mom sighed and blew her nose again. "Could happen to anyone. You just never know."

"Oh, my God. I can't believe this. How can Aunt Edith be…" I could not say "dead." "Gone? Do you want me to come over?"

"No. Your dad and I are at Mom's. She's devastated. This has hit her hard."

The shocking news made my pity-party seem so pathetic and childish. My dear, funny aunt was suddenly gone, and all I could think about was Ruby—my grandmother, and the devastating loss of her big sister. I desperately needed to wrap my arms around her and tell her how much I loved her. So, of course, I went over. How could I not?

———

Ruby is the executor for her sister's estate and will need to go to England to clear out and sell Aunt Edith's home. Mom wanted to go with her, but Pop is scheduled for a knee replacement. Several years ago, he got early retirement from the police force after taking a bullet in the knee. He offered to reschedule the surgery, but he's been putting it off for years and is in constant pain, so Ruby wouldn't hear of it. That means I'm going.

Aunt Edith had always said that under no circumstances would she want a funeral. The last time she visited, she told us that she had arranged to donate her body to forensic science. Edith said it made her happy knowing she would be doing one last good thing after she departed her old carcass, but it troubles me thinking of my great aunt's body being studied as she decomposes. She also promised me that it would be years before that happened. Instead, it had been just months.

Was It Murder?

is available on Amazon

Made in the USA
Columbia, SC
03 February 2022

55243257R00190